||||| |||||| ||| ||||||||| |||||| |||| |||||||
⟡ **W9-BYP-355**

Praise for Laura Abbot:

In *Mating for Life*... "I got touching
emotion...[and] tangible, thoughtful friends....
(Laura Abbot) can decorate the most ordinary prose
with the loveliest turns of phrase... A rich love story."
—*Tulsa World*

"(*This Christmas* is) a splendid heartwarming
romance."
—*Rendezvous*

"All the characters (in *This Christmas*) seem so real
it's almost impossible not to become immediately
absorbed in this romance."
—*Affaire de Coeur*

"(*Where There's Smoke*...) is a great novel with a
unique female lead who isn't afraid to stand tall in
the face of danger."
—*Middlesex News*

"Laura Abbot sets off fireworks (in *Where There's
Smoke*...)."
—*Affaire de Coeur*

"(*Where There's Smoke*...is) a grand tale with
resplendent characters that will remain in the reader's
heart for a long time after the last page is turned."
—*Rendezvous*

Dear Reader,

I'm one of the few people I know who can name each elementary and high school teacher I ever had. Why? Because they were extraordinarily gifted men and women who shared three characteristics: they valued learning, they cared for their students and they loved their jobs! They were my role models.

So it's not surprising that I joined their ranks, even completing college in three years so that I could teach at least one year before becoming a full-time homemaker. Funny how circumstances turned that one year into twenty-five! And I loved every single minute I spent among those lively adolescents. Well, almost every minute.

I was one of the lucky ones. I enjoyed a fulfilling career doing what I think I must've been born to do. Maybe it helped that I am descended from a long line of teachers, which now—I'm proud to say—includes my firstborn.

Is it any wonder, then, that *Class Act* was a story I had to write? If you enjoy it, you can demonstrate it best by doing me a special favor: Thank a teacher!

Laura Abbot

P.S.: I love hearing from readers. Please write to me at P.O. Box 2105, Eureka Springs, AR 72632.

CLASS ACT
Laura Abbot

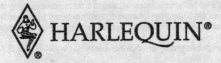

HARLEQUIN®

TORONTO • NEW YORK • LONDON
AMSTERDAM • PARIS • SYDNEY • HAMBURG
STOCKHOLM • ATHENS • TOKYO • MILAN • MADRID
PRAGUE • WARSAW • BUDAPEST • AUCKLAND

If you purchased this book without a cover you should be aware
that this book is stolen property. It was reported as "unsold and
destroyed" to the publisher, and neither the author nor the
publisher has received any payment for this "stripped book."

ISBN 0-373-70803-3

CLASS ACT

Copyright © 1998 by Laura A. Shoffner.

All rights reserved. Except for use in any review, the reproduction or
utilization of this work in whole or in part in any form by any electronic,
mechanical or other means, now known or hereafter invented, including
xerography, photocopying and recording, or in any information storage
or retrieval system, is forbidden without the written permission of the
publisher, Harlequin Enterprises Limited, 225 Duncan Mill Road,
Don Mills, Ontario, Canada M3B 3K9.

All characters in this book have no existence outside the imagination of
the author and have no relation whatsoever to anyone bearing the same
name or names. They are not even distantly inspired by any individual
known or unknown to the author, and all incidents are pure invention.

This edition published by arrangement with Harlequin Books S.A.

® and TM are trademarks of the publisher. Trademarks indicated with
® are registered in the United States Patent and Trademark Office, the
Canadian Trade Marks Office and in other countries.

Printed in U.S.A.

To my friend David

Heartfelt thanks to the Kansas City and Arkansas "porch gangs"; to the best critique partner ever, my father; and especially to my former colleagues and students, whose lives enriched mine in magnificent and humbling ways.

CHAPTER ONE

A BLAST of hot West Texas air, heavy with unchar-acteristic humidity, hit Connie Weaver in the face as she opened her car door. She lingered behind the wheel, reluctant to give up the cool, air-conditioned interior and this rare moment to herself. Transition time—easing from the frenetic back-to-school activity of her high-school students to the quieter, but no less demanding, atmosphere of home.

She gathered her things, then made her way across the sun-scorched lawn to her small brick ranch-style house, noting the drooping yellow chrysanthemums rooted in the parched soil bordering the porch.

Her skin registered oppressive mugginess. She glanced at the sky—cloudless. Yet she smelled the faint earth-moist hint of rain. With a resigned sigh, she pushed open the front door, awaiting the inevitable.

"Con-nieee, is that you?"

Like clockwork, the same hopeful question greeted her every weekday afternoon, as if she were thirteen instead of—she winced—forty!

Her mother's black cat, Yolanda, named for the fe-male in the Veloz and Yolanda ballroom dancing pair, brushed a welcome across her legs. Connie set her heavy canvas tote bag on the floor beside the living-room sofa, eased her aching feet out of her sensible schoolteacher pumps and forced a cheerful tone. "Yes, Mama, I'm home."

Adele Vail, wiping her wet hands on her faded apron and then fluffing her short, tightly permed white hair, stood in the kitchen doorway. "You're late."

Patiently, Connie reminded her of the after-school faculty meeting. "Burning questions today. The home-coming-queen election and enforcement of the student dress code." Connie smiled grimly. Every five or six years the identical issues, like pesky bugs, swarmed to the top of the agenda.

Adele eyed the clock. "Where's Erin?"

"She stayed late to work on the yearbook. A friend's bringing her home."

"For your birthday, I made that chicken dish you like." Adele paused, as if expecting applause. "I certainly hope it won't dry out before your daughter gets here."

"Your" daughter? At the base of her neck the pulsings that usually signaled an oncoming headache throbbed.

Adele continued. "After all, you only turn forty once."

How many times today had she been reminded? Her history department colleagues had hung a black wreath on her classroom door; her second-period world history class had surprised her with a sugary sheet cake; and after the meeting two of her closest faculty friends, Pam Carver and Ginny Phillips, had taken her to a nearby watering hole for a celebratory glass of wine. People meant well, but somehow she hadn't expected the actual day, September 17, to feel like such a milestone. As if she were stepping over a barrier between youth and middle age.

Wearily, she picked up her shoes and headed to her bedroom to change. Despite her exhaustion, after the family dinner a stack of exams had to be graded and two cheerleader parents expected her to return their calls. She'd hoped to avoid the cheerleader sponsorship, but when her good friend Ralph Hagood, the upper-school principal, had turned to her in desperation, she'd capitulated. The girls weren't so difficult, but in an attempt to hold on to their youth, some of their mothers seemed determined to relive high school through their daughters.

Shedding her denim shirtdress, she donned her cozy Keystone School sweats before going into her bathroom, where she swallowed two aspirin, then splashed cold water on her face. *Better.*

How old did forty look? She studied her features in the mirror. A few isolated gray hairs in her thick long brown hair; two faint vertical lines between her eyebrows, probably the result of fixing the teacher look on mischievous students; a slight sag of the skin at her jawline. And one redeeming feature—the laugh lines on either side of her mouth. No dramatic overnight changes. Not on the surface.

No, the changes were deep inside, where you asked yourself in a tiny scared voice, "Is this it? Is *this* all there is?"

Drawing away from the mirror, she chastised herself. After all, she had a lovely seventeen-year-old daughter, a relatively healthy mother, a fulfilling job

as history department chairman and several close
women friends. Behind her, thankfully, were the eight
chaotic years of marriage to Erin's father, Colin Weaver, charismatic American-lit professor; the devastat-
ing death of her own dad in the fall of 1989; and the
abrupt move from Oklahoma to Texas. Dwelling on
what might have been accomplished nothing. A
woman could be a lot worse off. Security, professional
satisfaction and caring students, friends and family—
they simply had to be enough.

She ran a brush through her loose hair, then gathered it at the neck with a large plastic barrette. A tap-
ping sounded on her bedroom door. *Erin?* She took a
deep, cleansing breath and stepped into the hall.

There were times—like this—when seeing her late-
bloomer daughter took her by surprise; when she realized that despite Erin's small breasts and thin frame
she was more woman than child. Still dressed in the
khaki slacks and dark-green print blouse she'd worn
to school, Erin had a classic appearance—intense
brown eyes, aristocratic nose and straight shoulder-
length auburn hair with full bangs.

"Gramma's beside herself. She says the chicken's
rubbery and the gravy is library paste."

Connie threw her daughter a long-suffering look.
"She still wishes we'd sit down precisely at the stroke
of six the way she and Dad did. Flexibility isn't one
of her strong points."

Erin smiled knowingly. "Tell me about it."

In the center of the dining-room table, set with the
good china and silver, was a three-layer coconut cake
sporting a blue-and-white plastic 4-0 candle holder.

Ramrod straight, Adele waited at her place until her daughter and granddaughter sat down.

"This looks delicious, Mama."

Adele took her seat. "It might've been, fifteen minutes ago."

Connie bit back her instinctive response. Though they'd lived under the same roof since her father's death, her mother had never adjusted to her and Erin's erratic schedules.

"It tastes fine, Gramma. Doesn't it, Mom?"

Connie, nodded emphatically, swallowing a forkful of chicken. "You went to a lot of effort."

Mollified, Adele's stiff posture eased as she daintily spooned gravy over her potatoes. "You deserve something special for your fortieth birthday, even if it was quite a bit of work at my age."

True, her mother wasn't getting any younger. Connie sometimes wondered, however, if such complaints weren't designed to provoke pity and guilt.

Erin, eyeing Connie over the edge of the napkin that barely concealed her conspiratorial grin, changed the subject. "Feel older, Mom?"

"Hey, I'm just *one* day older. Besides, it's fun being the center of attention."

"I heard the world history class brought a cake for you."

"A *cake!* Well, if I'd known that, I could have spared myself the trouble." Adele's lips puckered as if she'd just bitten into a sour pickle.

"I had only a tiny piece, Mama. The kids wolfed down the rest. Besides, it was store-bought—nothing like your homemade one."

"I should think not." As if realizing she was harping, Adele added, "I suppose it *was* thoughtful of the students to remember you."

Erin leaned forward. "Hey, Mom, maybe they were just trying to get out of listening to your lecture on the Crusades."

Connie widened her eyes in fake innocence. "Who would deliberately avoid such enlightenment?"

In unison she and her daughter answered, "Sophomores."

By the end of the meal, Adele grudgingly agreed the food hadn't turned out too badly. After Erin finished clearing the table, she lit the candles on the cake, then handed Connie a knife.

"Make a wish, Mom."

Connie rose to her feet and stared down at the white, coconut-encrusted dessert with the offending numerals standing in silent challenge. *Make a wish.* She hesitated. Inexplicably, this fanciful ritual had suddenly taken on overwhelming significance. A fortieth birthday wish required special attention, special honesty. But to wish for...*Jim?* An unforgettable, once-in-a-lifetime man?

For a moment, the present merged with the past, vibrant with detail—the savory odors of Wisconsin Avenue restaurants, the swirling waters of the broad Potomac, the awe-inspiring play of light and shadow on the Lincoln Memorial at night.

And deep, soulful eyes that saw right through her to the hidden part.

She lost herself in the flames dancing and flickering before her. Memories.

Finally, taking a deep breath, she leaned over. It was merely a tradition. Meaningless. So why not? She closed her eyes, heard his name echo in her heart and blew out the candles.

WELL, THAT HAD GONE better than expected, Adele reflected as she scraped the dinner dishes. Why was it, though, that those two were almost always late for dinner? She and Edgar, God rest his soul, had always eaten at six.

Edgar. She missed him every single day. It seemed impossible he'd been gone since 1989. And he would so have enjoyed celebrating Connie's birthday. But, then, he enjoyed almost everything. Especially the dancing. Adele caught her breath and stifled a sob.

They had met at a ballroom dance contest, and Edgar Vail had quite literally swept her off her feet. Love at first sight, no question about it. After their marriage when they'd opened their dance studio, she'd changed her name. From Delphia—awful sounding—to Adele. After Fred Astaire's sister. Adele and Edgar Vail—it had a nice ring to it. And they'd danced and danced, up until the day before he died.

After that, the music stopped. Now all she had was memories. And Connie and Erin, of course. She hoped she wasn't too much of a burden to them. Loneliness was a problem, but housework and watching old movies filled the hours. None of that senior-citizen-center stuff for her. Connie had tried to insist, but Adele had been adamant. No bingo, no shuffleboard, no crafts.

Besides, it was a couple's world. Who wanted some old widow woman?

SEATED AT HER DESK, red pen poised above the last exam, Connie stifled a yawn and, for the twenty-first time, read about the consequences of the Roman invasion of Britain. Rhett Mercer had an amazing gift for the dramatic, if not the accurate. She wrote a few suggestions on his test, then gratefully dropped the stack of papers into her tote.

Though it was after eleven, she ran a hot tub, deciding to indulge herself with her birthday gifts—bath salts from her mother and new pajamas from Erin. She eased into the steamy water, the cloying lilac scent reminding her, distressingly, of cosmetic counters favored by wrinkled dowagers. But there was nothing old or flabby, *yet*, about her body, except for faint stretch marks on her hips. Blessed with her father's lean frame, she prided herself on her firm abdomen and well-proportioned figure. For all the good it did her! Where did teachers meet available, decent men? Even if she stumbled across one, would he saddle himself not only with her but with Mother and Erin?

After dipping the washcloth into the water, she laid it over her face, letting the warmth seep into her pores. Well, Ralph Hagood would have—gladly. Her mother had approved. "Constance Ann, what are you waiting for? Ralph is a nice, steady man." Nice, steady, reliable…and dull.

Besides school, what did the two of them really have in common? Dates had consisted of chaperoning school dances, attending athletic events and taking in occasional movies. Yes, he had a good sense of humor. Yes, he'd earned her professional respect. Yes, she was genuinely fond of him—so fond, in fact, she knew he deserved more. He'd regretfully, but amicably accepted her no, though she had the uncomfortable sense that if she crooked her finger, he'd come running.

She sat up, vigorously soaping her body. What *was* she waiting for? Simple. Someone who set her on fire, whose smell and feel and taste transported her, who made her feel understood, desirable, passionate. Even as she thought about it, her body betrayed her with a telltale ache. Maybe she could have settled for Ralph, if only she'd never met a man…a man like Jim…who had made her feel those other things.

Darn it all, anyway. She quickly rinsed, pulled the plug and toweled off. Forty and mooning over ancient history! A self-indulgent waste of time. Water gurgled down the drain in a loud ''Amen!''

Rubbing lotion into her hands and soothed by the silky feel of her new jade green pajamas, she stepped down the hall to check on Erin. Light spilled out and the low strains of George Winston were audible. Connie entered quietly. Erin, her shapeless nightshirt tucked under her legs, sat hunched in front of the computer monitor.

''Much longer, honey?''

Erin smiled wanly. ''No. I'm just finishing this essay for English.''

Connie would have liked to insist her perfectionist daughter, currently ranked second in her senior class, go to bed. But since the deciding factor for Connie's taking a pay cut to teach at Keystone had been to provide Erin the advantage of small classes and a first-rate college preparatory education, she could hardly get on her case. "Thanks for the nice birthday. I love you."

"Love you, too, Mom. G'night."

Connie padded back to her room, set the alarm, turned out the light and snuggled into bed, feeling each and every one of her forty years.

The next thing she knew, someone was shaking her. Easing up from the pillow, she stared at the illuminated clock dial. One.

"Mom, wake up!" Erin sounded frantic.

Connie groped to turn on the bedside lamp, then shaded her eyes. "Honey, what's wrong?"

Erin sat on the edge of the bed. "Dr. Frankenberg is leaving."

"What do you mean 'leaving'?" She'd met with the headmaster only yesterday and he'd been discussing long-range planning.

"Right away."

Connie gripped her daughter's arm. "You're not making any sense."

"Listen, Mom. When I called Tara Farley to compare our calculus answers, she told me."

"Told you *what?*"

"At the board meeting tonight, Dr. Frankenberg announced his resignation. His wife is sick or something."

Virginia sick? "How would Tara know such a thing?" Then, dismayed and disgusted, she answered her own question. "That's right, her father's on the board." All too often trustees' kids scooped the faculty.

"Sorry I woke you, but I thought you'd want to know."

"You were right. I appreciate it." She eyed her daughter. "Bedtime?"

"On my way. G'night again."

"'Night, dear." Connie turned off the light, doubting she'd sleep much. Lee Frankenberg was an institution at the school. He'd been headmaster for nearly sixteen years, successfully managing the tightrope walk among the faculty, parents, students and alumni. Much of the credit for Keystone's excellent academic reputation belonged to him. She couldn't imagine the school without his wise, benevolent leadership. Resigning immediately?

Shivering, she pulled up the blanket. Something must be terribly wrong.

HER UMBRELLA scant protection for the autumn downpour, Connie hopscotched through the puddles in the faculty parking lot toward the upper school. Rain cascaded from the red tile roof overhanging the sprawling two-story southwestern-style building and splashed on the yuccas planted beneath. The gloom in the teachers' lounge this morning would undoubtedly match the weather as word spread about Dr. Frankenberg.

"'Morning, Mrs. W."

Brad Scanlon, one of her sophomore students and a dead ringer for Tom Sawyer, held the door for her.

"Thank you, Brad."

Puppylike, he trailed her down the corridor toward her classroom.

"Did I ace the test?"

"What do you think?"

"You won't tell me?"

When he stopped at his locker, she patted his shoulder. "All things with time. Second period, to be precise." Sidling past a gaggle of giggling freshmen girls, she fumbled for her keys, then unlocked her classroom door. Deliberately, she left the lights off. She liked these last quiet minutes before classes began. Something about the room—smelling faintly of chalk dust, lead pencil shavings, stale bubble gum and the mustiness of books—breathed promise and the challenge of the unexpected. After putting down her tote, she shook the wet umbrella, stowed it in the corner and opened the blinds.

She was writing the American history assignment on the board when Pam Carver, the attractive young head of the English department, came in, shutting the door behind her. She looked downcast.

"You know?"

"About Lee? Yes. Erin heard it from Tara Farley."

"That figures."

"Why is he leaving?"

"Virginia has a fast-growing cancer. Lee's going with her to Houston to the M. D. Anderson Cancer Center. Apparently, he had planned to retire after next year anyway. They've decided to make the most of their time together."

"The students?"

"They're starting to find out, and the teachers' lounge is Gossip Central."

Connie leaned back against her desk. "What a mess

for everybody, especially Virginia and Lee. Any official word yet from the board?"

"No. But in the lounge, Ralph is the odds-on favorite to replace Lee."

Connie knew of Ralph's ambitions, yet the notion had always made her uneasy. Nothing she could really put her finger on except a gut feeling he was too nice—soft?—for the politics of the position. "In that case, what happens in the upper school?"

Pam shrugged. "Who knows? But it would be easier to replace a principal quickly than a headmaster. At this time of year, any candidate who's available is someone not hired elsewhere. Slim pickings, I predict."

A shrill bell sounded in the hall. Connie stood. "Tara's in my first-period class, so I'd better get ready to defuse rumors."

As she left, Pam called over her shoulder, "Good luck."

Melissa Clayton, the first of Connie's senior advanced-placement students through the door, gasped dramatically, "Mrs. W., did you hear about Dr. Frank? Isn't it *awful?*"

Melissa was followed by thirteen other seniors, including Tara, all talking at once. "But our senior year will be ruined." "Wanna be headmistress, Mrs. W.?" "I feel *so* sorry for Dr. Frank."

Connie clapped her hands. "Seats, everyone. Quiet, please." Gradually, they slumped into their chairs, retrieved notebooks and texts from voluminous day packs and looked up at her expectantly. She came around her desk and, praying for the right words, plunged in.

"I know we're all concerned about Dr. and Mrs. Frankenberg. Tragedy and uncertainty are difficult, but we're lucky to have a caring school like Keystone. I imagine you want to help. The best way to do that is to act compassionately and responsibly. Rumors don't help. We all need to be patient until we get some facts."

Tara interrupted, "But I heard they're going to make Mr. Hagood headmaster." The class, as one, turned toward her. She continued in her voice of authority. "My father's on the board and—"

"Tara—" with effort Connie kept her tone neutral "—there has been no announcement from the board yet. I know your father is involved, but I would appreciate it if all of you—" she deliberately let her gaze fall over the others, as well "—would refrain from jumping to conclusions. You are seniors. The underclassmen will be looking to you for leadership. They need facts and support, not hearsay and idle speculation."

Jennifer Daly raised her hand tentatively. "Mrs. W., is there something, you know, that we could like *do* for Dr. and Mrs. Frankenberg?"

"That's a good suggestion. What do the rest of you think?"

His huge dark eyes luminous with concern, class president Jaime Hernandez spoke up. "What if the seniors did something like a quilt or a wall hanging? Each of us could make a square, maybe showing events in the school's history."

The class erupted with enthusiasm and ideas. Connie's eyes misted as she recalled the words of the wise teacher who had been her mentor early in her career: "Never underestimate kids. If you expect good things of them, they'll always come through."

DURING CONNIE'S last-hour planning period, she was summoned to Ralph's office. Rubbing a plump hand over his bald spot, he stood, tension evident in the set of his mouth. "Have a seat, Connie." Gesturing to one of the two upholstered wingback chairs, he settled in the other.

"Today must've been difficult for you, Ralph."

"Dreadful. I spent all morning with Lee. He's devastated. The phone's been ringing off the hook, and the teachers and students are in an uproar. I wish the board could have given us notice, but in fairness, they were blindsided, too."

"You probably feel overwhelmed. Not only will you lose Lee's guidance, but undoubtedly you'll carry a heavier load temporarily."

He nodded, then retrieved from his desk a single piece of paper, which he handed to her. "This will be distributed to the faculty after school."

She scanned the text: "The board of trustees announces with regret the resignation, effective immediately, of Dr. Lee Frankenberg. In this transition period, Ralph Hagood, upper school principal, will serve as acting headmaster. The board will proceed with an immediate search for an interim or permanent headmaster."

When she finished reading, Connie didn't look up,

feeling in the pit of her stomach Ralph's disappointment at not being immediately appointed interim head.

He leaned forward. "So what do you think I should do?"

"About…?"

"Putting my name in the pot."

He was watching her. "You've always had aspirations to be headmaster, Ralph. And you certainly know Keystone School inside and out." The words came out awkward, stilted.

"I'll count on your support, then."

She didn't know what to say. "You're a fine man, Ralph. One of the best."

When he rose, she stood, too. "You said it. 'Overwhelmed.'" His eyes, pain filled, found hers. "Connie, I wish—" He faltered, then looked away before picking up the faculty announcement and returning it to the desktop. "Thanks for stopping by."

Halfway back to her classroom the final bell rang, and she was swallowed up in an adolescent tidal wave and deafened by banging locker doors and shouted farewells. Brad Scanlon materialized alongside her.

"Thanks for giving me a B on the test, Mrs. W."

She turned a teasingly indignant look on him. "Who *gave* you anything? You earned it."

"Well, it'll sure help with *los parentos.*" He stopped at the exit. "Thanks anyway."

"You've set a precedent, Brad. From now on, I'm *expecting* Bs."

Threading her way through the crowd, she noticed broad-shouldered Kyle Drummond, the football team's center, lounging possessively near a locker, laughingly blocking the way of a girl. Startled, she recognized the red plaid blouse Erin had worn today. As she moved on down the hall, she caught a glimpse of Erin placing a hand on Kyle's shirtfront and smiling up at him adoringly. Connie tensed. Erin was flirting! Erin—who had always been too busy for boys, who thought schoolgirl crushes were beneath her, who had convinced herself popular guys wouldn't be interested in a scholar—looked radiant.

For Connie, it was a bittersweet moment—complete with the knowledge of the tender, wild poignancy of first love and the hurtful, crushing disappointment of love betrayed.

JIM CAMPBELL REMOVED his silver-rimmed glasses, rubbed his eyes, then stared out his office window at the boats moving up and down the Charles River between Boston and Cambridge, wishing he were once again a Harvard undergrad with nothing more serious to think about than a research paper. Then, as now, he'd known Campbell Courts, the family hotel business, wasn't where he wanted to spend the rest of his life. But, for the moment, here he was—board member and vice president for special events. He glanced at his desk calendar. September 24. With luck, this time next year he'd be back where he belonged. In a school.

After rolling down his shirtsleeves, he buttoned the cuffs, straightened his tie, then stood and shrugged into his suit coat. He wasn't looking forward to this luncheon meeting with his elder brother, Cliff, CEO of Campbell Courts. But in good conscience, he needed to inform Cliff he'd recently filed his creden-

tials with an educational placement agency. Cliff had
never understood his commitment to teaching; in fact,
he'd regarded it as a phase that would pass when Jim
"grew up." But his intentions couldn't have escaped
his brother, not after he'd recently completed his dis-
sertation and been awarded a doctorate in education.

He'd probably been a fool to leave teaching in the
first place. But when, as a young assistant headmaster,
he'd been passed over for a headship primarily because he lacked financial expertise, Cliff's job offer at
Campbell Courts had seemed providential. He'd figured he could gain the necessary business experience
before eventually returning to education.

However, he had reckoned without two factors: his
monumental dissatisfaction with the job…and Sondra.

She'd come along when he was most vulnerable—
craving stability, a wife, children. Why hadn't he recognized the inevitable? She'd married a hotel man, not
an educator. During their whirlwind courtship, he'd
assumed she understood his goals and shared his desire for a family. He'd assumed wrong. Sondra was a
good enough person, just spoiled by her creature com-
forts and comfortable niche in Boston society. Being
a headmaster's wife held no appeal. To appease her,
he'd stuck with his job for five tedious years. He'd
tried, really tried to make it all work. But when the
childless marriage kept drifting, becoming more a trial
than a sanctuary, they'd finally agreed to a divorce.
Over and out.

Jim took the express elevator to the elegant private
dining room of the chain's flagship hotel. Cliff, immaculately groomed, sat waiting at the small table

covered with snow-white linen and set with exquisite china and crystal. Lunch conversation centered on arrangements for an upcoming major convention. Over dessert, Jim dropped his bomb.

"Cliff, I appreciate everything you've done for me. But you know as well as I do that I'm simply not cut out for the hotel business."

"Now, hold on, Jim—"

"It's in your blood, Cliff. You were born to follow in Dad's footsteps. But, try to understand. I'm miserable."

Cliff set down his fork and leaned his elbows on the table. "We can transfer you, give you another assignment."

"No. I need a clean break."

Cliff rolled his eyes. "It's the school thing still, isn't it?"

Jim toyed with his coffee spoon before meeting his brother's gaze. "Yes. I'm circulating my résumé. With any luck, I should have a position for the next school year. I wanted to give you ample notice."

Cliff shook his head, aghast. "Why would you leave a lucrative family business? You've got it made, Jim. A country club membership, new company car every year, access to the summer place on the Cape, not to mention the stock options. And you'd leave all that for—for being a headmaster somewhere?" he sputtered.

"You love what you do and you're damn good at it. I'm glad. But it's not right for me." Jim knew full well his brother didn't regard teaching as a "real" job.

"What about the money?"

"It's not about money. It's about making a difference."

"Can't you do that here?"

"It's not the same, Cliff." His brother couldn't understand that Jim needed to feel what he did mattered in fundamental ways. And what was more fundamental than working with kids?

Cliff slumped against the upholstered chairback, expelling a deep sigh. "Am I wasting my breath to try to get you to come to your senses?"

"I'm sorry. This is something I have to do."

His brother sat in silence for a time, then leaned forward and gripped his hand. "Okay, then. I'll never in a million years understand how you can walk away from—" he gestured around the perfectly appointed room "—all this, from the family tradition. But if you're determined to do it, then I won't try to stop you. Go with my blessing."

Jim could hardly bear the disappointment in Cliff's eyes.

"And if you change your mind, you'll always have a place waiting here," Cliff added.

Back in his office after lunch, Jim found his mind wandering from the details of meeting-room assignments, menus and cost projections. Relief warred with...not regret exactly, maybe sadness. His brother's opinion mattered to him. Summoning his concentration, he turned back to his work and buried himself until his secretary buzzed him.

"Mr. Campbell, you have a call on line two. Shall I take a message?"

He checked his watch. A little before five. "I've got

time." He punched the button of the speaker phone. "Jim Campbell."

"Jim, Ollie Standish at Educational Placements. Sorry to call you so late in the day, but I'd like to run something past you."

"Shoot."

"Any chance you'd be available sooner than next summer?"

"What do you have in mind?" The possibility filled Jim with a burst of energy.

"The Keystone School in Fort Worth needs an interim head, like yesterday. It's a fine institution. I think you should consider applying. Interested?"

"I might be."

"I'll fax the school profile to you right away." Ollie paused. "Jim, I have a positive feeling about this. You and Keystone might be a very good match."

Jim listened intently as Ollie filled him in about the school and Lee Frankenberg's sudden resignation. Although Jim regretted the circumstances creating the opening, the longer Ollie talked the more appealing the situation sounded. An interim headship would get him out of Boston and position him well for seeking a permanent headship the following year.

Was he interested? Absolutely!

CHAPTER TWO

A WEEK LATER, after several productive phone conversations with Phil Buxton, the Keystone board president, Jim settled back in his aisle seat aboard a plane bound for Dallas-Fort Worth. With his knees bumping uncomfortably against the tray table, he concentrated on the information packet Buxton had couriered to him.

He'd already studied the financial statements. Sound information, although in his judgment a questionably large percentage of the program budget went to the athletic department. The curricula of the three divisions—lower, middle and upper schools—provided balance and continuity, and Keystone's impressive college acceptances upheld the claim of academic excellence.

Most appealing was the fit between the school motto—Caring, Character, Curiosity. Keystones of Excellence—and his own educational philosophy. Phil Buxton had particularly emphasized the character issue: "The board is concerned about the anything-goes attitude where youngsters feel little, if any, responsibility for their actions. Old-fashioned honesty, reliability and compassion should be valued, not ridiculed." Jim couldn't agree more.

"Something to drink, sir?"

The flight attendant stood at his elbow. "Black coffee, please." He knew he shouldn't get his hopes up, but so far everything he'd heard about Keystone—and he'd checked with several trusted contacts in the independent-school world—sounded promising.

As he sipped the coffee, he studied the agenda for his two-day visit. A campus tour, a series of interviews with key personnel and then a final session with the executive committee of the board of trustees.

He flipped open the school directory and studied the listings. Names. Always important. Twelve board members, three of them women. He scanned the faculty roster, noting a good balance of males and females, several with doctorates. He ran his finger down the page, searching for department chairs, deans, counselors. When one improbable name leaped out at him, he paused, stunned, his coffee cup poised halfway to his lips. Connie Weaver. Slowly he set down the cup, closed the directory and leaned back. Weaver was a common name. But *Connie?*

Georgetown University, 1989. The summer fellowship program for history teachers. What he remembered most was not the course work but the intensity with which he'd been drawn to the young woman from Oklahoma, whose idealism and enthusiasm had kindled a powerful response in him.

Seeing the capital from Connie's fresh perspective, he'd rediscovered it. "I wasn't prepared. It's so amazingly beautiful," she had said, her blue eyes dancing like those of an excited child. From that moment on, history had become insignificant. He'd studied Connie.

He'd never forgotten her, even though her rejection of him had puzzled and distressed him more than he'd cared to admit. Distressed him? Hell, that didn't begin to describe it. From time to time since, he'd pondered the "what-ifs." What if they'd had more time together? What if he hadn't accepted the reality of her Dear John letter? What if he'd gone to Oklahoma and demanded an explanation? Would his life have taken a different, more fulfilling direction?

"More coffee?"

The attendant's words jolted him upright. "No, I'm fine." *Fine?* Despite a fleeting acknowledgment of the need for caution, he was more eager than ever to get to the Keystone School. Connie? *His* Connie? But she lived in Tulsa. Or had lived there. Did she still have that lush long brown hair, those expressively graceful hands, the intellectual spark that could instantly enliven a discussion?

Searching through his packet of materials, he located an issue of the school magazine, realizing, belatedly and unashamedly as he thumbed through it, that he was searching the photographs for one particular face.

CONNIE DASHED into the gym, aware that Pam Carver expected to begin rehearsal by 7:15 a.m. Traditionally on the Friday of the football game between Keystone and their arch rival, Rangeland Academy, the upper-school faculty put on the pep assembly skit. This day was no exception. Though they made fools of themselves, the students always responded enthusiastically.

At least with this year's circus theme, she was a clown, not the rear end of a mule like last year.

Standing on the bleachers, Pam waved her arms for silence. "Everybody got your parts?" She looked over the group, counting noses. "Where's Ralph?"

One of the men responded. "He's tied up with another headmaster candidate. Some guy from Boston. Ralph said to tell you he knows the drill."

"Let's get started, then. This is our one run-through."

Afterward, walking back to the upper school, Connie, fell in step with Pam. "Our typical lousy rehearsal," she said.

"Which always means a smashing performance!"

"You'll look cute in that ringmaster's getup."

Pam cast her a baleful look. "The things we're willing to do for our students."

"They'll be wired today. Game days are bad enough—" she looked heavenward "—but *Rangeland Academy!*"

"This fella from Boston will probably succumb to massive culture shock. Big-Game Day in football country!" Pam shifted her bulging purse to the other shoulder. "Heard anything about where Ralph stands in the search process?"

"He's applied and been formally interviewed."

"I hope the board doesn't make a hasty decision. The safe 'known' suits me far better than an 'unknown.' Did you meet the candidate from Chicago?"

Connie frowned. "Unfortunately."

"That bad, huh?"

"Arrogance personified."

"Ralph should have a lock on it. I just hope he has the guts to run a tight ship, especially dealing with student discipline and parents with axes to grind."

They paused before crossing the entrance drive, waiting for a break in the steady stream of sports utility vehicles, vans and luxury cars delivering their charges. Pam snorted. "At any school, I can pick out the faculty parking lot at five hundred yards."

Connie poked her teasingly. "Surely you're not referring to our VW bugs, station wagons and vintage compact cars?"

"You know what I like about you, Connie?"

"What?"

"That doesn't even bother you. You're here for the kids. And we both know some at Keystone who are every bit as emotionally deprived as those in the inner city."

"I love them, Pam. If the price I pay is driving a used car with worn upholstery, so be it."

After parting from Pam at the entrance, Connie walked toward her classroom, reflecting on her friend's comment. Emotionally deprived? Oh, yes. Take Stanley Henderson in her sophomore world history class, for example. All the luxuries money could buy, but an absentee father, who spent most of his time in oil-rich Middle East countries, and an alcoholic mother known for making public spectacles of herself. No wonder the boy wore a scared-rabbit expression, had difficulty meeting her eyes and silently endured the occasional taunting of his classmates.

She'd tried to reach him. But even here it was hard to save them all.

"WHAT DO YOU THINK so far? Any questions?" Board president Phil Buxton, an earnest middle-aged investment banker, led Jim on a quick tour of the campus, impressive with its architecturally coordinated southwestern buildings and well-maintained, lush playing fields.

"You say most of the trustees are parents. How do they view their role?"

Buxton put his hands in his pants pockets as they strolled past the tennis courts toward the gym. "In theory or in practice?"

Jim grinned. Phil knew exactly what he was really asking. "Both."

"Theoretically, the board is a policy-making body and charged, of course, with financial oversight and fund-raising. The headmaster handles operations, personnel, curricula and programs."

Jim walked along silently, observing a group of middle schoolers sprawled on the grass with sketchpads, listening to their teacher explain perspective. She was interesting. He wished he could stop to listen.

Phil continued, "But in practice?" He shrugged. "Sometimes individual members ride a hobbyhorse issue or want us to stick our noses in where we don't belong."

Jim laughed, appreciating the board president's candor. "Sounds about par for the course."

"Sometimes the trustees need reminding they're overstepping their bounds. Generally speaking, though, they're a dedicated, hardworking group."

"What would you say is the major challenge facing the school currently?"

Phil held the gym door for him, then followed him into the foyer. Beyond, Jim could hear bouncing balls, the squeal of rubber-soled shoes and frequent whistles. "Bottom line, parents want a safe environment for their kids. They're scared to death of teen addiction problems, gangs, sexually transmitted diseases, and the list goes on. But Keystone has to offer more than safety and academics. We're teaching and molding tomorrow's leaders. We want our students to know the difference between right and wrong and to choose right."

He ushered Jim forward, lowering his voice as they skirted the physical education class. "Lately we've noticed a disturbing trend. Either students claim not to understand why an act is morally questionable or they don't care. Plagiarism, petty theft, lying about absences, disrespectful behavior—they're all on the upswing. We not only want them stopped, we want changed attitudes and values."

"That's a challenge I would welcome."

Phil looked straight at him. "I believe you." He held Jim's eyes, as if taking his measure. Then he pushed open a door leading from the gym to locker rooms and offices. "C'mon, I want you to meet Kurt Mueller, our athletic director and football coach. He was All-Conference at Tech. He's been at Keystone a long time. Takes his job very seriously." Phil knocked on the athletic director's office door.

"Come in."

Jim followed Phil into a darkened cubicle. A large man, with a graying blond crew cut and wearing a colorful short-sleeved madras shirt, khakis and cordovan loafers, sat leaning on his knees in front of a small television set, the remote control an appendage of his hand. He didn't look up. "Be with you in a minute." On the screen, a quarterback handed off to a running back, who plunged through a hole in the opposing line. "Damn," the coach mumbled. "Where the hell was our left tackle?" He reversed the tape and reran the play.

"Problems?" Phil asked.

The coach stood up and flipped on the lights. "Oh, Buxton. Sorry, I thought it was a kid." He turned to Jim, beaming almost too heartily, and stuck out his hand. "You must be Campbell."

Though Jim was two inches taller than Mueller, he sensed from the well-toned muscles and contrived smile that the man could come across as intimidating. "Nice to meet you. I understand you have a good team this year."

"So far so good. This week, though, the little peck-erheads are layin' down on me." He rubbed his palms together. "But I'll get 'em whipped into shape."

"Peckerheads" would not have been Jim's description of choice. "I'd be interested in a quick overview of the athletic program, if you have time."

"My pleasure. Have a seat, gents." Mueller settled back into his office chair, crossed his arms and, warming to his subject, reeled off win-loss records and league championships for any number of sports, dropping statistics and names along the way, obviously expecting Jim to be impressed.

When he paused for breath, Phil interrupted.

"Thanks, Coach. Jim's due at the administration building for another meeting."

Mueller rose to his feet and held open the office door. "Pleasure meeting you, Jimbo."

Jim shook the coach's hand. "This is obviously a very successful program. I noticed you have a sizable budget."

"Can't have quality without the cash. And we work hard on the quality." He gave Jim a punch to the left biceps. "Great school, Keystone. And you know part of why it's such a classy place? Aside, of course, from academics. It's because we've got loyal, generous boosters and alums. The kind of folks who want winners." He laid a hand on Jim's shoulder and smiled like a politician at a barbecue. "And that's what we give 'em, Jimbo. Winners."

Jim held his tongue. He'd never subscribed to the Vince Lombardi theory that winning was the only thing.

As Phil and Jim started down the hall, Mueller leaned out the door of his office. "Hey, Buxton, I'll give ya A&M and nine points tomorrow."

"No way. Thanks anyhow." Jim followed Phil out a side exit. "After this next meeting, we'll come back here for the pep assembly before your interview with the executive committee. Hope we haven't worn you out."

"Not at all. I'm very impressed." He didn't add that this was exactly the kind of school and type of professional challenge he'd been itching for.

"HEY, MRS. WEAVER." Holly Roth, the head cheerleader, bounced up to Connie as they walked to the gym for the pep assembly. "Do you think we should do our pom-pom routine before or after the skit?"

"It doesn't matter, but let the pep club president know."

"My mom has to leave at three and she wouldn't get us on video unless we go first."

"Fine." By all means immortalize the event.

Holly held the door for her. "See you later, Mrs. W."

In the girls' locker room, female faculty members scrambled into a peculiar assortment of makeshift costumes. From the shrieks and giggles, Connie judged they were nearly as keyed up as the football players. Ginny Phillips's Dolly Parton wig dwarfed her body; Pam looked splendid in her black ringmaster's suit; even rotund Jessie Flanders, the math teacher who'd been at Keystone since its founding, had risen to the occasion. In her bedraggled lion costume she looked appropriately ferocious as the mascot of Rangeland Academy. Connie quickly slipped into her baggy clown suit and tennis shoes.

"Over here."

Beckoning to her, Pam waited at the sink with her bag of stage makeup. Connie stood gamely while Pam painted her face white, smeared lipstick from one cheek to the other, put black smiley lines around her eyes and then pulled a red fright wig over her ears. "Perfect!" Connie looked in the mirror. Except for familiar blue eyes, she hardly recognized herself.

Huddled by the locker room door, the costumed cast watched while the pep band warmed the crowd to a fever pitch of clapping and stomping. Then a hush followed as Coach Mueller introduced the players, who stood awkwardly, shifting from foot to foot and tracing patterns with their toes on the gym floor.

With microphone in hand, the animated coach paced in front of the student body. "These boys have worked really hard and they're out for blood tonight. *Blood,* I tell ya. The last time the Rangeland Lions beat us was 1992. They're pussycats—*pussycats!*—and we're gonna stomp all over 'em." A huge roar interrupted his remarks. "But we can't do it without y'all. We need the crowd behind us." Some of the players nodded in agreement. "So whaddaya say?" Cheers filled the gym. *"Louder!"* The decibel level multiplied. "Okay, then, go get 'em, Knights!"

Next came the cheerleaders, and Connie noted that Holly's mother, Gleeanne Roth, was dutifully recording the carefully choreographed pom-pom routine.

Then it was their turn. Pam strode out first, cracking her ringmaster's whip and commanding center stage. An expectant hum rippled through the students. One by one the circus acts appeared: two young male coaches as tumblers; Ralph as the dancing bear; Ginny as a high-wire artist, holding a balancing pole and carefully placing one foot in front of the other, heel to toe, along an imaginary line; and then the clowns. Connie ran onto the basketball court, performed a couple of pratfalls, then collided with two male faculty members dressed as tramps, who picked her up and swung her to and fro between them.

When their act was finished, Connie stood, red-faced and out of breath, on the sidelines with the other performers. The grand finale was the lion tamer, the six-foot-four boys' basketball coach dressed in cardboard armor, easily subduing Jessie Flanders's lion.

Gratified by the student response and relieved her part was over, Connie gazed over the crowd in the bleachers, while the pep club president made her final announcements. Stanley Henderson, looking aloof, huddled in a corner reading a book. Jaime Hernandez sat among the energized senior guys, and a few rows down she spotted Erin sitting beside Kyle Drummond. Her daughter's cheeks were flushed. So far Erin hadn't mentioned Kyle to her and Connie knew better than to pry, but she couldn't help thinking, *Please don't let her get hurt.*

As a conclusion, the cheerleaders pranced out and led the crowd in the Keystone victory cheer. When the last yell died away, the students made a TGIF-beeline for the exits.

Perspiration oozing from under the scratchy red wig had turned Connie's makeup to grease. She couldn't wait to abandon the smelly costume, scrub her face and get home to wash her hair. She started gratefully for the locker room.

"Mrs. Weaver?" Someone put a hand on her shoulder. "Do you have a minute?"

Surprised to see the board president, she stammered. "Well, I...certainly."

"There's someone I want you to meet." He steered her back toward the stands. "One of our headmaster candidates thinks he may know you. Jim Campbell."

She faltered, her knees buckling. Had it not been for Phil Buxton's hand in the small of her back propelling her forward, she would have turned and fled. *Not* the Jim Campbell of her birthday wish. If so, the birthday fairy, though efficient, had a warped sense of humor to set this up when she looked like Ronald McDonald. Finally she dared to raise her eyes and look where she was headed. Her knees nearly failed her again.

There he stood. With the exception of a slightly receding hairline and glasses, he looked just as she remembered him. Maybe even better. Reddish brown hair, square-cut face, wide shoulders, long torso and legs. And oh, dear God, the smile, breaking across his face and accenting the wrinkle lines around his gray-green eyes.

"Connie?"

He peered down at her, as if trying to identify the face behind the makeup. She heard delight in his voice.

Phil Buxton rubbed his palms together. "So you *do* know this lady?"

"*Know* this lady?" Jim picked up Connie's icy hand and held it in his two warm ones, caressing her fingers. Connie, trembling, looked into his twinkling eyes, scarcely aware of the movement and noise swirling around them in the gymnasium. "I'd have known her anywhere!"

CHAPTER THREE

JIM CAMPBELL. Here. At Keystone. With shaking fingers, Connie unlocked her car door, then crumpled behind the wheel, her heart still thudding with surprise and something else—a girlish hopefulness. Her memories, however vivid, had ill-prepared her for Jim in person. His height, his breadth, the warmth of his hands, the humorous glint in his eyes. Swallowing back a rush of excitement, she tried to understand the immediacy and the power of her reaction to him. It was more than being so long without a man. It was Jim himself. This was silly. He had simply shaken her hand, not whisked her off to bed, for Pete's sake. Bed. A delicious sensation pebbled the skin of her forearms.

"Great skit, Mom!" Erin flung her day pack onto the back seat and flopped down beside her.

Connie donned her sunglasses to hide the flush of embarrassment caused by her unseemly fantasy. "What?"

"I said, 'Great skit.'"

Collecting herself, Connie concentrated on backing out of her space in the faculty lot. "Thanks, but I'm getting too old for pratfalls."

"You're not old. Look at Mrs. Flanders."

"Well, when you put it that way..." Connie drove

through the gates and onto the busy street in front of the school. "Lots of homework?"

"Tons. Why do you teachers pile it on over the weekends?"

"Why do you students procrastinate until the last minute?"

"Mom!"

Connie patted her daughter's shoulder. "I know. That was unfair. I'm proud of how you organize your time."

"Anyway, it's not all homework. Mrs. Phillips talked to the seniors today about college. She said applications needed to be mailed early, so I've brought home a bunch of catalogs."

Connie felt an ache that did not derive from clowning. "Honey, I want you to have choices, but we have to be careful about the cost. Even with a scholarship—"

"I know, Mom. Dad wants me to apply to Vanderbilt, and I'd love to go there. With student loans and stuff, maybe we can afford it."

Had Erin really examined tuition figures? "Texas has some fine state schools."

Erin scowled. "And cheaper ones, right? Are you saying I can't go to Vanderbilt?"

"No, but—"

"All right, all right. I'll look in-state, too. Are you happy now?"

Trying not to betray her frustration, Connie turned into their quiet residential neighborhood. "It's not a matter of happy. It's a matter of realities. Of course you can apply to Vanderbilt, but keep other options open. Tomorrow we'll check out those catalogs.''

"Okay." Staring straight ahead, her daughter sat quietly for a few blocks before speaking softly. "Mom?"

"Yes?"

"Kyle Drummond asked me for a date. Tomorrow night.''

Out of the corner of her eye, Connie saw Erin's face redden. She searched for the appropriately neutral tone, one that wouldn't convey her concern about the macho attitude of some of the football players Kyle ran with. "Oh?"

"Is that it? Just 'Oh'? I thought at least you might be pleased for me.''

Connie found her daughter's need for approval pathetically touching. "I'm sorry, honey. I am. It's wonderful!''

Erin relaxed against the seat. When she spoke again, her voice had lost its hard edge. "I'm kind of excited.''

"That's as it should be." Connie turned down the shady cul-de-sac toward her house.

And I'm kind of excited, too. She couldn't let herself think yet about Jim—about the implications of her wild reaction, after all this time, to the simple touch of his hand. Or about her fear that, once again, fate would intervene.

Pulling into the driveway, she forced herself to shift mental gears. Then, shutting off the engine, she retrieved her tote bag and followed Erin into the house.

"Con-nieee, is that you?"

"Yes. And Erin."

Her paisley caftan ballooning behind her, Adele walked into the living room and eased into an over-stuffed brocade chair. Yolanda jumped up and settled in her lap. "At last."

"Mama, are you all right?"

Out of the corner of her eye, Connie saw Erin duck down the hall to her bedroom.

"Just a little short of breath." Adele wheezed for emphasis.

"I'm sorry." Her mother's face was pale. Connie raised her head and sniffed. A spicy aroma emanated from the kitchen. "Did you fix dinner? You must've forgotten tonight's the Rangeland game. Erin and I planned to grab a hotdog there."

"Hotdogs?" Adele made a clucking sound. "Junk food." With gnarled fingers, she massaged her elbow.

"Have you been exercising as the doctor suggested?"

"I'm still your mother, young lady, and you don't need to tell me what to do."

First Erin and now Mama. Could she ever say the right thing? If only she could find a way to improve her mother's outlook. After her father's death, Adele had slipped into a year-long depression. Edgar Vail had been her mother's life. Their partnership, both in marriage and on the dance floor, was symbiotic. They had done everything as a twosome—dancing, bridge, movies, gardening. Now Adele's life revolved around Erin and her. Connie couldn't help missing her lively, energetic mother—all pompadour and chiffon, gracefully following her husband's lead as they swooped and circled across glossy wooden dance floors.

"I'm sorry, Mother." There was the "sorry" again. Why did she always apologize? To keep peace? "I'll set the table. Maybe if we hurry, we'll have time to eat."

Adele nodded uncertainly, suddenly looking very fragile. "Couldn't you stay home tonight? I get so lonely."

Connie didn't doubt it, but it was partly her mother's own doing for resisting all efforts to get involved with others.

"I know you're lonely. Tell you what. We'll spend tomorrow evening together. I'll rent a movie and we'll pop some corn and—"

"But what about tonight?" Adele wore her Bette Davis injured-soul look.

Her stomach cramping, Connie hesitated, torn by conflicting loyalties. "I guess the Keystone Knights can win without me."

AFTER DINNER, Connie dashed to the video store, settled Adele in front of the TV with Audrey Hepburn and Fred Astaire and at last hopped in the shower to wash her hair.

Later, stretched out on the sofa in her robe, toweling her hair dry, she observed her mother, watching the intricate footwork of the celluloid dancers. Since being widowed, Adele had simply given up, narrowing her interests and, at times, affecting martyrdom. Like tonight. *And emotional blackmail works because here I am—home, not at the game.* "Get a life." That's what her students would say. What kind of life could she get? Helping her mother and being a mother—that *was* her life.

Adele set aside her popcorn, then daintily wiped her fingers on a paper napkin. Connie sighed. Why couldn't her mother try? Her remaining years had much to offer. She and Erin shouldn't be the focus of her universe.

During the final scenes of *Funny Face* Adele's chin fell to her chest, then with a snort she reared back and stared blankly as the credits rolled across the screen. "Want to see another one, Mama?"

"No, I'm going to turn in." Adele heaved herself up and started slowly toward her bedroom, trailed by Yolanda. "See you in the morning."

"Good night."

Connie glanced at her watch. Only nine-fifteen. She stretched, then removed *Funny Face* from the VCR. Picking up the other movie she'd rented, she stared at it, considering. *Brief Encounter*. In the store she'd hesitated, knowing full well she was selecting it for its tear-jerking romance. As if the act of admitting her intentions absolved her, she shoved the tape into the slot and pressed Play. Turning the table lamp to its lowest setting, she lost herself in the black-and-white images of Trevor Howard and Celia Johnson, whose characters' unfulfilled longing left her breathless.

The bittersweet ending, as usual, reduced her to sobs. Pulling a tissue from her pocket, she blew her nose, unabashedly reveling in her cathartic sniveling. What had become of men like that? Men who listened. Men who craved in a woman, not just a partner, but a soul mate. *Soul mate.* That was how she'd felt about Jim that long-ago summer; it was why she couldn't fall in love with Ralph. That elusive quality of…boundless connection. Was she a fool to wait for it? To hope she could feel that way about someone again?

She sat clutching the damp tissue, legs tucked under her, tears still dampening her cheeks. Seeing Jim today had revived a part of herself she thought had withered away. She couldn't stall any longer. It was time to examine that summer, to revisit her feelings about Jim.

The decision made, she retrieved a cardboard box from behind the stack of sweaters on her bedroom closet shelf, brought it into the living room, turned up the lamp and slowly removed the lid. On top was an eight-by-ten photograph of the workshop participants, taken on the Capitol steps. She was in the second row, squinting into the sun. Jim stood behind her, his mouth cocked in an amused smile, his hands on her shoulders. She remembered being aware at the time of the natural affection of that gesture.

When she'd been chosen for the selective program, her excitement had been tempered by the thought of leaving nine-year-old Erin in Colin's care for four weeks. Despite her strained relations with him following their divorce, Colin doted on his daughter and she on him. There had been no reason not to accept the fellowship.

The course work had been grueling, but Washington was exhilarating. For four glorious weeks, she'd had no responsibilities except ones she'd chosen and no people more important than her colleagues. Most stimulating were the casual conversations, and sometimes wicked debates, she and the others engaged in over wine or beer in an intimate Georgetown pub. From recent Supreme Court decisions to Ulysses S. Grant's military strategy, anything was fair game.

From the beginning, Jim, genuinely likable, exuded quiet confidence. Others gradually began to defer to him, to ask his opinions, about which he was passionate. That was when she learned he shared both her lifelong interest in the Civil War and her conviction that history, taught correctly, could inspire students. Had she and Jim really been that young and idealistic?

From the box in her lap, Connie pulled the tattered program from a concert the group had attended at Wolf Trap. As memory took over, she drew in a quick breath. From the moment he'd asked to sit beside her on the bus, Jim had not left her side the entire evening. As they'd sat shoulder to shoulder under the canopy of stars, waves of symphony music breaking over them, she'd become aware of a thickness in her throat caused by the heady proximity of this deep-thinking, sensitive man.

One moment she'd been Connie Weaver, history teacher and adult; the next she'd blushed with sudden, incongruous thoughts and emotions. When the orchestra string section played a quivering vibrato, she'd barely refrained from touching his arm, draped comfortably on the armrest between them. Just when she'd thought she could stand it no longer, he looked down at her, winked affectionately and casually picked up her hand and cradled it between his. Her response had been immediate and embarrassingly sexual.

As long as she lived, that first time he had touched her would remain a magic moment. And the other times? The more intimate times?

She squirmed against the powerful need that crested within her. Dredging up these memories was maudlin self-indulgence. This afternoon had felt surreal, not only because she was dressed in that ridiculous clown outfit but because she'd convinced herself years ago that Jim Campbell was safely consigned to this keepsake box. Convinced herself that she had done the right thing in writing to him that long-ago autumn to end their relationship.

But the man who'd held her hand today was flesh and blood, not a faded, sentimental photograph.

She hugged the box, gazing into space. What if he were offered the position at Keystone? Could she walk the awkward line between professionalism and desire? Because she was drawn to him as strongly as ever. She shook her head, exasperated with herself. Nothing about this afternoon suggested more than a casual meeting between old friends—nothing except that spontaneous, warm smile conveying the hint of shared intimacy. Or was that wishful thinking?

She heard a car drive up outside, then the excited voices of teenagers. Erin. She quickly replaced the lid, hurried to her bedroom and stowed the box in its— She paused. She'd been about to say "hiding place." *Why?*

The front door opened quietly, followed by the click of the dead bolt. "Mom?" Erin stood in the bedroom door. "Guess what? We won in overtime. We're still undefeated!"

"Wow, I'm sorry I missed it."

"Me, too. Kyle played great. Even Coach Mueller complimented him." Her face glowed. "How was your date with Gramma?"

"She fell asleep before the end of *Funny Face*, but I watched both movies."

"Any good?"

"Entertaining."

"Well, g'night, Mom. Don't forget about tomorrow. The college catalogs."

"I won't. Good night, honey."

Boom! Catalogs—real-world stuff. Then another "real-world" thought hit her. Ralph so wanted to be the interim head. Yet, leaving her heart out of it and assessing the situation objectively, she knew Jim was the better candidate. If the board thought so, too...? Poor Ralph.

THE FOLLOWING TUESDAY evening, Jim threw down the latest *Smithsonian Magazine* and looked around his sparsely furnished apartment. After the divorce, he'd stored most of his personal belongings in anticipation of moving within the year. Or, now, maybe sooner. He stood, then paced to the window, where he stared out at the city, oblivious to the traffic noises blaring in the street below.

Over the weekend, he'd tried to rein in his enthusiasm for the Keystone School. He'd asked himself if he was too eager to bail out of Campbell Courts. But that wasn't it. He'd really liked the people and the place—to the point that he'd asked Phil Buxton about a contract option, in the event he was hired, permitting him to apply for the position permanently. Good things were happening there, though he wasn't fool enough to think any school was without problems.

Admittedly, an interim position was a calculated risk. On the one hand, it would give him leadership experience and an opportunity to assess his satisfaction. On the other hand, if he had to move on, he'd need a favorable recommendation from Keystone. If he screwed up...? Well, he'd make darn sure he didn't.

He turned, eyeing the telephone. When Phil had driven Jim to the airport, he'd told him the trustees would be making their decision within the week.

Jim sank into the leather armchair and tried again to read. Useless! The magazine fell to his lap. He really wanted this position. And, he admitted, he really wanted to see Connie Weaver again.

He *would* have known her anywhere, no matter what costume she'd worn. Her soft blue eyes sparkled with surprise and the same openness and intelligence he remembered. And her slender hands fit in his like a homecoming. That single moment in the gym had stayed in his mind, out of all proportion to the brevity of their encounter.

He laced his hands behind his head and leaned back. He'd never really forgotten her. Never overcome the nagging suspicion that his life could have been different. Better. Maybe if they hadn't gone to Gettysburg...but they had.

That balmy summer day, they'd rented a car, just the two of them, and driven into Pennsylvania to visit the famous Civil War battlefield. He could almost smell the grass-sweet scent of her hair, hear the haunting strains of "Golden Slumbers" from the Beatles' album playing in the tape deck, feel her hand tighten in his as they stood on Cemetery Ridge, aware of the profoundly haunting stillness of the fields where so many had died. Wordlessly, they'd shared those horrific days with scores of Blue and Gray ghosts.

And never, not with Sondra or anyone else, had he been so aroused or so fulfilled as that night, in the old inn, when Connie, her naked body melting beneath his, her eyes wide with wonder, yielded to him. He'd known, as surely as he'd ever known anything, that he loved her.

His words came back. "It doesn't seem fair. To find you, feel this way about you. And then to have only a few more days together."

"I know," she'd whispered, her breath warm against his chest.

He'd pulled her closer, tucking the light blanket around them. "It doesn't have to end here. Somehow we can work things out. Can't you just picture the two of us in a big old house overflowing with babies? Lots of them."

She'd acted skittish, he remembered. "Jim, don't. You've given me so much, but..." The "but" had had to do with her ex-husband's infidelities, her reservations about men in general and commitment in particular.

"I can understand why you'd be gun-shy. But, Connie, I'm not Colin. You can trust me."

"Jim, it's not that simple. These four weeks have been...I don't know...a lovely, unforgettable interlude. But not real life.'' He recalled her fingers, smoothing away the protest that rose to his lips. ''Let's not force it. Please. Not now.''

The summer had ended, but he hadn't given up. How could he when he'd met his other half? He'd written several letters. Had even scheduled a weekend trip to Tulsa. But then, out of the blue, had come Connie's letter. The letter that had left no doubt.

Was it masochistic to have unearthed it and reread it? But that's what he'd done upon his return from Fort Worth. He pulled the thin sheet of notepaper from his billfold, unfolded it and studied the faded blue lines:

Dear Jim,

Writing this letter is extremely difficult, but I'm convinced it is the right thing to do—for both of us. My month in Washington was an experience I will never forget, for many reasons, the most important of which is our friendship, which came at a time in my life when I most needed it. You helped restore that part of my womanhood that Colin had done his best to destroy. The affection and affirmation you offered me are gifts I will always treasure. I just hope, in my needfulness, that I didn't appear to use you. For that was never my intention!

Although I appreciate your warm, thoughtful letters and the suggestion that we might somehow continue from where we left off this summer, I believe the difficulties of a long-distance relationship, particularly with my personal responsibilities and your demanding job, present insurmountable obstacles.

I will always remember those four weeks as a golden time, and I will forever be grateful to you for helping me begin to heal. Let's leave our relationship at that. Please understand and honor my wishes.

                                        Fondly,
                                        Connie

He recalled mulling over the letter for days. Had he misjudged her feelings for him? Scared her off? Her tone, full of rationalizations, sounded forced, hollow. It was as if she were trying to talk herself out of happiness. As if she were willing to settle for…what?

But the "Fondly" had said it all. Finally, he had written her back, reluctantly acceding to her wishes. What choice had he had? And, upon reflection, perhaps she was right about the difficulties of a long-distance relationship. He'd left the door open, reaffirming his feelings for her, asking her to keep in touch from time to time. He'd never heard from her again.

He laid the letter on the table beside his chair. Eight years ago. A different lifetime. And as the months passed, ultimately he'd convinced himself. It *had* been an unforgettable interlude, not real life.

But now he'd seen her again. And longing had dealt him an unexpected blow straight to the solar plexus.

He removed his glasses, rubbed the bridge of his nose between his thumb and index finger and tried to control his runaway thoughts. What would he do about Connie if he *did* get the Keystone job? Forget the past? She'd obviously gotten on with her life. And he would have their professional roles to consider. But... He caught himself remembering the relief he'd felt when Buxton had confirmed her single status.

Yawning, he checked his watch. Ten-thirty. Nine-thirty Dallas time. This waiting was hell. But he might still hear. He thumbed through the magazine, the words blurring.

Concentrating at last on an interesting article, he was startled when, at eleven o'clock, the phone rang.

CONNIE SAT at the dining-room table that same evening, staring helplessly at income tax returns and other financial papers. Erin had brought home the financial aid form, which had to be completed before she would be eligible for college scholarships or financial assistance. The complexity of the form defied reason.

Worse yet, Colin had to be involved. He had verbally agreed to participate financially if Erin attended Vanderbilt, where he taught. With her academic record and strong test scores, she would probably qualify for some aid. But "some aid," even with Colin's help, and a full ride were miles apart.

Scooping up the papers in frustration and stuffing them into a folder marked "College," Connie rose, hunching her shoulders and bending her head from side to side to relieve tension. She flipped off the dining-room lights and headed toward her bedroom. A soft knock on the front door stopped her. She checked the wall clock. Ten-forty! Who in the world? One of Erin's friends?

When she pressed her eye to the peephole, she was

surprised to see Ralph Hagood. Quickly she unlocked the door and stood aside. "Come in."

He stepped across the threshold, took off his windbreaker and carefully laid it on the back of the nearest chair. "Sorry to bother you so late. I need to talk, Connie, and I know what I say to you will go no further."

Distress was written all over him, from his furrowed brow to the slump of his shoulders. "Sit down, Ralph. Would a cup of coffee help?"

He waved dismissively and collapsed into an overstuffed armchair. "Don't go to the trouble. I won't stay long."

Connie curled up on one end of the flowered sofa. Yolanda hopped into her lap and began purring contentedly. "Is something wrong at school?"

Ralph nervously flexed his fingers, then turned to Connie. "Not exactly." He bit his upper lip. "Connie, I...I didn't get the job."

"Oh, Ralph, I'm sorry. You must be so disappointed."

"I wouldn't say this to anyone else, but I really thought I had a good shot at it. I mean, I've been at Keystone for twenty years."

As the knowledge sank in, Connie felt her throat constrict. She deliberately unclenched her fists before speaking. "Then...who?"

"The fellow from Boston. Campbell. He's coming next week." Obviously trying to pull himself together, he continued. "It'll be up to me to introduce him around, orient him. Of course I'll do my best to support the man, but..."

"You've always been loyal to the school."

"I try. But this is hard."

She didn't know what to say to ease Ralph's disappointment at being passed over. Especially since she felt wild elation warring with sympathy for him.

Her fingers moved absently through Yolanda's sleek fur. In a matter of days, Jim would be at Keystone!

With effort, she stifled her excitement. Right now, Ralph was here, and in definite need of a friend.

CHAPTER FOUR

DURING HER LAST-HOUR planning period, Connie re-read the notice, her chest tightening: "Faculty members are reminded of the reception in the cafeteria after school Wednesday, October 15, to greet Dr. James L. Campbell on his first day with us. Light refreshments will follow a short program."

Today. She needed to carry off the event with dignity and...detachment. No way could she concentrate on the essays in front of her, not when her mind kept wandering to the handsome, encouraging face of Jim Campbell, who, she had learned from the bio distributed to the faculty, was still single.

With that one word, foolishly her spirits had soared. But Jim could be an entirely different person, her memories merely distortions of an idealized summer romance, where two people come together under unique circumstances. Or he might have resented the way she'd terminated their relationship. And yet...

Restless, she rose, walked to the windows, then stared vacantly at the colorfully dressed boys and girls clambering on the lower-school playground equipment. Oh, to be that carefree!

But right now she felt burdened with cares—for her mother, Erin, her students. Ever since her father's death only weeks after she'd returned from the Georgetown program, she'd had to put others first.

That fall of 1989 had been a nightmare—her father's fatal stroke, her own numbing grief, complex legalities and her mother's emotional collapse. As an only child, she'd had little choice. Resigning from her public-school job, she and Erin had moved from Tulsa to Fort Worth to care for Adele. When a position at Keystone had opened at the start of the next semester, she'd jumped at the offer.

And amid all the turmoil had been her agonizing deliberations about Jim. Jim, who had actually restored her faith that not only might some man one day want her, but that, after Colin's unspeakable betrayal, she might once again be capable of giving herself over to another human being. How tempting it had been to nurture the deep feelings Jim had ignited within her. But she'd resisted—somehow. Their relationship had been a fleeting summer romance. Could never be more.

Not when she was incapable of giving him the one thing he most wanted.

So she had reached her decision. Playing it safe, she had sent the letter. But she had never forgotten him…or the way he made her feel.

Sighing, Connie returned to her desk, gathered up the essays and slipped them into a folder. Enough already. She needed to marshal her emotions prior to the reception. Might-have-beens were useless and melodramatic. Reality awaited her in the cafeteria.

Detained briefly by Jaime Hernandez, who wanted to discuss the design for the Frankenbergs' wall hanging, Connie barely made it to the meeting in time. Wrinkling her nose at the lingering odor of macaroni and cheese, she slipped into a back-row seat next to Pam Carver just as Phil Buxton began his introduction. *Dr. Campbell.* The title sounded so…distancing. She watched Jim stride toward the microphone to the accompaniment of polite applause from the still shell-shocked teachers.

Gripping the sides of the podium, he nodded in acknowledgment of the welcome. Connie crossed her legs, then stared down at her clenched hands, waiting for the sound of Jim's deep, familiar voice.

"Thank you for coming. After a long relationship with Lee Frankenberg, it can't be easy for you to greet a replacement, especially someone you don't know."

Connie glanced at Ralph, who was sitting impassively, fiddling with a ballpoint pen. She noticed several others eyeing him circumspectly, as well. The decision to hire an outsider had received outspoken criticism in the teachers' lounge. Even Jim's impressive résumé, complete with glowing recommendations, hadn't swayed those who'd openly preferred Ralph.

After a few moments, she permitted herself a second look at Jim. He stood tall, comfortably gesturing and making eye contact with his audience. Her stomach flip-flopped. Why did an immaculately groomed man in a business suit project such…presence? Confidence? Sexuality?

The rims of his glasses glinted in the lights, and then his eyes found hers. She stopped breathing. When he turned away, she released a pent-up sigh and tried to concentrate on his words.

"...I don't expect to make many changes. My door will always be open, and I'll welcome all the help I can get." He chuckled self-deprecatingly before continuing.

"I hope to provide strong leadership, commitment to students and adherence to Keystone's philosophies. I pledge you my wholehearted support.

"But—" his voice dropped and he embraced the room with his eyes "—I can't do any of that without your backing. So my first priority is getting acquainted. To that end, I'll be sitting in on classes, holding one-on-one conversations with each of you and plunging into campus life.

"Caring, Character, Curiosity. Those are worthy goals not only for our students but for all of us. Goals I take as personal challenges. Thank you."

Applause, more enthusiastic this time, echoed through the room. As Jim stepped away from the podium to shake hands with the teachers clustered around him, the others gravitated toward the food table, decorated with pots of gold chrysanthemums tied with crimson bows.

Pam nudged her in the ribs. "What did you think?"

"About what I expected." They queued up in the refreshment line. "He said all the right things."

"Who's talking about what he *said?* What about the way he *looks?* Peter Jennings, step aside! I loved Dr. Frank, but you have to admit Dr. Campbell's easier on the eyes."

"Do I take that as a thumbs-up?" Connie couldn't

help grinning. Intelligent and earthy, the top-notch English teacher, thirty-five and on the prowl, never minced words about men. Connie found Pam's reaction to Jim both reassuring and disturbing.

"Most definitely, but lest you take me only as a shallow, man-hunting female, I did like what he had to say, too. Just the right mix of deference, loftiness, approachability and pep talk. I think people will give him a chance."

"After they move beyond feeling sorry for Ralph."

"How long that lasts depends on Ralph."

They both glanced at the upper-school principal, who stood awkwardly balancing his food while Jessie Flanders, with fluttery hands and mother-hen mannerisms, chattered away.

Connie picked up a cup of watery fruit punch. "Then I'm not worried. Ralph's a team player." Placing a jelly-filled doughnut on a napkin, Connie searched for a place to sit.

"Over there." Pam gestured.

Suddenly ravenous, Connie bit into the confection as she trailed after Pam. Just before they reached two vacant chairs, Connie felt a tap on her shoulder. She whirled around to stare straight up at Jim. She cringed. First the clown, now the lady with the powdered-sugar mouth. Pam hovered at her elbow. Jim spoke first.

"It's nice to see you again, Connie."

Pam, edging closer, shot her a we'll-talk-about-this-later look. *"Again?"*

Jim smiled. "Connie and I go back several years. But most recently, when I was here interviewing, I saw her in the pep skit." He studied Pam. "And if I'm not mistaken, you were the ringmaster."

"You have an embarrassingly good eye." Pam extended her hand. "I'm Pam Carver—"

"English department, right?"

"Give the man an A," Pam quipped.

Jim shook her hand. "I'll be interested in visiting with you soon. Now, though, if you'll excuse me, I need to say hello to the coaches before they leave for practice. Nice talking to you." He smiled again before sauntering off.

"Connie Weaver, you've been holding out on me. You 'go back several years' with that hunk?" Pam made a hurry-up gesture with her fingers. "C'mon, give."

Connie couldn't believe it—she was blushing! To calm her trembling nerves, she lifted the punch cup to her lips before trusting herself to speak. "It was 1989. We both participated in a summer program in D.C."

"You could have told us you knew him."

Yes, I could have. Why didn't I? "It was a long time ago."

"Long time or not, how could you keep quiet about somebody like him?"

"It didn't seem like a big deal. Besides, I don't want people thinking that relationship entitles me to any special consideration."

Quirking her mouth, Pam gave Connie a knowing look. "He can give *me* all the 'special consideration' he wants." She wadded up her napkin and stuffed it into her paper cup. "I have errands to run. Better scoot."

"See you tomorrow," Connie called after her. *Special consideration?* Her worst fears—or her highest hopes—had been confirmed. Jim was exactly, excitingly, as she remembered him. Special consideration was the least of what she craved from the new headmaster. And, for sound professional reasons, the last thing she was likely to get.

WHEN JIM LEFT the cafeteria at five-thirty, he paused on the sidewalk to survey the campus. Only a few cars remained in the faculty lot. On the football field, young men in grass-stained practice uniforms executed plays. Long shadows dappled the well-tended grounds. Instinctively, he knew he needed to savor this moment.

Today had been frantically busy but exhilarating—meeting the people who were the heart and soul of the school, acquainting himself with the most pressing matters on his desk and feeling his way through the obstacle course of faculty expectations. He felt rather like a sprinter coiled in the blocks the second before the starter's gun fires.

The clanking of metal on metal interrupted his reverie. Turning, he saw Ralph Hagood lowering the flag in front of the upper school. On short acquaintance, the upper-school principal seemed like a good man. Seizing the opportunity to sound him out, Jim started across the lawn. "Need some help?"

Startled, Hagood looked up. "Thanks." He handed Jim one end of the emblem to fold.

"You on your way home?" Jim gave his section of the flag to Ralph. "I don't want to keep you, but if you have a minute—"

"Sure. C'mon back to my office. The coffeepot's still on."

Inside, Jim settled into a wingback chair, hoping the principal would feel more comfortable on his own turf. Ralph poured two mugs of coffee, offered one to Jim, then sat down behind his desk.

Leaning forward, Jim rotated the mug slowly between his fingers, then looked Ralph in the eye. "Let me come straight to the point. I'm aware you applied for this interim job. It must've been a helluva shock when they brought me in." Ralph blinked but held Jim's gaze. "You've served this school capably for a long time. I can't answer why me and not you. But I can acknowledge your disappointment and the awkwardness that might arise between us if we let it. That's why I'm here now. To get off on the right foot in our working relationship."

Ralph shrugged. "No point mincing words. I *was* upset. I thought I'd demonstrated both my ability and loyalty. A headship has always been my goal. I'd have liked it to be here." Ralph paused, as if considering his next words. "But that has nothing to do with you. I'd be a damn fool to resent you personally."

Settling back, Jim took a sip of the strong, bitter coffee. "I appreciate your candor."

Ralph ran a forefinger around the rim of his cup. "Hell, it's in my best interests to help you any way I can. Good for you, for me and for the school." He reached in a file drawer and pulled out a student handbook. "Let's start with student discipline procedures."

Two hours later, Jim left the upper school, pleased with the conversation. Stopping by the administration building, he stuffed his briefcase with reading materials. There was so much to learn, and because of Lee Frankenberg's abrupt departure, no time for a gradual transition. He'd be up well past midnight.

Driving through the dark campus, he was surprised to see lights still burning on the football field. He turned off the main road and pulled into the parking lot between the gym and the stadium. Several boys, still in pads, their socks drooping over their shoes, were jogging wearily around the track. *Running laps?* Jim checked the clock on the dash—7:50. *What the hell?* Surely there were policies about the length of practices. These kids still had to shower, eat dinner and study. Maybe tonight was an exceptional circumstance. But they should've been home long before now. Jim made a mental note to check the situation with Kurt Mueller the next day.

Easing the car back onto the main drive, he headed for the town house he'd rented near the school. Hunger gnawed at his stomach. The one glazed doughnut at four-thirty hadn't been enough. *Doughnut.* He grinned in the dark. He wondered if Connie had any idea how transparent her reactions had been when he'd touched her and she'd wheeled around with sugar on her lips.

Sugar on her lips. He felt a familiar but unexpected stiffening in his groin. What business did the distinguished headmaster of the prestigious Keystone School have imagining those soft, sweet, remembered lips brushing his own?

"MOM!" Erin's voice rose in a wail. "What am I gonna *do?* Why is Dad being like this?"

Connie briefly shut her eyes, laid aside the textbook she'd been reading, then patted the place on the sofa next to her. The busy day, the awkward reception, a frantic dash to the pharmacy to pick up her mother's medication and now Colin, whose timing, as usual, was unerringly diabolical. "Like what, honey?"

Erin's eyes filled with tears as she sat down, crossed her legs and hugged a sofa pillow against her chest. Connie prayed for patience. "I take it that was your father on the phone?"

"Yeah. Calling to give me the third degree. Am I still getting As? When will I know my SAT scores? Have I finished my Vanderbilt application?" She punched the pillow. "Why can't he ever just say 'How are you?'"

Connie bit her lip. Her former husband saw life as a reflection of himself. An imperfect daughter would never do, not for Colin Weaver, Ph.D., whose scholarly publications earned international acclaim. But, darn it, as daughters went, he couldn't ask for better than Erin. "What specifically upset you tonight?"

Erin punched the pillow. "If I go to Vanderbilt, he wants me to live with him...."

Connie released the breath she'd been holding. "I see." Control. That had always been Colin's game.

"Mom, I don't want to live with Dad. I might as well stay home. I mean, he's okay, but it's not like being in the dorm, having freedom."

"What did you tell him?"

"I didn't know what to say. He *is* my father. But he's forcing me to do something I don't want to do."

"*Forcing* you?"

"Yes. He said he'd help with my tuition, but only if I lived with him to save on room and board."

Connie's fingernails bit into the flesh of her palms. "Are you saying he's not going to contribute to your college expenses unless you go to Vanderbilt?"

Erin lowered her head. "That's what it sounded like."

A suffocating rage engulfed Connie. He'd promised. And dumb her, she'd believed him when he'd said he'd help with Erin's college expenses. He'd help, all right. In *his* way, on *his* terms. It was so—she fumed, searching for an appropriately damning epithet—so Colin! She could almost hear his voice oozing the kind of patronizing and irrefutable arguments against which she'd always felt impotent. Not until she'd discovered, seven years into their marriage, that she wasn't the only gullible coed upon whom he'd worked his charm had she gathered the courage to take Erin and leave him. Never mind that he'd left her emotionally devastated, questioning her femininity and sexuality!

Connie tipped Erin's chin up, noting the trembling of her pale lips. "Listen to me, honey. Nobody—not your father, not Gramma, not me—can make this choice for you. When we studied the catalogs, you found other schools you liked. You have time. You needn't rule out Vanderbilt, but you don't have to rush a decision."

"What'll I tell Dad?"

From the vulnerability in her daughter's eyes, Connie knew Erin didn't belong trapped in the middle. "Leave that to me."

"But, Mom, you know how Dad can be."

"Stop. Your father is a man of definite opinions. But he *does* love you."

"Right now that love feels more like blackmail."

Connie reached over and gently swiped Erin's bangs aside. *This is going from bad to worse. And the heck of it is, Erin's only saying what I'm thinking.* "Leave your father to me."

The pillow slid to the floor as Erin gave Connie a quick hug. "Sometimes I don't think I want to grow up."

Me, either. "I'm afraid there's not much we can do about that." Connie tried a small grin, although inside she was seething at Colin.

When the phone shrilled beside them, Connie jumped.

"I'll get it in the bedroom, Mom." Erin dashed down the hall.

It was probably Kyle Drummond, whose senior photograph had recently appeared on Erin's dresser. At least he'd make Erin feel better. Connie had no such relief. She struggled to her feet and headed for the desk in her bedroom. She couldn't face phoning Colin; he had a clever way of twisting words to his advantage. No, she'd write him. Lay out Erin's concerns—and her own—logically and forcefully. She should have taken Colin back to court to have college expenses negotiated into the child support. But lawyers cost money, and Colin had assured her he'd help.

Hot tears suddenly prickled her eyelids. She sagged into the desk chair, picked up a tissue and blew her nose. The day's demands assaulted her: "You could have told us you knew Dr. Campbell." "Con-nieee, I forgot to renew my prescription.'' ''Why is Dad being like this?'' She rubbed the muscles coiled at the base of her neck, bowed down by the weight of all the hats she was trying to wear—and judging by tonight, not very successfully.

She pulled out her bond stationery, picked up a pen and studied the blank page. Finally, after wiping her eyes with the back of her hand, she began: ''Dear Colin, Although you undoubtedly believe you are looking out for Erin's best interests, she and I are both uncomfortable with your suggestion that she live with you her freshman year....''

THE NEXT MORNING after a brief appearance at the fourth-grade musical program and a budget session with the business manager, Jim headed toward the athletic director's office to follow up on the late football practice.

He found Kurt Mueller, feet propped on a desk stacked with requisitions and invoices, studying a play book.

''Hope I'm not interrupting anything.''

Dropping his feet to the floor, Mueller swiveled around. ''Just figuring what we can run against Holton Hall inside the ten-yard line.'' He set the play book aside. ''Have a seat.''

''Holton a tough opponent?''

''If we beat 'em, we've got a chance for our third consecutive undefeated season. But their interior line outweighs us by a Texas mile. Our kids are gonna have to suck it up.''

"Phil Buxton said you have a heck of a quarterback."

"Yep, Tommy Ben Watson. Kid has a good chance of bein' recruited for Division I ball." Mueller folded his hands behind his head and eyed Jim assessingly. "Is this a social visit?"

Clearly, small talk wasn't the coach's forte. "I'm playing catch-up trying to familiarize myself with things around here. Do you have a handbook of athletic department policies?"

Mueller's eyes narrowed slightly. "Lemme see." He pulled open a desk drawer and rummaged through some dog-eared files, then finally extracted a faded blue booklet. "Help yourself."

"Thanks. And good luck with Holton Hall."

"We'll need it."

Jim stood and then, as if it were an afterthought, posed the question. "I noticed some of the players still on the field after seven-thirty last night. Late practice?"

Scowling, the coach leaned back in his chair. "Right before this big game, if you can believe it, a few fellas were doggin' it. Had to get their attention, so to speak."

"What about their studies? Those kids couldn't have gotten started on homework until after nine."

Mueller rose to his feet, folded his arms across his chest and leaned companionably against the edge of his desk. "Look, I see to it they're gettin' by in the classroom. Absolutely. That's important. But during football season, winning's what counts around here. Ask anybody."

Jim held the coach's stare. "I have some trouble with that point of view. I enjoy football as much as the next man, but the athletic department needs to meet the faculty halfway in encouraging academics."

The coach moved forward and opened the door to usher Jim out. "Which we do, which we do. But lemme tell you a fact of life. You're in Texas now, son. And for our parents and alums, that means capital friggin' 'F' football. Catch my drift?"

Jim stared into flinty eyes. "I read you." He waved the blue pamphlet. "And I'll read this. So long as you're running a clean program in harmony with the school philosophy and league rules, I'll be your biggest supporter."

"I'll count on that, Jimbo."

Jim started out the door, then paused and turned back to face the coach. "One other thing. I'd prefer you call me 'Jim' or 'Dr. Campbell.'"

Mueller aimed his index finger pistol-style at Jim's chest. "Gotcha, *Jim*."

When he reached his office, Jim shrugged out of his coat and rolled up the starched cuffs of his dress shirt before scanning the handbook. There was the clause: "During the regular season, practices shall be confined to two hours' duration and shall be completed at or before six-thirty p.m." What was going on? Those kids had been on the field more than an hour after the prescribed deadline.

He drummed his fingers on the desk. Kurt Mueller was obviously a force to be reckoned with.

CHAPTER FIVE

HURRYING DOWN THE HALL toward the teachers' lounge the following Wednesday noon, Connie figured this was just one of "those" days. First, her hair dryer had gone on the fritz; next, just as she and Erin were leaving home, Adele had sent them on a frantic search for her misplaced glasses; and just now she'd spilled copy machine toner down the front of her frumpy plaid flannel dress.

"Hey, Mrs. W., wanna buy a spirit ribbon?"

Smiling hopefully, Tara Farley blocked her way. Connie never turned down the pep club girls who sold the ribbons as a fund-raiser, but right now she was tempted.

"Oh, sure." She dug in her purse for two quarters.

"Thanks. Homecoming week's so exciting!" Tara headed down the hall in search of her next customer.

Exciting, all right. Taking the straight pin and attaching the gaudy streamer to her shoulder, Connie registered the irony of the crimson script overlaying the gold ribbon: "Stay cool, Knights!" Terrific!

Later, in the lounge, Connie sat quietly at the work table, munching on a carrot stick while she recorded grades. She preferred eating elsewhere—the smell of stale coffee and the sight of crusty day-old cinnamon rolls were unfailingly accompanied by unappetizing servings of gossip. Today, however, she'd had no option; her classroom was being used for a lunchtime meeting.

Making a dramatic entrance, Pam Carver burst into the room. "Of all times!" She flopped onto the sofa, spread her arms and threw her head back. "Not when the juniors were having a mature discussion of symbolism in *The Scarlet Letter* or even when the seniors were tolerating T. S. Eliot. Oh, no! He had to come while the sophomores were whining about grammar."

"The head?" asked the geometry teacher.

"Who else?"

Jessie Flanders daintily laid aside her plastic container of beef stew and, preening like a peahen, offered her opinion. "Pamela, Dr. Campbell is just trying to learn about the school. I'm sure he didn't expect your students to behave perfectly."

The unspoken "as mine did" was louder than if she'd actually uttered the words. Connie snapped a rubber band around the test papers, closed her grade book and made her way toward the door.

"Hey, Connie." Pam looked right at her. "Peter Jennings caught your act yet?"

"No." She sidled around the refrigerator.

"He will." Then Pam had the audacity to wiggle her eyebrows suggestively. "He will."

That's exactly what I'm afraid of. She stepped into the hall and ambled toward her classroom. Maybe the meeting had ended. It was bad enough keeping up, around the faculty, the pretense that Jim was nobody special, but Connie couldn't imagine how she'd survive the scrutiny of her hawk-eyed students.

Well, she'd better start imagining. Because there, leaning against the wall outside her door, studying the contents of a file folder, was the headmaster. Another triumph for Murphy's Law! She'd be lucky if Jim didn't mistake her for Forrest Gump's mother.

Slowing, she observed how relaxed and confident he appeared, even in repose. As she approached him, he looked over the top of the folder, smiled warmly and stood erect.

"Connie."

She liked the way he made something soft and melodic of her name.

"Mind if I visit your sixth period?"

Mind? Offhand, she couldn't imagine a worse fate. After lunch, her juniors—thirteen boys and four girls—were on sugar highs and required all her management skills. She grinned wryly. "Do I have a choice?"

He sobered. "Sure. Is this a bad time?"

Any time is a bad time. "Only if you're not prepared for an *active* group. Just so you're forewarned, they call themselves the 'six pack.'"

He followed her into the vacant classroom. "Sounds like fun."

"All that and the Constitutional Convention, too."

"Great! How can we miss?"

Let me count the ways.

FOLDING HIS LEGS under one of the larger student desks, Jim watched the voluble students, exchanging postlunch banter, surge into the room. Their reactions—from "Shh, there's the new head" to "You're in for it now, Mrs. W."—amused him, while at the same time he remained aware of the pressure his presence put upon any teacher. From the affectionate, boisterously respectful greetings the students gave Connie, he guessed she was every bit as effective in the classroom as he'd always assumed.

Spots of color high on her cheeks and the way she avoided his eyes betrayed her nervousness. He wanted to tell her it would be all right, to confess how eagerly he'd anticipated seeing her again. Often in the past few days, sudden, vivid images of her had intruded upon his work, distracting him. Keeping their personal relationship in perspective wasn't going to be easy. And looking at her now as she smilingly coaxed from the students the factors delegates to the Constitutional Convention had had to consider, he wasn't sure he even wanted to.

He cupped his chin in his hands, watching the way a shaft of sunlight highlighted tendrils of her hair as she wrote an impressive number of volunteered responses on the blackboard. With satisfaction, he noted how deftly she included most of the students. Then, when she turned to face the class, he found himself distracted by the way her generous breasts formed soft peaks beneath her dress. Somewhere above the hammering of his heart, he heard her ask the class to sort the factors by subject—agriculture, trade, manufacturing, religion, etc.

"Okay, let's divide into smaller groups." She walked up and down the aisles, having the students draw slips of paper from a basket. "Each of you will represent the interests of the colony you've drawn. But since there are seventeen of you, some will have a slip labeled 'rabble rouser.' Your job is to play devil's advocate."

A mischievous-looking redheaded boy in the front row pumped his fist in the air. "Yeah! That's me." The other students groaned loudly. The fellow behind him punched his shoulder. "Jamison, *you?* That's all we need! Mrs. W., did you rig this?" The class laughed. Jim, feeling like a randy teenager with a crush on the teacher, couldn't take his eyes off Connie.

"Ten minutes. Jot down the points you want to raise. I'll be available to help and—" she paused, then smiled questioningly in Jim's direction "—perhaps Dr. Campbell would offer his services, as well."

"Wh-what? I'm afraid I wasn't paying attention." The girl next to him snickered.

"He's a former history teacher."

Reluctant at first to approach him, the students relaxed after he stood and wandered among them. Soon he was fielding a barrage of questions. The room was chaotic—students comparing notes, forming alliances, scratching outlines of their arguments. Jim grinned. Who said a quiet classroom was the most productive?

"Time!" Connie waved her arms back and forth referee-fashion. "Circle the desks and make a label to designate which colony you represent. I'll serve as moderator." Another rush of noise and activity ensued as the students moved furniture, book bags and themselves. "The first session of the Constitutional Convention is called to order. Rules of debate are as follows.'' Connie stipulated the procedures. ''The chair now recognizes—'' searching the room, she responded to a demure young woman ''—the delegate from Delaware.''

When the bell rang, Jim couldn't believe he'd spent the entire period in one classroom. He'd been transfixed. History had come alive, and not merely for the juniors.

Connie dismissed the students, who stampeded from the room. Jamison, grinning impishly, lingered. He cocked an eyebrow at Jim and Connie. ''You were sure giving Mrs. W. the once-over. Did she pass inspection, Doc?'' His double meaning was inescapable.

Connie, a flush rising from the neckline of her dress, laid a hand on the student's shoulder. ''*Dr.* Campbell.''

''Dr. Campbell,'' he repeated.

''Son, this was not an 'inspection.' This was good teaching. You're lucky to have Mrs. Weaver.''

''Yeah. I never liked history till this year. She's way cool!'' He slung his book bag over his shoulder, then he gave Jim a thumbs-up before strutting into the hall.

Connie laughed self-consciously. ''I really didn't hire him as my press agent.''

Jim looked down into her dancing eyes. ''You didn't need to. You *are* cool!''

Her expression changed, first becoming vulnerable, then opaque. With a sudden return to reality, he acknowledged the delicate line he'd crossed between professional respect and personal feelings. *Damn, this was hard!*

"I don't know about 'cool,' but I hope you enjoyed the class."

"I did. So much so I couldn't tear myself away."

"I was nervous."

He told the gentlemanly lie. "I would never have known."

"I'm glad."

He glanced at his watch. "Say, aren't you off this next period?"

"Yes."

"Since I'm here, why don't you go ahead and fill me in about the history department?"

"Well..."

"Unless you're busy."

"I'm never too busy for you."

Her words took his breath away. He knew she meant "never too busy for the headmaster." Still... The thinking he needed to do about Connie couldn't be deferred. Either he had to risk a personal relationship or he had to endure the loneliness and need she intensified in him. Could he afford to jeopardize his professional ambitions?

Could he bear not to?

DRY-MOUTHED, Connie ushered him to a chair beside her desk. His eyes, warm and twinkling, turned her brain to mush.

He cleared his throat. "We haven't really had a chance to visit yet. I can't tell you how surprised I was to learn you're on the faculty."

"I... You were a surprise for me, too."

"A pleasant one, I hope?"

"Keystone is lucky to have you."

He cocked his head appraisingly. "That didn't exactly answer my question."

Uncomfortably warm in the flannel dress, she forced an honest reply. "A very pleasant one."

"Good." The word hung in the air like a benediction. He took a pen and a small notebook from his inside jacket pocket. "Let's take care of business first. Then I want to hear more about you."

Was it her imagination or had he put special emphasis on 'you'? Already the subtle scent of ocean breeze aftershave had transported her a thousand miles and several years into the past. Frantically, she summoned solid, dependable, no-nonsense Connie Weaver who had mysteriously deserted her, leaving behind a tongue-tied stranger.

Aware of his gaze, she somehow fumbled through a recitation of course offerings, faculty profiles and the successes and challenges of the department. Occasionally, he interrupted with perceptive questions. He'd always been a good listener—it was one of the traits she'd liked best about him—and his interest prompted her to elaborate in greater detail than she'd intended. He made her feel as if he had all the time in the world, that at this moment she was the only person who mattered. *Purely professional, Connie.*

He leaned back in his chair, stretching his legs. "Students here seem to enjoy a healthy mix of academics, extracurricular activities and athletics. Are they ever stressed out trying to do too much?"

"That happens. The debaters who play basketball, the student council president who sings in the chorus, the natural tension between coaches' and teachers' demands. Some overextend themselves, either because of their own drive, their parents' expectations or both. My daughter is an example. She tries to do it all. I worry about her perfectionism.''

"Uh...Erin? Isn't that her name?"

Connie relaxed. "How nice of you to remember."

"I remember quite a bit."

A momentary awkwardness came over her as she considered the possible allusion in his remark. "She's a fine young woman. I'm proud of her."

"As well you should be." He shifted forward in his seat. "Tell me how you think the athletic program complements the curriculum."

Looking into his eyes, she found no leeway for evasion or gilding the lily. She weighed her words. "Obviously, the school is committed to the sound-mind-in-a-healthy-body concept. But in practice...?" She paused, then, encouraged by his slight nod, went on. "I think we sometimes send kids mixed messages."

"Meaning?"

"Philosophically, Keystone's priority is educational excellence, but to some teachers it seems athletics is the tail wagging the dog." She stopped, startled that she'd blurted out her feelings, that she so implicitly trusted him.

"What are we talking about? Money, influence, what?"

"All of the above. The majority of our substantial donors give first to the athletic program. Then we have the parents with delusions. You know, 'my son the NFL player.' So when coaches pull students out of class too often or when the weight room gets a new training machine while the science department makes do with inadequate lab equipment, we academic types wonder what the priorities truly are.''

"But—"

"Hey, it's the way of the world, especially in Texas. We've learned to live with it." Connie realized she might have gone too far. "And as Dr. Frank was always quick to point out, the success of our athletic teams enhances our public relations efforts. Helps admissions. Parents enroll their children here so they can participate instead of sit on the sidelines at some larger school.''

"How do the students handle the pressures?''

"Actually, amazingly well. Most are resilient and have figured out how to work the system. But then…'' She trailed off, thinking of a couple of seniors who often straggled into her first-period advanced-placement class exhausted, blue circles rimming their bloodshot eyes. "The others? The ones stretched to the limits? They concern me.''

"Me, too.'' His familiar compassion struck a responsive chord.

They fell silent for a moment before he abruptly put his notebook away, pulled his chair closer and covered her hands with his. "I appreciate your insights, but whaddaya say we give Keystone a rest and concentrate on catching up?''

She looked down at Jim's hands, which rested on hers. She might as well be Celia Johnson sitting in *Brief Encounter*'s railroad station tea shop feeling sparks every time Trevor Howard touched her. When she glanced up, Jim was staring at her with...pleasure? Affection?

She began by telling him more about Erin. He smiled approvingly when she mentioned her daughter's goal of graduating first in her class. "I'm not surprised she's bright. She has a bright mother."

The shift from small talk into the personal caused a fluttering of nerves. What to say? *Yes, I'm very bright, but right now I'm having carnal thoughts?* She opted for the simple and obvious. "Thank you."

"What about *you?*" There was no mistaking the emphasis this time.

"Me? Well, I've been at Keystone seven and half years."

"Why did you leave Tulsa?"

Connie gave him a short account of her father's death, the subsequent move to Fort Worth and her mother's situation.

"That must've been a rough time for you and Erin."

"It was."

He withdrew his hands. "I wrote."

She lowered her eyes. "I know."

"I never really understood about your letter."

The silence screamed.

"Why, Connie?"

The flannel dress turned scratchy. "I... I'm sorry. I didn't mean..." She couldn't tell him the real reason. Not then. Not now. "We left Oklahoma in a rush, it was such a confusing time, you were so far away, I—"

"Hey, not to worry." He took her hand again. "It

happened. It's behind us. But, as I said the other day to Phil Buxton, I've never forgotten you.''

Her flesh was surely burning imprints into his palm. How was she supposed to interpret all this? A display of warm professional interest? Or...? Lord, the 'or' was overwhelming.

''Nor I you.'' Safe and truthful.

He grinned lazily. ''I'm glad. We had a lot of fun together.'' His expression turned serious. ''More than fun. That was a special summer for me.''

''For me, too.'' She must sound like the village idiot, echoing everything he said as if she hadn't an original thought in her head.

''Connie, my guess is you're uncertain how we should act now because of what happened in the past.'' He raised on eyebrow questioningly.

''The situation *is* a bit awkward.''

''Well, it needn't be. I'm not going to behave as if I don't know you, don't have feelings for you. That would be dishonest. Renewing our friendship is a natural consequence of my being here. We'll be friends, do our jobs. There's nothing to be concerned about.''

Nothing! That one word summed it up. She felt the professional mask sliding over her face as she gathered the loose papers on her desk. ''I appreciate your openness, Jim.'' She rose to her feet. ''It's one of the things I always admired about you, and it's a quality Keystone needs. We've pretty much gotten in a rut, accepting the status quo and taking one another for granted. You'll offer a breath of fresh air.''

''I may stir things up, too.''

''That wouldn't be all bad.''

He stood up. "Connie?"

"Yes?"

"Thank you for your honesty and support."

"Any time."

He started toward the door. Before she could stop herself, she laid a hand on his sleeve. "Jim, I know some of the other departments are having get-acquainted functions for you. Would you be free Sunday evening for potluck with the history department?"

"I'd be delighted. What time?"

"Let's say five-thirty at my house. I'll send you directions in the interoffice mail."

"I'll look forward to it."

She felt heat rise from her collar. "So will I."

He paused in the doorway and seemed to be studying her, a bemused expression on his face. "And I'll look forward to seeing you, Connie." Then he turned and strode down the hall, leaving her with confused, unteacher-like thoughts.

DRESSED IN KHAKIS and a worn Harvard sweatshirt, Jim sprawled in the huge leather chair in his office Saturday morning reviewing plans for the annual fundraising drive. Sunlight streamed through the window. The welcome absence of ringing phones and whirring copy machines should have made it easy to concentrate. But he was restless, agitated. And, for the life of him, he couldn't figure out why.

He had a sudden longing for home, for a nonschool voice. On impulse, he picked up the phone and dialed Cliff's private number, hoping to find him at his office.

"Cliff Campbell speaking."

Bingo! "Hi, buddy. It's your long-lost brother."

"About time." Cliff sounded delighted. "How's it going out there on the range?"

"Busy, but great. You wouldn't believe the hoopla last night for the big homecoming game. Low-key eastern enthusiasm didn't prepare me for the sheer Texas energy of the event." He chuckled. "You've never seen so many banners and crepe-paper streamers in your life! And you could cut the tension in the locker room with a knife."

"Did 'y'all' win?"

"Talk about your nail biter. Our hotshot quarterback, kid by the name of Watson, completed a Hail Mary pass in the final seconds to pull it out."

"I suppose they carried the kid off the field?" Cliff sounded amused.

"Not the kid, the coach."

"That figures. Maybe it'll be your turn next."

"In your dreams. I know my place."

"The big question is, do you actually like your place?" Cliff sounded dubious.

"Yeah, I really do. You should have seen me last night, glad-handing the crowd. I heard more suggestions about how to run the school in three hours than I ever learned in any education course. Even had one wealthy Lubbock alum hint at making a major donation to the football program."

"I guess you're telling me that for the foreseeable future, I can't convince you to come back to Boston."

"Frankly, Cliff, I don't know why you'd want me."

"Hell, you've always sold yourself short as a hotel

man. Besides—'' his voice mellowed ''—we miss you.''

''I appreciate that, Cliff. The hard part is being so far from family. But it's a trade-off.''

''I can tell from your voice it's a good one for you. I'm glad, Jim. Really.''

More relaxed after he hung up, Jim settled over the sheaf of papers on his desk. Talking with his brother had been a good idea. Amazingly, Cliff had seemed genuinely pleased for him.

Fifteen minutes later, he was surprised to hear the front door of the administration building open. He walked into the entry hall. ''George?''

''Sorry, Dr. Campbell, hope I didn't alarm you.'' The youthful-looking business manager raked his longish brown hair out of his eyes. ''I need to finish some end-of-the-month computations. It's always quieter on the weekends.''

''Sure is. I'll be here most of the day myself.''

''In that case...'' The younger man paused, as if coming to a decision. ''Would you have some time this afternoon?''

''Sure. Whenever you're ready.''

''I've finished—'' he hesitated again ''—preparing the figures you asked me for. About the athletic department.''

Concerned, Jim returned to his office. George Carey had been the Keystone business manager a little over a year, and he was thorough and conscientious. But today he seemed tense.

Shortly after two, Jim looked up to see George

standing in the doorway, with a bulging folder tucked under his arm.

Jim gestured to the conference table. "Have a seat." Picking up a yellow legal pad and pen, he sat down beside George, who fanned out sheets of budget figures. "What's up?"

The business manager nervously turned his pencil end over end between his fingers. "I hope nothing."

"But?" Jim raised his eyebrows, beginning to wish he'd never initiated this investigation.

"But...there are some financial irregularities."

"Irregularities?"

"I've been over and over the figures. Made comparisons with previous years and—" his Adam's apple bobbed "—I think there's a significant shortfall."

Jim straightened, all ears. "How significant?"

George cleared his throat. "Eight to ten thousand dollars."

Jim blew out a breath of air. "Whew. That's quite a chunk of change. Do we have that many accounts receivable or unpaid pledge contributions?"

"I wish."

"Oh?" Jim felt prickles of tension work their way up his spine.

"I've looked at this thing from every angle. But I'm afraid there's only one conclusion."

Jim was faintly aware of a cloud moving across the sun, subtly dimming the light in the room.

"Someone is embezzling school funds."

Oh, Lord. "Who?"

"The evidence points to Kurt Mueller."

"Son of a gun! That's a pretty serious charge."

The younger man looked worried. "Believe me, I know."

Jim laid a hand on George's shoulder. "Sorry. I expected some problems. Just not this one." Picking up his pen, he arranged his pad so he could take notes. "Okay, start through the numbers. And don't hold anything back. I need the full picture."

An hour and a half later, the business manager gathered up the spreadsheets and arranged them neatly in his folder. To Jim, the case appeared cut-and-dried. What a way to have to apply his hard-earned business experience! "One last question, George. Did you ever have occasion to discuss this matter with Dr. Frankenberg?"

"When I first came, I was pretty green about school finances in general and Keystone's in particular. Dr. Frank told me that the athletic department historically had had more financial autonomy than other departments and that although bills were sometimes late getting paid, eventually everything worked out."

Jim grimaced. No point faulting his predecessor. He was the one in charge now. "Concessions revenues? You think that's what we need to investigate first?"

"Yes, sir. That and gate receipts."

The two men stood. "Then get after it. Meanwhile, this is between the two of us."

"I understand."

After George left, Jim paced to the window, where he stared out over the grounds, barely taking in the profusion of chrysanthemums and pansies blooming around the flagpole. *Kurt Mueller. That's all I need. A full-blown scandal.*

Maybe, just maybe, the athletic director wasn't involved. Yet in his gut he really didn't believe it could be anyone else. Why had Mueller done it? That was the big question. And, God help him, one he had to pursue.

CHAPTER SIX

LATE SUNDAY AFTERNOON Connie aligned the napkins and silverware beside the flowered china plates on the sideboard. In the kitchen, Adele was garnishing the sliced ham. The coffee was made, the punch refrigerated and each tiny sandwich roll sliced. Standing back, Connie surveyed the effect, appreciating how artistically Erin had arranged the floral centerpiece before dashing to her church youth-group meeting.

Until this moment, Connie had busied herself with preparations, occupied her mind with details. Now she had no defense against the fluttery anticipation of Jim's arrival. Had it been only six weeks ago in this very room that she'd wished him here?

Forty was too old to feel giddy each time she saw him, too old to become blushingly aware of an involuntary, primitive, decidedly physical need. The same birthday fairy who'd arranged for her to be dressed in a clown costume at the big moment must be enjoying a knee-slapper right now—when every potent urging had to be denied.

Hugging herself against a sudden chill, Connie resolved to carry off this party in style. She would conceal inappropriate emotions and act the confident history department chairman and hostess.

"Con-nieee, can you help me?"

Sighing deeply, Connie ran her hands down the soft

wool of her red tunic sweater, then returned to the kitchen.

Promptly at five-thirty, Jim arrived, followed shortly by the department members, bearing assorted hot and cold dishes. Connie arranged the food on the dining-room table, grateful for an excuse to avoid the animated chatter filling the crowded living room. Bustling officiously among the guests, Adele refilled punch cups and responded with put-upon grace when several politely inquired about her health. "Anything I can do to help?" Connie whirled around at the sound of Jim's voice.

A cream-colored turtleneck and brown tweed blazer highlighted the ruddiness of his skin, the reddish brown of his well-groomed hair. When he smiled down at her and clasped her elbows, she couldn't control the automatic attack of nerves. "No...thank you. I'm finished."

He glanced at the table. "Looks good."

She nodded distractedly. "Everything's ready. Shall we join the others?"

Except for her mother's monopolizing Jim at dinner, the party went well. Over dessert and coffee, he responded informally to questions, and by the end of the evening, her colleagues went away seemingly reassured about the interim headmaster.

When it became obvious Jim had no intention of leaving before the last guest, Connie grew edgy. After loading the dishwasher, Adele, pleading exhaustion, excused herself. Connie was alone with him, tremblingly aware of his masculinity...and her own discomfiture.

In an effort to pull herself together, she collected the few remaining coffee cups and carried them to the kitchen. To her dismay, Jim followed. After removing his jacket and pushing up his sleeves, he selected a tea towel from the rack. He nodded at the crystal stemware and stacked china. "You wash, I'll dry."

"That's not necessary. I'll attend to this later."

"I insist. It's the least I can do."

He stood beside her, leaning casually against the counter. Her breath caught in her throat as she filled the sink with hot soapy water. Moving clumsily, she nearly dropped two goblets. After carefully washing and rinsing them, she handed one to Jim. While he wiped the piece with painstaking thoroughness, he enthused about the history teachers he'd met. She couldn't concentrate…acutely aware of the clink of fine crystal and the strong citrus scent of the detergent.

"Tell me about your mother."

"My mother?"

"She strikes me as a lonely person."

There it was again—his perceptiveness. Placing her palms flat on the counter, Connie sagged forward, fighting back unexpected tears. "Oh, Jim, she is." She swallowed hard. "I wish I knew what to do about it."

He reached out, traced a finger along her cheek, then turned her head toward his. "I'm sure you've tried."

The understanding in his eyes was achingly welcome. "Everything. Church circles, the senior citizens' center, AARP. She refuses to go unless I go, and most activities occur while I'm at work. She totally fell apart when Dad died. For the first few months, I assumed her depression was a normal expression of grief. But instead of getting on with her life, she's become increasingly dependent and resistant to change. Erin is the light of her life."

"And you?"

"And me. But it can be...suffocating sometimes."
The instant the words were out of her mouth, guilt
clawed at her. "I...didn't mean that. It sounded petty,
self-serving."

"And accurate?" He'd slipped his hand to her
shoulder, where it rested comfortingly.

"I don't know what to do anymore." She stared at
her feet. "She's getting more and more reclusive."

He tilted her chin so that she couldn't avoid the
sympathy in his gray-green eyes. "And you keep trying to make everything okay, don't you? Even at the
expense of your own needs."

"She's my mother. That's what daughters do."

"At what cost, Connie? You can't be responsible
for her happiness. Only she can."

She turned back to the sink, mechanically resuming
her task. "I suppose you're right, but I sure keep trying."

He chuckled, breaking the serious mood. "It's the
teacher in you. 'Just give me one more chance to make
a difference.'"

Staring into the suds, she smiled wryly. "I guess
I'm a born optimist."

"That's not a bad thing to be if you don't take
yourself too seriously."

There it was. Not only sensitivity, but that same
common sense she'd found so endearing years ago.
How tempting it would be to unburden herself to him,
to lean into his strength. She cut off that thought. She
felt altogether too vulnerable.

He stood beside her in comfortable silence, the only
sounds the swish of dishwater and the squeak of the
towel against glass. Occasionally when she handed
him a cup or goblet, their knuckles grazed or his shoul-

der accidentally brushed hers. The quiet kitchen, the steamy water and the domesticity of their chore created an intimacy she both craved and rejected.

She glanced at the kitchen clock. Nine. Jim would be leaving shortly, and Erin was due back soon. She forced herself to focus on the evening's remaining tasks—removing the leaves from the dining-room table, writing utilities checks, typing a quiz for the seniors. She pulled the stopper out of the sink, carefully dried her hands on a paper towel and rubbed on hand cream as, out of the corner of her eye, she watched Jim put the finishing touches on a pitcher.

He set it aside and faced her. "You've got bubbles on your cheek." He lifted a finger to her face and gently wiped away the airy foam. A tiny, innocent gesture—that's all it was. Blinking, she turned away and began screwing the lid on the hand cream jar, rearranging the sponge and pot scrubber.

"Are you avoiding me?" He hadn't moved.

She felt light-headed, confused. "Wh-what do you mean?" She swiped the sponge over the faucet handles.

Then she felt an arm encircle her waist.

"Look at me, Connie."

His soft eyes held tenderness, truth, memory. "Are you afraid of me?"

Her throat thickened. There was challenge in his gaze. "Not...not of you...exactly."

He drew her closer, his eyes unflinching. "Of what, then?"

She looked to her left toward the kitchen window. "You know. Don't make me say it."

"What?"

"What can never be."

He recaptured her chin and forced her to look at him. "You feel it, then? That same attraction we had before?"

She tried to twist away. "Don't, Jim. It's unproductive...and dangerous."

"So you do." He framed her face in his large warm hands. "I do, too. I won't ignore it."

"But..."

"I did some serious thinking today about you. You know what I concluded?"

"No, what?"

"We're lucky. Life gives very few second chances." His hands fell from her face, over her shoulders, down her arms, the trail of his fingers etching pinpricks of yearning. "I don't intend to squander ours."

He pulled her against his chest and parted her lips with his. She was powerless! The din of obstacles, arguments, consequences were silenced in an instant by the hot pressure of his mouth on hers, by the safety of his strong embrace. As she arched into him, the spasm of her desire matched the thrust of his hips against her. She couldn't think. It had been so long...so long since she'd felt raw passion. She'd even questioned if she was still capable of such emotion. She stood on her tiptoes, running her fingers through his hair, aware that somehow, sometime, he'd removed his glasses.

Finally, he pushed her to arm's length and studied her. "Wow! That was a pretty definitive answer."

Avoiding his eyes, she turned in his grasp. He encircled her from behind, his arms curling her against his chest. When he rubbed his jaw along her temple, she shivered at the delicate rasp of his face against her skin.

"You're afraid of my position? What people will say?"

She nodded and hung her head, knowing full well that wasn't all she feared.

He moved her long hair aside and nuzzled the base of her neck. "There's no question it's awkward. But we're responsible adults who have a right to a private life."

"But... I don't see how... Keystone is a fishbowl."

He took hold of her shoulders and squared her around to look at him. "One step at a time. This pretense that we're merely colleagues isn't working. Does it feel right to you?"

"Well, no, but..."

"We need time—time to examine the past, to discover what's between us now. Without feeling pressure. Connie, I'd like to see you socially. We can be discreet about times and places, but I refuse to risk losing you again."

The joy of knowing he cared was tempered by professional caution and by what still lay unspoken between them—the real reason she'd written the letter, the one reason she should stop this right now. "Jim, you don't know what these people are like...."

"Yes, I do. I'm a realist. There'll be talk. But I know we aren't the first faculty members to explore a relationship. And neither of us is a fool." He lowered his head and stared into her eyes. "Is it worth the risk to you?"

"I'm worried about *you*, your reputation."

"That's not what I asked."

"Jim…" Her emotions were tumbling, just like mementos spilling out of a keepsake box. "Yes."

That single syllable whooshed into the silence like a piston engaging the drive wheel of a powerful locomotive.

Then he smiled that wonderful warm-cocoa-and-cookies smile that melted her through and through. "Good," he said.

He picked up his glasses before leading her into the living room, where they settled on the sofa. "Remember Gettysburg?"

She closed her eyes. Her heart stopped. Gettysburg—the beginning…and the end. "One of the loveliest days of my life. And one of the saddest. All those tombstones and memorials."

"I remember your hair blowing in the breeze. The way you traced the names on the Virginia monument with your fingertips. How we said we could almost smell the gunpowder."

She looked up at him. "Was it just a magic summer—or real?"

He pulled her close. "That's what we're going to find out. I hope it was real."

The slamming of a car door nearly drowned out her "We'll see." Connie sat up. "It's Erin."

Jim stood. "Good. I want to meet her."

Erin breezed in the door, her brown eyes glowing with a happiness that, to a mother's practiced eye, had nothing to do with meeting the headmaster. Her daughter's flushed cheeks and dewy eyes suggested she and Kyle had not come straight home from the meeting. But, then, who was *she* to talk? She ran one hand absently through her hair. "Jim, this is my daughter Erin. Erin, I'm sure you recognize Dr. Campbell."

Erin grinned and stuck out her hand. "Nice to meet you, sir. You visited my physics class last week."

"Mr. Klem was really putting you through the paces."

"He's tough, but I'm learning lots." Erin surveyed the tidied room. "How'd the party go?"

"Fine," Connie said.

"Any cookies left?"

"Plenty." Erin excused herself and headed for the kitchen. "While you're there, would you retrieve Dr. Campbell's jacket? He was just leaving."

Jim leaned over and whispered in her ear. "Chicken."

Connie registered the sudden confusion of roles—responsible parent and flustered romantic. "It's not just reactions at school I'm thinking about." She nodded in Erin's direction. "There are other considerations. What are we beginning?"

"Trust me, Connie."

Holding a cookie between her teeth, Erin returned and gave Jim his jacket. He thanked Connie for the party, then departed.

"Mo-om?" Erin grinned mischievously.

"What?"

"He's kinda cute. For an old guy." Connie squirmed as Erin studied her with amusement. "And you know what? I think you agree."

Connie bent to rearrange the sofa pillows. "I suppose you could say that."

"He looks kinda like that anchorman, you know. What's his name. Not Brokaw. The other one."

"Peter Jennings?"

"Yeah, that's him. Mom, Dr. Campbell could be a hot prospect for you."

Connie straightened. "Now, see here—"

Erin started down the hall toward her bedroom. "Think about it," she called over her shoulder.

Embarrassed, Connie stood quietly staring into space. If her reactions were that transparent to Erin, how could she possibly carry off business-as-usual at school?

Suddenly restless, she walked into the dining room, pulled on the end of the heavy table, separated the leaves and manhandled them into the hall closet. Oh, God, Gettysburg. It wasn't only the day she'd never forgotten. She sank onto the sofa, aware that the mere memory of that one night with Jim had triggered an upheaval deep within her.

Their B-and-B, a picturesque white clapboard farmhouse nestled in rural Pennsylvania, had been shaded by gigantic maple trees. The room—furnished with Shaker-style antiques, a colorful handbraided rug and a spotless white Martha Washington bedspread—had opened onto a private back porch where climbing roses, fanned by gentle breezes, emitted a delicate fragrance. To this day, the scent of roses stirred Connie, just as she'd been stirred that glorious night by the tenderness, then the passion of their lovemaking.

Before that night she'd never truly known orgasm. Colin rarely concerned himself with her pleasure, only his own. With him, she'd been controlled, detached. But one moist brush of Jim's lips over her abdomen and she'd exploded—instantly, shockingly, deliciously.

Connie, her eyes filling with tears, leaned her head back. One night. But it had made all the difference. If

Gettysburg had never happened, maybe she could have settled for Ralph…or someone. If Gettysburg had never happened, if Jim hadn't said those words, maybe… She wiped her eyes. But he had said them, and they'd killed her. Spent, he'd crumpled on top of her, his fingers tenderly twining through her hair, his breath hot against her damp skin. "Can't you just picture the two of us in a big old house overflowing with babies? Lots of them."

She'd wanted to scream, shake her fist at God. Babies! The one thing she'd never be able to give him. Erin was the only baby she'd ever have, thanks to the emergency hysterectomy necessitated by the difficult birth. While her insides turned to ashes, Jim had rambled on about his love of children, his dream of being a father, his amazement at finding her, his beloved Connie.

Somehow she'd pulled off the two remaining days of the seminar. When the plane carrying her home took off from Dulles, a part of her had died. The letter had seemed the cleanest way to end things.

Lord, what had she and Jim started tonight? Was she being fair? At forty-three, did he still want children? Was she premature in supposing he hoped something permanent would come of their time together? Would it be so terrible to enjoy feeling like a woman again—even for a little while?

Hope, arousal, fear—these were powerful emotions…and ones she found impossible to ignore.

A COLD PRAIRIE WIND whipped the flag outside the administration building the following Friday morning. Inside, Jim slumped at his desk, removed his glasses and rubbed his bloodshot eyes. Last night's board meeting had lasted well past midnight. An unproductive discussion of the food service operation, prompted by the complaints of a handful of parents, had delayed more pressing agenda items such as the fund-raising campaign and the search for a permanent headmaster.

When he'd finally collapsed into bed at two-fifteen, he'd been too keyed up to sleep. Just as his eyes would close, he'd remember another chore he had to get done before leaving for tonight's away game in Midland. He stared at the open file folder on his desk. The athletic department. With a deep sigh, he put on his glasses and bent over the confidential memo from George Carey.

The school's fiscal year ended June 30. Figures for the past five years revealed that up to and including the past year, the athletic department had run at an occasional significant monthly deficit, but that by year's end, the figures balanced. George had explained that under his leadership the financial records had been put on a new computer system. Prior to that, all monies from activities—orchestra, debate, school newspaper, athletics, etc.—had been held in separate accounts, to which the sponsors or coaches had access and over which they exerted control.

In George's judgment, such a system not only lacked accountability but was a financial disaster waiting to happen. He'd gradually been bringing all school accounts under the umbrella of the business office. The athletic director, however, had been vocal in his resistance, insisting his system worked and that changing over would be a time-consuming and complicated process. At the very least, he'd argued to Dr. Frankenberg, the other piddling accounts should be converted before adding the complex athletic department figures.

Dr. Frankenberg had reluctantly concurred, giving Mueller a one-year grace period. Jim rubbed his temples. *This year.*

George's report also outlined the general cycle of embezzlement, in which an employee "borrowed" institutional funds for personal use, sometimes with the expectation that such sums could be repaid before audits revealed a problem. In this particular case, George suggested, the fact that any shortfalls culminated in satisfactory end-of-the-year accountings fit that pattern. Jim stared at the figures before him. Currently, the athletic department was $8,517.02 in the hole.

Pushing back from the desk, Jim stood and planted his palms in the small of his back, then bent to relieve his tired muscles. Time for a chat with his athletic director. But not on game day. He wasn't that big a glutton for punishment.

At least he had Sunday to look forward to. He'd called Connie Tuesday evening to invite her to go antiquing. His decor was pure "bachelor," and although his furniture was adequate, he still needed a few pieces. For somebody who'd always longed for a big home with kids and dogs underfoot and a huge backyard with hundred-year-old shade trees, the austerity of his treeless town house community was depressing. He definitely needed a woman's touch. He stretched his arms over his head and grinned at his slip—Freudian? It wasn't only his home that needed a woman's touch.

He did. One particular woman's!

CURLED UP on the sofa, an afghan wrapped around her legs, Connie absently picked up a handful of candy corn from the dish on the end table and, one by one, put the morsels in her mouth as she punched numbers into the calculator on her lap desk. Adele sat across the living room engrossed in the Saturday night television movie classic—*Dial M for Murder*. Connie glanced at the flickering image of Ray Milland—far more sinister than the goblins and monsters who'd roamed the neighborhood trick-or-treating the night before.

The first-quarter's grades were due in the office Monday. Erin, her big eyes shadowed by dark circles, had driven herself, staying up into the wee hours every night this past week studying for tests, completing papers, updating her physics lab book. Her naturally cheerful disposition had taken on an edge. When Connie had urged her to relax and put life into perspective, she'd snapped. "Relax! Right, Mom. You think Bruce Silverstein's relaxing?" Bruce, currently ranked number one in the class, was Erin's friend but also her academic rival. "You don't get it yet, do you? I'm going to be valedictorian. Somehow!"

Connie ripped the long strip of tape out of the calculator and began transferring her seniors' quarterly marks into her grade book.

Tonight Erin and Kyle were at a Halloween party hosted by three sets of senior parents. Connie cringed. These were parents who believed it was safer for kids to drink in their homes, under adult supervision. Connie knew she should have confidence in Erin, who had always proved responsible and claimed drinking was stupid. But, then, Erin had never been in love before. What might she do to impress Kyle and his cocky football buddies and their sophisticated dates? Sometimes Connie wished she were one of those parents who hadn't a clue what teenagers were up to—or chose not to know. But the facts confronted her every day at work.

As if reading her mind, Adele muted the TV during the commercial. "Connie, when is Erin coming home? I worry about those youngsters and how they drive— roaring up and down the street at all hours of the night."

"Her curfew tonight is one."

Her mother sniffed. "I can't imagine what you're thinking of. Why, I never let you stay out that late. Nothing worthwhile goes on after midnight, I always say."

"Erin will be off at college next year, Mama, where there are no curfews. She needs to learn to handle herself."

"Well, anything could happen. I can't understand why you're not worried."

Not worried? The term *carefree mother* was an oxymoron. "She'll be fine."

Clucking disapprovingly, her mother gave a self-righteous shake of her head and restored the volume just as a close-up of Grace Kelly filled the screen. Connie observed the thin line of her mother's lips, her total absorption in the screen. When was the last time she'd heard her mother laugh?

After the movie, Adele dragged herself off to bed. At midnight, Connie wearily began grading the world history tests. Sophomores. Honestly. If it weren't for the creative spellings—Maggiellen for Magellan, as an example—she'd be beyond boredom.

Her eyelids drooped, and with difficulty, she roused herself. She had to finish. She wanted no ugly papers hanging over her head tomorrow when she spent the afternoon with Jim. During this past week she'd caught only fleeting glimpses of him—once in the library, another time in the parking lot. Tomorrow! Her heart raced.

But doubt had reared its ugly head. Did she have any right to complicate his situation at Keystone? For that matter, to risk complicating her own? Did she have any right to forget why she'd ended their relationship eight years ago? Down deep, though, she knew it wasn't a matter of "rights." It was a matter of...what had Jim said?—a second chance. If only briefly.

Redoubling her efforts on behalf of the sophomores, she realized halfway through the papers that it was after one. Where was Erin? She stood and walked over to the window, where she parted the drapes. The street was deserted. She knew she shouldn't be alarmed. It was only a quarter past, but Erin had never missed a curfew. Where could they be? Maybe they'd had car trouble or something. Sure! The old "flat tire" routine.

She dropped the drape back into place and returned to the sofa, where she forced herself onward through the papers, one by one. Finally—the hum of a motor, the scrape of a tailpipe on the inclined driveway, the slam of a car door. She sagged against the cushion in relief. She heard the metallic click of Erin's key in the door, the whispered "Me, too. G'night."

"Erin?"

Her daughter stood just inside the living room. "Mother? What are you doing still up?" She lifted her chin with a hint of defiance. "Waiting for me?"

"Yes and no. Grading papers. But when one o'clock came and went, I began to worry."

"You didn't need to. It's no big deal."

"Well, it's a big deal to me, young lady."

"Mo-other. I'm not a baby. The time just got away from us."

"Did you ever stop to consider what you might be putting me through?"

Erin chewed on her lip. "I 'spose I should've phoned."

"That would've been thoughtful." Connie laid her papers aside, forcing the sarcasm from her tone. "Tell me about the party. Did you have a good time?"

Erin perched tentatively beside her. "I guess. Some of the kids got whacked, but most of us played pool, ate, watched TV."

Got whacked? "And you wonder why I worry?" At least she didn't smell any alcohol on Erin. She put her arm around her daughter's waist. "You've had a pretty exhausting week. Maybe you can sleep in tomorrow."

Erin yawned and stretched her arms over her head. As she did, Connie stared, transfixed, at the tiny red spot blooming at the base of her daughter's neck. "I'd love to." She leaned over and kissed Connie's cheek. "'Night, Mom. Sorry about being late."

Late? Connie had almost forgotten that infraction at the shock of seeing her daughter's delicate skin clearly and unmistakably adorned with a hickey!

"What's that on your neck?"

Erin stopped in her tracks, her teeth clenched, while crimson colored her flawless complexion. "How should I know?"

"It looks like a hickey to me."

"So what? It's hardly in the same league with pregnancy."

Erin had never looked at her with such disdain. "Just be careful, honey."

"Jeez, Mom. Get a clue. For your information, Kyle and I aren't 'sexually active.'" Then, as a parting shot before she stormed to her room, she added, *"Yet."*

Connie tried to understand. Her daughter was exhausted. She was in love for the first time. It was natural to express affection. And maybe, just maybe, Connie was overreacting because of her own recent arousal.

How would Erin receive a well-intentioned mother-daughter chat? When they'd been over this ground before, it had been in the realm of the hypothetical. A hickey was *not* hypothetical.

Her body ached for bed, but her mind raced with all kinds of questions about Kyle, about Erin, about hormones.

She reached for the world's best-known insomnia cure—another sophomore test paper. Stanley Henderson's. She flipped to the third page and looked at the space for the answer to the essay question. Drawn in the blank was a huge black question mark, traced over and over with what appeared to be savage intent. She could feel an actual indentation in the paper. At the bottom of the page, in his tiny pinched printing, he'd written a brief note: "Mrs. Weaver, I'm sorry. I know I flunked. But it doesn't matter. The hell with it! Nothing matters anymore."

Dread stopped her breath. "Weirdo." That's what the unkinder sophomore jocks called him. The recollection of his body, withdrawn from the pep rally crowd and hunched over a book, as if he were cringing from anticipated onslaughts, came to her. *Nothing matters anymore.* A plea for help if she ever saw one. Poor Stanley! She'd have to go to the guidance coun-

selors' office first thing Monday morning to alert
Ginny Phillips.

She thrust the papers aside, turned off the light and,
too fatigued to move to the bedroom, drew the afghan
up over her. She snuggled into the throw pillows.
Mother. Jim. Erin. Stanley. Insomnia guaranteed.

CHAPTER SEVEN

"HEY, MOM, Peter Jennings just drove into the drive-way."

Connie glanced up from the full-length mirror in which she was studying the effect of the floral scarf she'd clumsily knotted at the neck of her ivory blouse. Accessorize. Right. She never could get the hang of tying these fool things. She ripped the scarf off. "Darn."

In the reflection she caught Erin's amused smile. "Let me do that, Mom." Like magic, her daughter's nimble fingers took the scarf and created style. Obviously a good night's sleep had worked wonders on Erin's surliness. " 'Darn' the scarf or 'darn' Dr. Campbell?" Erin patted the knot, then stood back, studying her handiwork.

Embarrassed by the transparency of her jitters, Connie looked down to be sure her leather belt had caught each loop of her navy slacks. "The scarf. Thanks, honey."

When she'd announced this afternoon's outing with Jim to her mother and Erin, Adele had reacted predictably. "Do you think it's wise to see the headmaster socially?" she'd asked. When Connie reminded her she'd seen Ralph socially, her mother's response had been curt. "That's different."

Different? Connie reluctantly conceded her mother might have a point. She and Ralph had been peers, not employer and employee. And with Ralph there had been only friendship on her part, not the tantalizing sense she had with Jim of something momentous about to happen.

"Mo-om." There was urgency in Erin's voice. "He's coming up the walk."

Connie's hand went automatically to her hair, curling loose and full on her shoulders. "How do I look?"

"Fine. Now, come *on*." Erin pushed her toward the living room. "Everything's cool. Go for it!" She gave her a high sign, before tactfully slipping into her bedroom. At least Erin approved, Connie reproached herself. She was a grown woman. Why was approval even an issue?

When she opened the front door, her breath caught. Jim, dressed casually in a crimson Henley shirt and tan cords, looked less like a dignified headmaster and excitingly more like the relaxed young history teacher she'd never forgotten.

"Ready?"

"Let me grab my purse." She shouldered the bag, then shut the door behind her.

Jim cupped her elbow as he guided her to the car. "Beautiful day."

Pausing before getting in the dark-green sedan, she took in the mild November afternoon—the vast autumn-blue sky; the warm breeze lulling her against the reality of approaching winter; the elms and oaks, still sporting a few die-hard gold and brown-red leaves. She sighed with satisfaction. "Gorgeous. Probably one of the last."

"We'd better make the most of it, then."

As he drove down the street, he looked over and smiled. "Okay, navigator. Where to?"

"What exactly are you looking for?"

"If I knew 'exactly,' I'd tell you." He braked for the stop sign and gave her a mischievous look. "But, of course, this trip was never really about antiquing."

"No?"

He accelerated down the block toward the major thoroughfare. "No. Call me devious. I wanted to spend time with you. The rest is pure subterfuge, for which I refuse to apologize."

She looked over at him. He faced straight ahead, the merest hint of a grin quirking the corner of his mouth. "I'm flattered, but so long as we're out, we may as well give the antique stores in Grapevine a whirl." She pointed at the intersection. "Turn right, then get on the interstate."

Traffic was light as they headed east past acres of mustard brown land, periodically sprouting houses under construction in such developments as "Hacienda Grande" and "Sleepy Meadows." The barrenness, relieved only by high power lines and garish billboards, struck Connie as neither "grande" nor meadowlike. She hoped, though, that Jim would like the quaint, small-town atmosphere of Grapevine, where property on the main street had been converted to gift and antique shops.

"I'm curious, Jim. Why didn't you stay in the hotel business?"

"I never should have left education. I've loved school ever since I was a kid. With few exceptions, I was always happy there." He fell silent.

"And the hotel business…?"

He glanced over at her. "Was never happy."

"Then, why?"

"Why did I go into it?"

She nodded, pleased that they seemed able to communicate by verbal shorthand.

"It's a long story."

"And it's miles to Grapevine. I'm interested, Jim."

"From the beginning, my father groomed my brother, Cliff, and me for the family business. The proper prep schools, social clubs, university—everything. 'Contacts, boys. It's all about contacts.'"

Connie watched his jaw twitch.

"So I did all the expected things, met all the 'right' people, worked summers in the hotels. On the fast track to the inevitable end—Campbell Courts."

"But you didn't start out there."

"Thank God, or I might still be there."

"I don't understand…"

"How I got into education?"

"Yes."

His brow furrowed in concentration, he pulled out to pass a lumbering RV. "Two reasons. The headmaster of my boarding school persuaded my father to indulge my desire to teach. Dad figured after a year or two I'd get it out of my system."

She smiled. "Obviously he was wrong."

"*He* was, but Gaffer wasn't."

"Gaffer?"

"Reason number two. My grandfather on my mother's side. A true Down East character. The only gifts of the sea, he used to say, are fish, salt and sense. And he had no use for the man who lacked sense."

She shifted closer and laid a tentative hand on his knee. "He must've been a strong influence in your life."

Smiling wistfully, he looked at her, his eyes mellow. "Gaffer was the greatest. Before I was old enough to work summers, I spent every July at his cabin in Maine. He didn't talk much, but as he said, not much a man needs to say to a pine tree, a gull or a campfire. Those were some of the best times of my life."

"He's dead?"

His right hand settled on top of hers. "Died twelve years ago. Just the way he wanted to. Went to sleep one night and that was it."

"You miss him, don't you?"

He squeezed her fingers in assent before raising his hand to point out a road sign. "This our turn?"

"Oops. Guess I'm not doing my job."

He swerved onto the exit ramp and, taking a cue from her nod, turned left at the bottom. She rode quietly for a few minutes, replaying the conversation in her head. "Jim, you mentioned two reasons. What was it about your grandfather that prompted you to return to education?"

He leaned back, stretching his left leg. "Something he said and lived. 'You only go round once, son. Make it count.'" He relaxed against the seat. "The hotel business was right for my father. It's right for Cliff. I couldn't 'make it count.' Not after being in teaching.''

"And what about Keystone? Does *it* feel right?''

He plucked her hand from her lap, then brushed his lips across her knuckles. "Better than right.'' And then, as he lowered their clasped hands onto his firm thigh, he sent her a heart-stopping grin. "Perfect.''

She shouldn't feel this happy. It was dangerous. Here in the cocoon of the car, carefree for the moment, she could delude herself that anything was possible. That, against all the odds, she and Jim had been brought together to…"make it count.'' A river of longing flowed through her. This man, this day…a mirage, shimmering on the horizon of the future. "Fish, salt and sense.'' She needed a good dose of the latter.

She pulled her hand away to gesture at the water tower in the distance. "We're nearly there. Follow the markers to the business district.''

IGNORING THE STRIDENT play-by-play of the Sunday NFL game, Adele reached across Yolanda's back and fumbled with the TV remote, her arthritic fingers refusing to do her bidding. Fiddle. She squinted at the tiny channel numbers and repeatedly pressed 6. Nothing. Finally, in exasperation, she located a pencil on the end table and, using the eraser, punched the 6 again. Ah! She set down the remote and leaned back, watching with satisfaction the opening credits of *Magnificent Obsession*. Rock Hudson and Jane Wyman. Pity about Rock. He'd died, let's see, six or eight years ago. And that cute Jane, used to be married to Ronald Reagan. Well, before Nancy, of course. She'd always loved this picture—poor blind Jane and valiant, steadfast Rock. Now, *this* was a love story, not like those explicit sitcoms of today where people jumped in and out of each other's beds. The very idea!

Fortunately, Erin didn't watch many of them. Connie ought to have some rules about the TV. Not much on it fit for young girls. And the soap operas? Even worse. In her day, on a Sunday afternoon, the family had sat around the old Westinghouse radio listening to *One Man's Family*. Now, *there* was some decent entertainment.

She worried about Erin. That young man—what was his name? Curt, Lyle?—seemed nice enough, but you couldn't be too careful. All this talk on the news about teenage drugs, drinking and date rape, of all things—why it was enough to make a person frantic. She wished Walter Cronkite were still broadcasting. She could trust him. As it was now, she couldn't tell fact from fiction.

She shifted her hips to get more comfortable and lost herself in the movie. But then, suddenly, something Jane said reminded her of Connie's date with Dr. Campbell. What could the child be thinking to go out with the headmaster? Mercy, it just wasn't done. Connie had assured her it was an innocent outing with an old friend. Old friend? Since when? Why had Connie never mentioned she'd known Dr. Campbell before? Something smelled fishy.

The poor thing. Connie so rarely saw a man that it would be petty to butt in. But it would have been so nice if she'd accepted that pleasant Ralph's proposal. Treated her like a queen, he did. Erin and herself, too.

She shook her head to clear the cobwebs. Enough of Connie. She couldn't live her daughter's life for her, though she had some strong opinions about it. And then there was the big question. What would happen to her if Connie met someone? Thought about getting married?

She rubbed her aching knuckles. She'd have no place to go. A lonely old albatross. Not a pretty prospect. She wouldn't think about it. She'd watch the movie. Yolanda stretched, kneaded her lap, then curled into a ball.

There—Rock was leaning over Jane, their lips drawing closer. With a forefinger, Adele adjusted the glasses on her nose, then settled back, eyes focused on the screen lovers.

JIM CAUGHT Connie's eye across the small wrought-iron table in the courtyard of the quaint Grapevine coffee shop. "Another cappuccino?"

Connie smiled wickedly. "I shouldn't, but—"

Catching the waiter's eye, Jim held up two fingers. "Done."

"I'm feeling truly indulged. Two cappuccinos and the lovely cameo. Thank you."

"My pleasure." To put it mildly. She'd been in another world in the antique shops—each new discovery bringing a lilt to her voice. She'd swoop ahead of him, then linger over a special find, her lovely long fingers delicately tracing the wooden inlay of a game table or the intricate surface of a cut-glass bowl. He'd watched her covertly, taking delight in her good taste and unselfconscious enthusiasm.

He'd managed, with her help, to select a fine oak
library table, a sturdy bentwood rocker and a brass
table lamp, all of which the proprietor had agreed to
deliver. But the cameo was his favorite purchase. The
feminine ivory profile set in coral reminded him of
Connie's creamy complexion, aristocratic nose, reed-
like neck. When she'd paused and then leaned over to
study it more closely, he hadn't hesitated. "It's you."
He gestured to the clerk to unlock the display case.
"And it's yours."

She'd looked up, a faint flush coloring her cheeks,
"Jim, you don't have—" He'd laid a finger on her
lips.

"To buy you a gift? No, I don't. And that's exactly
what makes it a gift. Please."

Their eyes had met, and, in that moment, he'd
sensed a yielding in her that went beyond the cameo.
She'd held the gaze, then a fragile smile bloomed
across her face and shone in her eyes. "Thank you,
Jim. Thank you very much."

Now, her tapered fingers dangling from the armrest
of her chair, she sat telling him about the wall hanging
the seniors were making to present at the schoolwide
Lee Frankenberg Appreciation Day. She spoke with
the same animation he'd witnessed that day in her
class. How could anyone fail to be drawn to her?

The waiter brought their steaming cappuccinos. Jim
raised his cup in silent toast, took a tentative sip, then,
setting down the cup, said, "Tell me more about Erin.
Has she decided on a college yet?"

With her napkin, Connie wiped the corner of her

mouth. "She's usually an absolute delight. But this college business may be the death of us."

"Oh?"

He noticed Connie's hands clutching the wrought-iron arm of her chair.

"She wants to go out of state."

"Why?"

"You know. The idea that you haven't really left home if you stay too close. Also, she's ambitious, so challenging schools appeal to her. But I seriously doubt we can swing any of them. Except maybe Vanderbilt."

"Why Vanderbilt?"

"Colin, Erin's father, is on the faculty there. He wants her to live with him."

"So she'd be off campus?"

"Right. That's part of the problem. She wants the full experience—dorms, roommates, independence. I can't blame her."

"And the other part?"

She fingered the knot of her scarf and looked uncomfortable. "Besides the steep tuition, Colin himself. I can't remember how much I told you about him that summer…"

"Enough for me to know he's a Class A jerk. Wasn't he the English department Casanova?"

"You have a good memory." She lowered her eyes to the cup on the table.

"Based on what you said about him then, these days he'd be up on harassment charges."

Her voice was small. "I suppose."

Jim scooted his chair around the table and put his

arm around her. "I'm sorry. It was thoughtless of me to mention that."

She sat quietly, neither encouraging nor discouraging his casual embrace. "No, it's all right. It's just...when I think of that time, how betrayed and humiliated I felt..." She looked up, honesty and pain showing in her expression. "As if there was nothing—" she paused, seeming to search for the exact word "—*feminine* about me."

He wished they weren't in public, wished he could let his emotions sweep them both away to a place where she'd have no doubts about her femininity—or about her sexuality. But he knew he needed to proceed carefully. "I'd hoped our time in Washington proved that Colin, not you, was the one with the problem."

She brushed her fingers across his cheek in an intimate gesture. "Oh, Jim, it did. You made me feel like every woman wants to feel—adored, special." Her hand fell back into her lap.

"Then why...why did we lose what we had?"

She smiled crookedly. "I desperately needed to believe in the fairy tale. To cling to it. I was too afraid of reality."

He ran his hand gently over her tense shoulder. "Fairy tales have happy endings. Maybe we're still in the middle of the story."

She sat forward, reaching for her cup. "Jim, I—"

"You think I'm coming on too strong?" He left his arm draped across the back of her chair.

"Not exactly, but—"

"You're still afraid."

She nodded. "If even for a minute I let myself look toward the ending..."

"You see obstacles. The ugly stepsisters, the wicked witches, the dragons."

She took a sip of the cappuccino, then held the cup in both hands, studying the contents. "What would *you* call an aging mother and a lovely daughter who are my responsibilities, a group of parents and teachers who might disapprove even of what we're doing right now?"

"I'd call them roadblocks you're throwing in our path."

She whipped her face around to stare at him. "That *I'm* throwing?"

"Yes, you. What we're doing isn't scandalous. It's perfectly natural. And if this goes where I think it might, what makes you think I wouldn't welcome your mother and Erin as part of the package called Connie?"

"It's just... Colin—"

"Forget Colin." Jim removed his arm from the chair back and thrust both hands deep into his pants pockets. "That sorry fella really did a number on you."

"Present tense. *Does.*"

"What do you mean?"

"Erin."

"Is this back to Vanderbilt?"

Connie set her cup down decisively. "Oh, yes. Dr. Wonderful Weaver is holding Erin hostage. He'll help with her tuition only if she lives with him and goes to Vanderbilt."

"Helluva guy. Do you think he means it?"

"With him, you never know. He enjoys keeping me off balance."

"What's Erin going to do?"

"She'll apply to Vanderbilt, and she's reluctantly agreed to consider some Texas schools."

"Sounds reasonable. Erin's a bright girl. I'm sure Ginny Phillips is working with you on scholarships and financial aid packages."

"Ginny's great. But—"

"I know, you can't count on it. But have confidence in Erin and wait until the results are in. You may be surprised."

"I hope so." She glanced at her watch. "And speaking of 'surprised,' where did the afternoon go? I need to be getting home."

He signaled the waiter and paid the bill. When she started to rise, he grabbed both hands and gently pulled her back into the seat. "You have a turn, too, you know."

She frowned in puzzlement. "A turn?"

"In life. It can't always be the other person's moment. But you have to be willing to try."

She lifted her lashes and looked straight into his eyes. "Are you talking about...?"

"Yes. *Us.*" Still holding her hands, he returned her gaze, nearly oblivious to the group of young people settling noisily into the adjacent table.

"Don't press me, Jim."

Damn, she was lovely...and too selfless for her own good. "Okay. Slow and easy. But are you willing to try—"

"Try?"

"To see how the story ends."

She hesitated, then gave a brief nod. A lock of hair fell across her cheek. "Yes, I'll try."

With his fingers, he brushed her soft brown hair back. Her whispered promise filled him with a contentment he hadn't experienced in years.

AFTER DINNER, Connie sat on her bed running her fingertip over the lovely cameo, recalling the unforgettable afternoon. Erin and Adele had both quizzed her about the outing, but she'd sidestepped them with a "Fine. We had a nice time," deliberately ignoring Erin's out-with-it look. She didn't want to talk about Jim, to diminish the glow she still felt. It had been so long—when?—since she'd gone weak in the knees as a husky masculine voice whispered an endearment. She wanted to take the experience and wrap it in soft lamb's wool, keep it in a safe place where only she had access to the precious memory.

Get a grip. What in the world was she doing harboring these romantic notions? Possibly jeopardizing both their professional futures? Letting her fantasies obscure her real responsibilities under this very roof? This afternoon had been an interlude, like a scene in one of Adele's old movies—Katharine Hepburn in Venice or Deborah Kerr on an ocean liner. Beautiful, memorable, heart stopping...but illusory. Indulging herself was easy in the courtyard of a Grapevine coffee shop, impossible in the spotlight of Keystone, where subtleties, nuances, even seemingly inconsequential actions were seized upon and made fodder for the gossip mill.

She'd been content enough before Jim's arrival, reconciled to life without a man. In a way, she wished he'd never come, never upset her ordered routine. And yet, she'd promised him. She'd said, "I'll try."

Gently she laid the cameo on the bed. She hugged herself to ward off a sudden shiver. What might trying involve? Did she have the courage? And what if she did and Jim still wanted children?

The phone on her desk rang. She made no move to answer. It would be for Erin anyway. But, no. "Mo-om, for you. Ms. Carver."

Connie plucked a sweater from the desk chair and pulled it around her shoulders before picking up the receiver. "Hi, Pam. What's up?"

"A couple of things. The bad news first. Don't you have Stanley Henderson in class?"

"Yes, why?"

"Ginny asked me to call. She's been notifying all his teachers that his house was the target of vandals last night."

"Toilet paper? Plowing his lawn?"

Pam sighed. "Worse, I'm afraid. Lime on his grass spelling out 'Wuss.'"

Slumping into the chair, Connie tried to collect her thoughts. "That's awful. The poor kid has enough problems without harassment from...who? Do they know?"

"No. But Ginny's been concerned about some incidents at school. Stuff like Stanley's notebook disappearing in geometry class, somebody putting Vaseline on his locker padlock. And who knows what's happened in the boys' john? She wants us to keep our eyes and ears open.''

"Were Stanley's parents around?"

"What do you think? His dad's still in Saudi or somewhere and his mother is at a spa in Houston. Ginny just happened to drive down his street on her way to church this morning. When she saw the lawn, she stopped and talked with Stanley. Didn't get much out of him. But she said he's obviously angry and scared."

Reflecting on the note he'd written on his test, Connie decided to call Ginny immediately instead of waiting to see her tomorrow. Stanley definitely needed help. "I can imagine." She paused. "I hate to think any of our kids are involved."

"Who else could it be?"

"Does Dr. Campbell know?"

"Ginny tried to reach him this afternoon but had to leave a message on his answering machine." Pam cleared her throat. "Which brings me to my second reason for calling."

Inexplicably, Connie felt a premonitory chill. "Which is?"

"When are you going to come clean about our handsome new headmaster?"

"Wh-what do you mean?" Connie could kick herself for stammering.

"You weren't the only one in Grapevine this afternoon. I went out there to do some early Christmas shopping." Pam gave a throaty, self-satisfied chuckle.

"Way to go, friend. Even from a distance I could see how he was looking at you."

"Pam, it's not what you think." Or was it? She hated having to play games.

"Why not? Are you stupid or just so out of practice you don't recognize when a man's crazy about you?"

Connie's defenses crumpled. "You think...?"

"No question about it, sweetie. And I think it's great!" She continued, her voice rising with excitement. "You two knew each other a lot better in Washington than you let on, right?"

"Pam, I don't know what to say. I feel embarrassed, but it's also such a relief to be able to talk about it."

"I suppose you're whipping yourself up one side and down the other because you think you have to be proper at school and Joan of Arc at home." As if Pam could sense Connie's hesitation, she rattled on. "Well, screw that. You deserve some fun. When do you suppose another hunk like Jim Campbell is going to come along? Forget about what people think. It's not like you're doing anything wrong."

"I know. Still..."

"Muzzle that little censor in your head right now. Read my lips. Go for it!" She paused. "You want to, don't you?"

"Yes, I do." The words had popped out so automatically they surprised her.

"Then quit worrying about the rest of the world. It will keep spinning even without your hand on the controls." She lowered her voice. "Connie, I'm really pleased for you. And don't worry. This is just between you and me."

"Thanks. I know I can depend on you. And something tells me I'll need a friend."

"Then count on me. See you tomorrow."

Connie replaced the phone in its cradle. She felt an uncharacteristic aliveness, a sense of anticipation. There was no turning back. She really did want to know the end of the story.

CHAPTER EIGHT

AT THE START OF second-period world history the next morning, Connie stared at the empty seat, first row, fourth desk. Sophomore girls chattered about their weekend activities, Brad Scanlon scaled several desks to reach his, a wadded-up piece of notebook paper sang past her ear on its way to the wastebasket. "Settle down" came automatically out of her mouth, but her attention was riveted on the vacant chair. Stanley's.

Raising her eyes toward the back of the room, she saw Jerry Rutherford and Hale Metzger lolling in their seats, long legs stretched insolently into the aisle. Hale glanced toward Stanley's desk, cocked his jaw in a wiseacre grin, gave Jerry a surreptitious thumbs-up and then turned innocently attentive baby blue eyes to meet hers. She honestly tried to like all her students, but there was something about these two—glib, devious, unctuous. The outer trappings of decency were all there—the salon haircuts, the orthodontist's dream teeth, the designer jeans, the graceful movements of born athletes. But a sinister, almost amoral, aura made her distinctly uncomfortable around them. Even afraid. She shuddered, then opened the textbook on her desk. For Pete's sake, they were only kids.

Teaching the Spanish Inquisition to this group on a

Monday morning was like slogging through mud in hip waders. And it didn't help that her gaze kept straying to the ominously empty seat. Stanley might be a loner, but he never missed school.

By the time the class ended, she'd made up her mind. Catching one of her juniors as he entered the room for third period, she asked him to start the class on their discussion of Andrew Jackson's presidency. She ducked into the teachers' lounge, grateful she was alone, scanned the student directory and dialed Stanley's home. No answering machine, just a succession of hollow rings. With increasing dread, she waited. Finally, on the ninth ring, she heard the click of a receiver being lifted. Trying to talk calmly, she said, "May I speak to Stanley?" Silence. She tried again, more urgently. "Stanley, this is Mrs. Weaver. Is that you? Answer me." A groan. Then again, silence... shattered by the sound of a phone crashing to the floor.

Connie slammed the receiver down and raced for Ginny Phillips's office, aware both of the irrationality of her act, based on so little evidence, and of the absolute conviction there was no time to waste. *Hang on, Stanley. Just hang on!*

"HARRIET, please cancel my afternoon meeting with the cheerleader mothers. Something's come up." Jim hung up the phone, then stared at the deli sandwich on the paper plate. It was nearly three. He should be ravenous. Glancing around Ralph's office, he watched the principal nibble on a pickle, Ginny Phillips toy with a chip and Connie stare vacantly out the window, her face ashen. Thank God for Connie's intuition. Alerted by Ginny, he'd immediately called the police to check the Henderson home. Then he and Ralph had driven to the boy's house, followed by Connie and Ginny.

When no one answered the bell, a uniformed officer had entered the residence through an unlocked patio door. The rest was a blur—the discovery of Stanley's limp body and the empty pill bottle; the frantic and, fortunately, successful resuscitation efforts; the harsh two-tone ambulance siren; the frustration of waiting for word in the emergency room; then the attempts to locate phone numbers for next of kin. And, of course, the pathetic and disturbing note found on the boy's neatly ordered bedroom desk, the words not scrawled but precisely printed: "I'm not being selfish. Nobody'll miss Stanley the Wuss. Mother and Father can do whatever they want now, and those jerks at school won't have me to kick around anymore."

Halfheartedly, Jim bit into the pastrami on rye. After interviewing a neighbor, the police had finally reached Stanley's mother in Houston, but there was still no word from his father, whose oil company was tracking him down somewhere in the Mideast. No wonder the kid had wanted out.

Jim knew he couldn't overlook the school's responsibility. The "jerks at school" may have pushed the young man over the edge. He forced the food down his throat, then spoke. "It goes without saying we owe Connie a great deal of credit." She turned toward him, her eyes luminous with unshed tears. "For the moment Stanley's out of danger. But we have to consider how

Keystone may have contributed to the problem and what we're going to do about it.''

Ralph nodded in agreement, then turned to Ginny. "Can you give us any background?"

Ginny set the potato chip down, then wiped her hands on a napkin. "There's no question he was being harassed. Little things. Ralph, you remember my telling you about the time some of the sophomore guys deliberately knocked his books out of his arms, then stomped on his papers."

"I called those fellas on the carpet. Thought I had them all straightened out." His shoulders slumped. "Apparently not."

"Don't be too hard on yourself, Ralph," Jim said. "This isn't the first time something like this ever happened in a school. We'll always have our bullies."

Connie spoke softly. "Stanley was more vulnerable than most. Where was his support system?"

Jim's heart ached as he looked at her; her concern and silent accusation were evident in the worry lines creasing her forehead. "Connie's right. Obviously the kid couldn't turn to his parents."

"He sent us a loud, clear signal on Connie's test," Ginny reminded them.

"Too bad we didn't have time to follow up," Ralph said. "And you talked with Stanley yesterday."

Ginny sighed. "Talked *at* him was more like it. He was polite, but extremely withdrawn. I expressed my availability for help, gave him my home phone number, but he just sat there looking as if he was ready to explode. I could feel his anger."

"What *did* he say?" Jim asked.

"Only that he didn't need any help. That nothing mattered anyway."

"Jeez." Ralph rubbed his hand over his forehead.

"We'll offer his parents whatever resources we can," Jim said. "But what about our students? Any idea who's been making Stanley's life miserable?"

Ginny spoke through pursed lips. "The 'in' jocks."

Connie turned to Ginny. "Jerry Rutherford or Hale Metzger included?"

"Top of the list. Why do you ask?"

Connie briefly related the boys' suspicious reactions to Stanley's absence.

Ralph groaned. "That figures. Leadership at its worst. And the hell of it is, I have never been able to catch those two in the act."

Jim balled up his sandwich bag and tossed it into the wastebasket. "I think we can begin by having a chat with those two. Sounds as if they may be a little short on caring and character."

"It's a place to start," Ralph mumbled doubtfully.

Jim stood. "These fellas on the football team?"

Ralph looked up at him. "Yes, why?"

"Maybe Kurt Mueller can put some pressure on them."

Jim sensed a sudden chill in the room. Ginny studied her lap, Ralph simply stared into space and Connie looked at him as if he'd suggested Martians had invaded the school. "What's the matter?"

Ralph sighed. "Rutherford and Metzger are Mueller's fair-haired boys, the great hope for the future of Keystone football."

Jim clenched his hands. "Are you saying football players get special treatment?"

Connie, glancing at Ralph, who was nervously twisting his paper napkin, filled the awkward silence. "Jim, watch your step."

Jim fought the anger sweeping over him. "We'll see about that." Picking up Ralph's desk phone, he dialed the athletic office. "Coach, Jim Campbell here. Rutherford and Metzger will be late to practice." He waited while the coach offered vociferous objections. "I won't keep them long, but I *will* keep them. You and I need to discuss this matter, as well. I'll be in my office after you finish practice. See you then." He hung up before the coach could object.

Checking his watch, he turned to Ralph. "We have ten minutes before the end of last period, right? Would you bring the two young men in here and join me for this discussion?" Ralph nodded, then departed.

Ginny and Connie gathered up the remains of their half-eaten lunches and prepared to leave. "Thank you both," Jim said. "Remind me never to take woman's intuition lightly."

Connie's gaze lingered on his face. "Good luck."

After she and Ginny left, Jim leaned dejectedly on Ralph's desk, pondering his approach to the young men. He hoped for all their sakes that schoolboy mischief, not malicious cruelty, was at the root of this incident.

CONNIE STOPPED at the upper-school office to thank the secretary for locating a substitute on such short notice, then returned to her classroom. Emotionally drained, she sank into her desk chair and mechanically began reading the note left by the sub. Tomorrow the students would be asking where she'd been. What could she say? All she could think about was poor lonely Stanley, an obvious and natural victim. She was tired, but not too exhausted to be furious—furious with Stanley's self-absorbed parents, furious with adolescents who preyed on the weak to enhance their misguided manhood, furious with herself for not making greater efforts to befriend Stanley.

And now Jim was in the middle of the mess. She didn't envy him having to confront Jerry and Hale...or Kurt Mueller. For everyone's sake, she hoped he could defuse the situation.

"You okay?"

Connie looked up. Pam stood in the doorway.

"Not really. C'mon in."

Pam closed the door behind her, drew a student desk close to Connie and sat down. "What's going on? Frankly, you look like hell."

Her friend's honesty drew a tired smile from her. "That's how I feel. Mangled."

"Tell me about it." Folding her hands on the desktop like an expectant student, Pam waited.

"It's Stanley Henderson."

"Oh, God," Pam intoned.

"He tried to commit suicide this morning." Connie felt the tears she'd been fighting all day gather behind her eyelids. "He's out of danger. His grandparents are with him. But I can't stop thinking how close a call it was." She pulled a tissue out of a desk drawer and carefully wiped her eyes before telling Pam the disturbing details.

"Jeez, Connie. What if you hadn't decided to call?"

"I know. I don't even want to think about it."

"I hate suspecting any of our own kids might be involved."

"Me, too. But you and I weren't born yesterday."

"Especially where adolescent testosterone is concerned," Pam added dryly. "Does Dr. Campbell have any idea what he's wading into?"

"I don't know." The tears threatened again. Connie looked into her friend's eyes. "Pam, I'm scared for him. You know how Kurt Mueller's made the football players a law unto themselves."

"Oh, honey." Pam stroked Connie's forearm. "Your Jim's a strong man with good instincts."

"I know you're right, but—"

"But you care so much?" Pam's questioning gaze left no room for equivocation.

"Am I being irrational?" Connie lowered her eyes and waited for Pam's usual tell-it-like-it-is response.

"You're bushed. But irrational? Not likely. Fragile, maybe. You've had a brutal day and you're worried about the man you love."

Connie's head snapped up. "The man I—"

"Love, babe. It's written all over you."

"Oh, Pam. What am I going to do? He's got enough troubles without me."

"Do? Maybe get some rest. Let the headmaster make his own decisions. About you. About Stanley. About the school. He's a big boy."

"I just don't want to be a complication."

Pam shoved the student desk back and stood. "Maybe you should be." She smiled sympathetically. "He's not only a big boy, my friend, he's a virile man who looks at you the same way you look at him."

"But...the school?"

"Keystone be damned." Pam's voice rose. "For once, Connie, think about yourself." She gave Connie a sisterly hug. "Now, go home, for God's sake, and get some rest. It'll all look better in the morning."

"I hope so. Thanks, Pam, for listening."

"Maybe someday if I meet Mr. Right, you can return the favor."

"Gladly."

Pam left the room, and Connie, with the force of habit, began gathering up the books and papers she needed to take home. Yet she knew she'd never be able to concentrate tonight, not with everything that had happened, not with the confusion she was feeling—regret and anger about Stanley; concern for Jim; and, despite all her attempts to rationalize away the obvious, the uncertainty and joy of acknowledging that she was indeed, at forty, in love.

At that moment, she heard a knock at the door. She looked up as Erin sailed in and settled in the desk just vacated by Pam. "Mom, isn't it awful?"

"What?"

"Stanley Henderson. He tried to kill himself." Erin's eyes were rounded in horror. "Do you know him?"

"Yes, but where did you hear such a thing?"

"Kyle. Some of the football players were talking

about it. One of the guys lives near Stanley. His mother called him at school to tell him.''

Connie felt tension knife through her. "What did the boys say?''

"Only that they'd had a little fun with him and he couldn't take it. Said it served the little wuss right.'' Big tears pooled in her widened eyes. "That's horrible.''

Handing Erin a tissue, Connie fought for control. "Yes, that *is* horrible. Insensitive and cruel. How widespread is this knowledge?''

Erin wiped her eyes, then blew her nose. "Pretty much all the kids who were hanging around after school. You knew about this?''

"Yes, honey. The good news is Stanley's going to be all right.''

"But how can he ever face coming back here to school?''

"I don't know. Time will tell.'' Connie picked up her purse, abandoning any intention of taking work with her. "Let's go home and collapse.''

As they walked toward the door, Erin added with a sigh, "I can't collapse. Big physics test tomorrow.''

Concerned, Connie studied her daughter. Her complexion was sallow and big bags underscored her eyes. Erin was driving herself way too hard.

EARLY THAT EVENING, Jim closed the blinds in his office and settled behind his desk to sign letters. Mueller was scheduled to appear in half an hour, but Jim fully expected the coach to keep him waiting. Bearing down with his pen, Jim felt frustration travel through his arm, into his fingers and onto the typed pages as he scrawled his name.

He couldn't erase the picture of those two cocky kids sitting in Ralph's office, looking for all the world like Sunday-school perfect-attendance honorees. The obsequiousness, the calculated blend of innocence and outrage, the smoothly rehearsed answers. "No, sir, we have no idea who might have trashed Stanley's yard. Maybe someone from Rangeland Academy." "With all due respect, sir, I don't think it's any of your business where we were Saturday night." "Too bad about Stanley, but what's the big deal?"

Jerry Rutherford had finally had the grace to look uncomfortable, but the Metzger boy had been all bland sophistication, playing the unjustly maligned victim. Neither one of them had broken under questioning. Jim hadn't really expected that to happen, but he hoped he'd worried them.

Jim set aside the last letter. Now for the next unpleasant duty. He dialed Phil Buxton's number. On the off chance the story made the morning paper, he didn't want his board president caught unawares. Buxton was genuinely distressed to hear about Stanley but guarded when Jim raised the possibility that Keystone students' actions might have precipitated the suicide attempt. "Be sure you get all your ducks in a row, Jim. Hale Metzger's father is a big donor and quite influential in the community. I don't know the Rutherford kid, but we don't need this incident blowing up in our faces."

Politics. It always comes down to politics. "At this point, I'm not suggesting these two kids were directly involved. From Ralph and others, I've learned that several of our athletes, especially football players, have a history of harassing their fellow students. Are you suggesting we look the other way?''

''Hell, no. That's exactly the kind of crap the board wants stopped.''

''At what cost?'' Jim knew what he wanted to hear.

''What exactly are you implying?'' Shrewdly, Buxton hedged, forcing Jim to clarify.

''As I understood my job description, I am to stand firm in helping students develop character and show compassion.''

''Right.''

''No matter whose kids are involved?'' Jim clutched the receiver, waiting.

''Yes.''

''Thank you, Phil. That's what I was hoping you'd say. I'm soliciting Kurt Mueller's cooperation in applying some pressure.''

''I wish you well.''

''I'll keep you apprised. Good night.'' Jim hung up the phone, relieved that he had Buxton's support, because all his instincts suggested the situation could get ugly.

He pulled up the football roster on his computer. Metzger was a wide receiver, one of five sophomores on the varsity. He wrote down the names of the other four, including Rutherford. Possibly kids whose early stardom had gone to their heads.

Hearing the outer door of the administration building open, he shut down the computer and crossed the room to greet the athletic director. One look at Mueller's face, and Jim knew this wasn't going to be easy. The man scowled beneath his ball cap. When he shook Jim's hand, it was more a competition than a greeting. "Couldn't this have waited till tomorrow?"

"No." Gesturing at the wooden armchair, Jim said, "Have a seat." Then he rounded his imposing desk and sat down, hands folded on the surface. "Have you heard about Stanley Henderson?"

"Kid who tried to commit suicide? Yeah, I heard."

"From whom?"

"My players." Mueller remained impassive, eyes never wavering from Jim's.

"Specifically?"

"Hell, what difference does it make?"

"Just answer the question, please."

"Some of the sophomores. Maybe Rutherford."

"Do you know Stanley?"

"No. Just what the kids say about him."

"Which is?"

"What a wimp he is. More interested in chess than sports or girls."

"How long has that kind of locker room character assassination been permitted?"

Mueller leaned forward. "What're you suggesting?"

"I'm suggesting that's exactly the kind of labeling we're supposed to discourage. Athletes above all should be setting a positive example."

Mueller shrugged. "They do fine on the field. What more do you expect me to do?"

Barely concealing his irritation, Jim sat back in his chair, forcing his hands to rest on the arms. "I expect you or any faculty member to help our students understand that all human beings are to be treated with respect. As a coach, you have great influence with your players.''

"So?"

"So, Ralph and I have reason to believe that some of your players have been making young Henderson's life pretty miserable. But no one seems willing to come forward—either to acknowledge responsibility or blow the whistle."

Mueller's expression hardened. "Look, I'm sorry about the kid. But you're barking up the wrong tree making these half-assed accusations. Hell, these are high-strung fellas who might get a little out of control occasionally. But you got no proof."

Jim said nothing, simply waited, his eyes locked on Mueller's.

The coach stood abruptly. "I'll do what I can. But you gotta understand this is play-off season. We don't need these kinds of distractions. Kids have a lot more on their minds than some pansy—"

Jim leaped to his feet. "Stop right there. That's exactly what I'm talking about. Stanley Henderson is a student at this school, and his well-being is every bit as important to me as any other student, football players included. I'm no longer asking for your help. I'm telling you. I want the young men under your influence to know, beyond any doubt, that you will not tolerate demeaning talk or harassment. Do I make myself clear?"

Mueller glared at him, then removed his cap, ran a paw through his cropped hair and replaced the cap with authority. "Loud and clear."

"Good night, then."

The coach lumbered toward the door, then paused with his hand on the knob. "One thing, Jimbo. Be damn sure you know what fights are worth pickin'."

The empty building echoed with the sound of the outside door slamming shut. Jim pounded a fist against the wall in frustration. That last remark was a threat if he'd ever heard one. Schools were crazy places. Power was seldom held by those with titular authority. One challenge for any headmaster was learning whose fingers manipulated the strings. Today he'd discovered two of them: Kurt Mueller, whom he'd suspected, and Hale Metzger's father. With ironic clarity, he realized this interim position was a double-edged career sword.

SITTING ON HER BED in her pajamas, Connie reread Colin's letter—another example of his impeccable timing. Today, however, Colin on top of Stanley was merely anticlimactic. "I am not happy about your intransigence in this matter," Colin had written. "I suppose it won't hurt to allow Erin to apply elsewhere. However, financially, it's a frivolous decision." Connie's fingers cramped around the heavy vellum stationery. Frivolous! To permit your gifted daughter to explore her options?

She laid the letter aside to turn down the bed. The cool sheets and downy pillows looked incredibly inviting. As she crossed the room to turn off the overhead light, the phone rang.

She grabbed the receiver. "Hello?"

"Hi, it's Jim. Am I calling too late?"

She picked up the phone, sank to the floor and

leaned against the foot of the bed, aware of a delicious warmth enveloping her body. "Not at all."

"You had a rough day. I wanted to thank you for being on top of things with Stanley."

"I just wish my sixth sense had kicked in sooner."

"Don't second-guess yourself. Are you okay?"

"Tired, yes, but fine. How about you?"

"I'll manage."

"How was the rest of your afternoon?"

"You mean the boys? About as I expected. Innocence personified, and Mueller was only minimally cooperative."

"I'm sorry you're having these problems."

"Problems come with the territory. Don't worry about me."

Had he read her mind? Whatever thought she hadn't given to Erin, Stanley and Colin this evening had been focused on Jim. And now he was worrying about her. Exactly what was wrong. She couldn't sidestep the ramifications of their roles at the school, the impossibility of just being two people who...

"Are you there?"

She coiled the phone cord around her finger. "Yes."

"This isn't an official call, you know. I needed to hear a friendly voice."

Professional objectivity drained away with every word. "Mine is."

"Was it only yesterday that we had the whole afternoon to ourselves?"

"What a difference a day makes, huh?" She hugged the phone to her chest.

"Yes and no." His voice sounded lower, more intimate. "I know what you're thinking. That you and I...that it's all too complicated."

She hesitated. "Yes."

"Well, you're wrong. You're the only thing that makes any sense at a time like this."

Unbidden, tears surfaced. It had been so long since anyone had made her feel this important. Especially a man.

He continued. "Don't let me down, Connie. I need you."

"Jim, I..."

"Don't say anything. Just let the future unfold as it will. Please?"

"I'm worried."

"That's my department. Tuck yourself in and get a good night's sleep. See you tomorrow."

She held the receiver in her hand long after he'd hung up. This was insane. She had to get her emotions in check. She'd spent her life doing what was expected, prudent, selfless. And all she wanted to do right now was cast her carefully constructed persona aside and rush into Jim's arms.

And risk disgrace.

CHAPTER NINE

THE FOLLOWING Wednesday evening Jim stood along the side wall of the cafeteria, listening to the tributes being paid Lee Frankenberg. Decked out in their Sunday best, lower-school students sang; the faculty performed a *This Is Your Life* skit; and Phil Buxton, on behalf of the trustees, gave the Frankenbergs airline passes. As the grand finale, the seniors presented their wall hanging, with each contributor relating the school history depicted in his or her square.

A productive, fulfilling career ending with well-deserved recognition. Jim envied the man and hoped, in some way, to make a positive contribution himself to Keystone. Currently, his tenure was growing rockier by the minute—thanks to Kurt Mueller and Hale Metzger, whose influential father had already phoned with a high-handed complaint about his son's being singled out for questioning. Regrettably, the Stanley Henderson incident had delayed his discussion with Mueller about the athletic department's finances, a meeting he feared might quickly become confrontational.

Jim could understand a certain amount of Texas distrust of a Yankee. After all, they did things very differently back where he came from. The first time he'd

mentioned having played college lacrosse, several
folks had eyed him warily, as if he'd announced a
preference for quiche instead of barbecue. Mueller,
too, had let him know he was in alien territory, where
football ranked right up there with the flag, Mom and
apple pie—a perspective reflected by the sports cov-
erage in the local media. Nor, despite having watched
old episodes of *Dallas,* had he been prepared for the
freewheeling, extravagant life-style of some school patrons. Acceptance obviously involved mastering cul-
tural intricacies beyond purchasing a pair of hand-
tooled cowboy boots.

Had he been too eager to bail out of Campbell
Courts and get back into education? Glancing around
the room at the beaming parents, the excited students,
the dedicated faculty, he knew the answer was no. He
just needed time to adjust. And so did they. After all,
he already spoke "school," and he could learn
"Texas."

"Quite an event. Are you enjoying yourself?"

Jim hadn't noticed Pam Carver sidle up to him.
"Immensely. This evening has given me a renewed
appreciation for Keystone. And for Dr. Frankenberg."

"He's quite a guy."

"I'm honored to be in the same company with
him."

"And with *her?*" Pam nodded at Connie, seated,
listening attentively as Tara Farley pointed to her embroidered square and explained the senior luncheon
tradition initiated by Dr. Frankenberg.

Momentarily flustered, Jim stared at Connie and the

cameo pinned to the ribbon encircling her neck, before turning to Pam. "What do you mean?"

"It's okay. I'm on *your* side. Don't worry about public opinion. It's notoriously fickle. I'd hate to see Connie sacrifice her happiness on the altar of propriety. And no matter what others say, my lips are sealed."

"Are we that obvious?"

"Yep, and I wholeheartedly approve." She winked, then eased away from him.

Thrusting a fist deep into his pants pocket, Jim leaned against the wall, furious with himself for feeling so unsettled. He'd given lip service to Connie about the—what was Pam's word?—"propriety" of their relationship. But with Pam's overt reference to the ethical dilemma, he realized he'd perhaps underestimated the conservatism of the school community.

So where did that leave him? Torn between Connie's transparently obvious emotions, his reborn attraction to her and his responsibilities to protect not only her but the school from any breath of scandal. The Keystone honeymoon period was definitely over...along with his naive notion that a headmaster's private life was his own business.

He glanced back at Connie, surprised to find her beaming a radiant smile meant for him alone—as if she'd sensed his thoughts and had reached out to steady him. What she didn't realize was that she was inadvertently advertising their situation to the assembled group. Damn, had he misled her or simply fooled himself?

Just then the school orchestra struck up the opening

strains of the alma mater. The crowd rose, joining voices in a tearily sentimental farewell to the retiring headmaster.

Jim hung around briefly for the reception before discreetly retreating to his office to work on the draft of his remarks for Friday's upper-school assembly. In the wake of the recent harassment incident, he'd chosen the topic of character. "A man's true character," he had written, "lies in what he would do if he could be assured no one else would ever know."

Studying those words, he threw down his pen. Was he a hypocrite, deluding himself that he and Connie could exist separate and apart from the institution that employed them both? But what had they done to be ashamed of? Absolutely nothing. His only error in judgment, he was beginning to believe, was underestimating the small-town mentality of the school community and the standard of behavior to which he was held. But what about his needs? What about eight empty years? Eight? Hell, more like twenty!

Frustrated, he tossed the speech aside and wandered to the window. The parking lot, empty except for his own vehicle, was cloaked in the blue white haze of the mercury-vapor lamps. In the distance, floodlights illuminated the main entrance of the upper school. A reddish-orange harvest moon climbed above the horizon in heart-stopping splendor. A wave of loneliness, unexpected and powerful, swept over him. He sighed. Surely things would look better tomorrow.

Agitated voices jarred him out of his funk. He looked up to see Kurt Mueller and a smaller man, dressed in a black overcoat, passing outside the window, walking briskly toward the gym. Suddenly, the coach stopped, then shook a fist in the man's face before stomping off. The other man paused, casually lit a cigarette, glanced warily around and then followed Mueller.

Alarmed, Jim grabbed his jacket, locked the administration building and quickly followed them to the darkened gym. Cautiously, he eased open the outer door and moved down the dark corridor toward the athletic director's office. Pale light was visible under Mueller's closed door, and Jim could hear the mumble of angry conversation.

At first, all he could catch was a phrase here and there. Mueller saying, "Just three more weeks." Then an unfamiliar menacing voice replying, "We've heard that too many times before."

"But I've always made good." The coach sounded desperate.

"Mueller, time's up. We're calling you."

A scraping noise, like a chair being shoved across the floor, followed. More mumbling. Then, as crisp and final as a referee's whistle, came the words "Pay up or shut up, Coach."

Mueller bellowed, "Goddammit, Mancuso, read my lips. I don't have five grand. You gotta give me till after the weekend. I can clean up on the NFL games."

The sinister voice cut through the coach's words like a stiletto slicing tendons. "No dice. The man says Friday, the man means Friday."

After backpedaling to the corridor light switch and flipping on the entire bank, Jim advanced to the office door and knocked loudly. Silence—sudden and ominous. "Mueller, open up."

Seconds passed. Jim held his breath. Then abruptly the door opened, and Mueller stood blocking Jim's entry, glaring.

"What the hell're you doin' here?"

"Heard some noises. Just checking." Beyond the coach, Jim saw the smaller man, sleek and dapper, standing quietly, a smirk on his face. "A friend of yours?"

Mueller hesitated, then nodded at his visitor. "Him? One of my suppliers. We, er, had a little business to transact."

"Well, school's out for today. Tell your supplier goodbye."

The "businessman" skirted Mueller without a glance. "I was just leaving," he said. "But—" he pointed an index finger at the coach's belly "—I'll be back."

Jim and Mueller stood eyeballing each other until they heard the click of the exit door. "Sit down," Jim barked, moving forward into the office.

"Who asked you to barge in here in the middle of the night?"

"Suit yourself, then. Don't sit." Jim stood toe to toe with the man, smelling the sour odor of perspiration. "But be in my office at ten o'clock tomorrow morning with all the financial data for the athletic department from July through October."

"No way! We gotta big game Friday."

Jim stepped back, his jaw rigid. "Ten o'clock sharp!" Then he turned, slowly shut the office door and breathed deeply. All the way down the hall he tried to get hold of himself, to quit seething. He could see the headline now: Keystone AD Embezzles Funds To Cover Gambling Debts. And that irresponsible son of a bitch was working with young men, molding character? Not anymore!

He shoved the bar to open the outside door so hard his palm stung. The cooler air hit him like a shock wave, the full implications of the scene he had just witnessed only now surfacing. Somehow he had to handle this without compromising the school's reputation. He'd permit the coach his hearing, but given the circumstances, the sooner Mueller was gone from Keystone, the better.

Adrenaline still boiling in his veins, Jim hurried back to his office. The wind had picked up, chilling him. He was in for one helluva night!

THE FULL MOON SHONE right in her eyes, keeping her awake. Finally Adele threw back the blanket, struggled to a sitting position and turned on the bedside lamp. Her entire body ached, and no matter how she rolled and shifted, she couldn't get comfortable. Yolanda stretched beside her, yawning.

Adele plucked up her glasses and peered at the clock. Three a.m. The old waltz "Three O'clock in the Morning" played in her head. Many a time she and Edgar had danced the whole night through. For a brief instant, she pictured herself in his arms gliding across a spacious ballroom floor. Well, her days of gardenias and moonlight and dancing were long gone.

Ben-Gay was *not* a romantic scent and hobbling to the bathroom was hardly a waltz!

She swung her legs over the side of the bed and fumbled for her house slippers. Maybe with any luck, tonight she'd only have to make one trip.

Later, as she climbed back into bed, she thumped her pillow in frustration. Her body was betraying her. She couldn't even get to and from the bathroom without shortness of breath. Maybe Connie had a point about exercising. But how could she take long walks when merely crossing the room was an adventure?

She groaned, relaxing back onto the unforgiving mattress, knowing she'd be awake for quite a spell. Thinking about days gone by was little comfort. Only reminded her of how much had changed since Edgar had died. It seemed like part of her had gone with him. It was harder and harder to be cheerful. For Connie's and Erin's sakes, though, she tried.

But they were worries, too. Erin was getting skinny as a rail, picking at her food or grabbing an apple and rushing off without a proper breakfast. And she stayed up too late studying. That school ought to be ashamed of itself, giving those poor children so much work. Just tonight, she'd heard Connie telling Erin to turn out her light and go to sleep. Erin, all weepy, had sassed her mother, telling her she had to finish some fool project. Adele rolled onto her side, dislodging Yolanda. She hadn't liked Erin's tone of voice. Snappish-like.

Then Connie. Something was going on with her. Last evening she'd spent more time than usual getting all gussied up for the do for Dr. Frankenberg. And she'd had a sort of glow about her. Adele jerked the covers up over her shoulders. Once again, she hoped Connie didn't have any foolish notions about that new headmaster. He might be likable enough, but trouble lay down that road. Why, whatever in the world would people think?

And that cameo! Connie had outright blushed when Adele had asked where it came from. "Jim insisted," Connie had said. A full feeling in Adele's chest caused her to grope on the bedside table for her antacid tablets. Lying awake worrying wasn't bad enough; now she had heartburn, as well!

RUBBING A HAND over his just-shaved skin, Jim peered through bloodshot eyes at the list on his desk and, with a sinking feeling, dialed the phone. It had taken the rest of the night to contemplate strategy and review George Carey's athletic department financial report. He'd raced home about six in the morning to have a quick shower and grab a change of clothes before heading back to his office. Mueller's actions defied reason, though clearly the man needed help.

"Phil? Sorry to bother you so early, but we have a problem here that's sensitive and potentially controversial. Any chance you could come by here on your way to work?... No, I'd rather not discuss it on the phone.... Thanks. Eight will be fine."

Next he left a message on Carey's voice mail requesting him to clear his schedule for the afternoon. At this point, the fewer people involved the better, but Buxton's input was vital. He reviewed the notes he'd made early this morning—a formidable list of decisions. How to wrest the checkbook and financial records from Mueller. What, if anything, could be done about the danger the athletic director faced from his bookmaker. Whether the man should coach tomorrow's game. The extent to which any other faculty members might be involved. And, most critical of all, how to protect the school's short- and long-term interests. Handled improperly, this affair could be become a sticky media and legal issue.

When his secretary arrived, he asked her to cancel several engagements, including the rescheduled meeting with the cheerleader mothers. Two appointments, however, couldn't be missed. A noon one with Stanley Henderson's grandparents and a five o'clock meeting with Hale Metzger's father.

He slumped back in his chair and removed his glasses, dangling them by one earpiece. *Well, Campbell. You asked for it, you got it. You're the headmaster. Dr. Frankenberg escaped just in time.*

He set the glasses on his desk and ambled to the window, where he could watch the students stream into the upper school—happy, oblivious to the trouble brewing. It was their character development and well-being he had to keep in mind, not the sordid actions of adults.

Across the way he spotted Erin, parting company with her mother and joining a group of girls huddled beside a Jeep Cherokee. Connie, long hair lifting in the breeze, made her way purposefully toward the entrance, her cheeks pink with cold. A throbbing sensation pulsed through him. Her loveliness, her goodness, that long-limbed graceful walk of hers—Lord, he wanted her. And he needed her. Desperately.

He raised his arms, resting both hands on the window frame, his forehead pressed against the cool pane of glass. And now he had to set her aside. She was right. A school could be vicious. He had to protect her by staying away from what he craved most—her warmth, support and comfort.

If he screwed up with Mueller, he could just about kiss goodbye any hope of a positive recommendation from the Keystone board. He pushed away from the window, paced to the phone and buzzed Harriet to bring him more coffee. It would take more than caffeine to keep his wits about him today, but another hit sure couldn't hurt.

GEORGE CAREY, a thick file on his lap, sat in the corner of Jim's office. Phil Buxton had suggested having a witness present for this and any future meetings with the athletic director. Probably a good idea, Jim thought. A lawsuit was the last thing Keystone needed.

Drumming his fingers on his desk, Jim eyed the wall clock. Mueller was late. His opening offensive play? Undoubtedly, the man would try to bluster his way through this interview. The board president had reacted to Jim's suspicions with undisguised alarm. The school couldn't have a compulsive gambler and embezzler on staff, but personnel issues had to be kept in strictest confidence. Suspending or firing the athletic director would provoke upheaval, especially among those who thought the man walked on water.

At ten-fifteen, after a soft tap, the door opened. "Coach Mueller to see you." The secretary stood aside as the athletic director brushed past her. "Can I get you gentlemen some coffee?"

Jim rose. "That won't be necessary. Hold all my calls, Harriet." When the secretary closed the door behind her, Jim looked directly at Mueller, who held one slim folder. Still dressed in the Keystone jogging suit he'd had on last night, he stood legs apart, the stubble on his chin and his puffy eyes suggesting he'd never left campus. "Have a seat at the table. I've asked George to sit in on this meeting."

Mueller glared at the business manager, slammed his folder on the table and slowly sat down. His expression could have stopped an entire defensive line. Jim leaned over, palms flat on the table, his face inches from Mueller's. "Looks as if we have the serious matter of a shortfall in athletic department funds to discuss. It will be in your best interests to cooperate fully in our investigation. Understood?"

The coach curled a lip and remained silent.

"I'll take that as a yes," Jim said as he seated himself at the head of the table. "What can you tell us about why bills aren't being paid on time?"

"They always get paid."

"When? How much is interest on late payments costing us?"

"I don't have those figures."

I'll bet not. Jim could feel his jaw working. "And where has the cash from concessions and gate receipts disappeared to? Or do you have deposit slips—" he nodded at Mueller's folder "—to account for that income?"

The coach glanced over at George, who waited impassively. "Here." He shoved the folder at Jim.

Jim opened it and studied the contents, letting the athletic director stew while he took his time interpreting the obviously doctored figures. Gate and concession income far below those of previous years; only a few of the many creditors reflected. A far from thorough or accurate accounting. So the man was going to stonewall. Well, Jim hadn't really expected him to confess. His ego was far too big for that. Closing the folder, he turned to the coach. "Effective immediately George will handle all financial business of the athletic department." Jim stood and held out his hand. "Give me the checkbook."

Mueller's eyes bore into Jim's. "I don't have it."

"Then we'll have to go get it."

The coach shoved back his chair and launched to his feet. "You can't do that!"

"Yes, Mueller, I can. In fact, I've been directed by Phil Buxton to do exactly that. Furthermore, I've been asked to set up a meeting at two o'clock Sunday afternoon to determine your future, if any, at this school."

"Look, Jimbo, I don't need this crap. I've got a game tomorrow night. An important one. You're in way over your head here. I've got friends in high places."

Jim busied himself gathering up the coach's papers, then spoke mildly. "I'm sure you do. Let me caution you. It would not be in anyone's best interests to make public what I observed last night. And it might be advisable for you to bring your attorney Sunday."

When Mueller looked up, his expression was venomous, nor could Jim ignore the menace of the coach's clenched hands. "George and I will walk back to your office with you to retrieve the checkbook, unpaid bills and anything else necessary for an internal audit. Meanwhile, you are to keep this matter under wraps. Buxton and I have agreed it's too late to make any coaching changes for tomorrow's game."

Mueller exploded. "You've got that right!" He strutted up to Jim, poked a finger in his chest and hissed, "Hear me, boy. Don't dick around with me. And if you know what's good for you, don't dick around with my program, either."

Jim stepped aside and nodded to George, who looked uncomfortably from one man to the other before slowly rising to his feet.

"I'm afraid the dicking around has already been done." Jim opened the door. "Between now and two o'clock Sunday, you'd better give some serious thought to your personal situation and to Keystone's best interests."

As Mueller, accompanied by Jim and George, stomped out, Jim took a few deep breaths to calm his roiling stomach before acknowledging his board president's insight.

No doubt about it—the situation was going to get ugly.

THE AUDITORIUM ECHOED with the slamming and banging of seats, the shuffle of feet and the uproar of teenagers calling across the room to one another. Connie and a couple of other faculty members stood at the

back shooing reluctant students inside for their
monthly assembly. As the student council president
called the group to order, Connie sought out a vacant
seat, along the way reminding several students to put
aside their homework and pay attention. Today was
Jim's first address to the upper school. Most of the
kids seemed willing to give him the benefit of the
doubt, provided he didn't make any radical changes.

After Ralph's obligatory announcements, Jim approached the podium. Keeping her emotions bottled
while being around him like this seemed artificial, but
necessary under the circumstances.

When he cleared his throat, she noticed pronounced
worry lines around his eyes and uncharacteristic tension in his body. Strange. It wasn't like him to be
nervous.

He began with a story of two long-distance runners,
good friends as well as competitors, who had spent an
entire season in fierce head-to-head competition, first
one winning a meet, then the other. In the state championship, after a grueling race, the two approached the
finish line in a dead heat. One held out his hand to the
other. Grinning in spontaneous agreement, they
clasped hands and crossed the line together. And were
disqualified for breaking meet rules by touching each
other!

Jim paused, before challenging his audience, "What
might we learn from this incident? And how might
each of us have reacted under similar circumstances,
particularly if we were convinced no officials were
watching our actions?

"Long after the championship trophy rested discolored and dusty in the back of some display case," Jim suggested, "that moment of friendship, mutual respect and dignity ennobled them. Each young man cared about the other and recognized and affirmed the other's talent and merit." He made eye contact with the youngsters. "Losers? Or young men of character?"

Scanning the audience, Connie could tell Jim's anecdote had captured their attention. With flashes of humor and a noticeable lack of preachiness, he spoke of the importance of honoring not only your fellow human beings but yourself.

Connie's attention strayed to Jerry Rutherford, who fidgeted with a pencil, and to Hale Metzger, who, with arms folded across his letter jacket, lounged back in his seat, affecting bored indifference.

Jim leaned forward over the podium. "First and foremost, we have to live with ourselves. Perhaps the most telling question of all is this—what would you do if you could be assured no one else would ever know?" He paused, then concluded, "The answer defines not only your sportsmanship but your character."

Connie sat a moment, stunned by his question, feeling a flush spread beneath her collar. Around her, students clambered noisily toward the exits. If no one would ever know? She'd pursue Jim shamelessly, ignoring family and professional considerations, jeopardizing reputation, livelihood.

"Mrs. W., you sick?" Brad Scanlon had stopped in the aisle, eyeing Connie with concern.

She tried a smile. "No, Brad. Why?"

He tilted his head. "I dunno. You just looked kinda...dopey."

Rising to her feet, she recovered her sense of humor. "Why, Brad, you say the sweetest things."

He grinned. "I'm just glad you're okay. See ya later."

She stooped to pick up a gum wrapper, then moved quickly to the door, where Jim waited. "Nice speech."

His eyes were warm. "Thanks. Maybe it made a dent."

"It did with me."

"How so?"

Before she could answer, Ralph walked up. "Jim, I'm available now if you want to fill me in about...that other matter."

"Be right there." Before he followed the principal, he turned back to Connie. "Could I pick you up for breakfast tomorrow. Say around eight-thirty?"

Connie smiled. "I'd like that."

"Okay, then." Jim backed away. "We need to talk."

Was she overly sensitive or had his shoulders slumped at those final words?

CHAPTER TEN

"CON-NIEEE." Adele's voice rose. "You can't be serious."

Connie calmly poured herself a cup of coffee. "Mama, be reasonable. It's breakfast in broad daylight in a public place."

Her mother frowned over the top of a cookbook she'd been studying. "But he's the headmaster. It just isn't done."

"This is not 1890. We are professional colleagues who happen to be old friends." Her cup rattled in its saucer when she sat down at the table. "I'm an adult." She blew on the hot liquid, trying to dispel the defensiveness her mother, with uncanny effectiveness, had provoked.

"All I can say is, I hope you know what you're doing." Adele sniffed, then flipped the page of the cookbook.

Connie fumed as she quietly drank her coffee. Irritatingly, her mother had pricked her conscience. *Did* she know what she was doing? Or was she fooling herself? Jim wanted children. She had to keep this whole thing casual. Anything else wasn't fair to him. Meanwhile, was it so terribly selfish to squeeze a little happiness out of this one year?

When she heard the doorbell, Connie set the cup and saucer in the sink, retucked her embroidered chambray shirt into her jeans and planted a kiss on her mother's head.

Flinging open the door, she was unable to stifle the enormous grin that broke across her face the minute she saw him, tall and rugged looking in thigh-hugging Levi's, a crimson-and-navy plaid flannel shirt and... cowboy boots!

"Good morning." She surveyed him. "Well, look at you. You could pass for a born-on-the-ranch Texan."

Humor glinted in his eyes. "The Stetson's next." He placed his hands on her shoulders. "Truthfully, now. I don't look ridiculous?"

When he made her heart race like Clint Eastwood in full gallop? "No, Jim. You do not look ridiculous." She grabbed her denim jacket. "'Bye, Mama."

"Great. Because I'm taking you to Ranger Jack's for the biggest country breakfast this side of the Pecos."

Ranger Jack's was an institution—red cracked-vinyl banquettes, chrome-and-yellow Formica tables, food-stained plastic menus and a patina of grease glazing the branding irons and rodeo posters decorating the walls. The smells of bacon and coffee filtered out some of the tobacco odor as they waited in the doorway for a table. From the speaker over their heads, Patsy Cline belted out "Crazy." Jim chuckled. "Any place you have to stand in line for breakfast has got to be good."

Connie looked at the grizzled men at the counter

slumped over their newspapers, slurping coffee—then at several elderly couples sitting mutely in booths, shoveling their forks to their mouths. "Have you been here before?"

"No. Something this classic needs to be shared."

"Next thing I know, you'll be taking me to a cattle auction."

He stroked his chin as if in deep deliberation, then caught her eye. "Might be something to consider."

A redheaded waitress with the wrinkled face of a boiled cabbage jerked her head at them. "Yonder." They made their way to a window booth, where another waitress swished a wet rag over the table surface. "Know whatcha want?"

"Coffee and menus, please," Jim said.

"Back with y'all in a sec."

They had trouble deciding among the Davy Crockett, the Sam Houston and the LBJ—all, Connie joked, destined to keep cardiologists in business. Over coffee while they waited for their food, Jim told her about his meeting with Stanley's grandparents, who had agreed to secure counseling for him. Ginny would work with his teachers to ease his return to school.

"I don't think we'll have much more trouble from Jerry Rutherford," Jim added. "His parents plan to monitor his friendship with Hale Metzger. That kid, however, is another story."

"Too much money, too little attention and no discipline."

"You got it. Plus a father who's on the warpath."

She moved her elbows off the table to make room

for the waitress to set down a platter-sized omelette with hash browns. "About what?"

"Picking on his kid."

When Connie gathered up her napkin and pantomimed wiping away a tear, Jim laughed. "Too bad all parents aren't as cooperative as the Rutherfords," she said.

"What? And hold a child responsible for his actions?"

His grim look belied his light tone. She swallowed a bite of omelette, gooey with melted cheese, before speaking. "What in the world can we do for kids like Hale?"

"We fight for 'em. God knows adolescence is rarely anyone's finest hour. We chip away. We let kids, and sometimes their parents, know that discipline is part of love. If enough good adults can love kids at their worst, then we run a chance of turning some young lives around." He attacked his pancakes. "Sorry, I didn't mean to climb on my soapbox."

She regarded him thoughtfully. "Your caring is showing. I like it."

"That's all that got me through the appointment with Metzger Sr. He wasted no time in reminding me that parents' tuition dollars pay my salary. I just bit my lip and kept thinking about Hale. No wonder he's the way he is." He speared a piece of sausage. "Hey, I didn't mean to dump on you like this."

The soft look in his eyes warmed her better than any coffee. "I don't mind."

"I know you don't. Back in Washington, I felt I

could say anything to you. That you'd listen. And, best of all, you'd understand."

Connie ducked her head and wiped her mouth. Understand? She understood, all right. Soon, very soon, she'd have to find out if he still harbored his same dream—a house filled with children. But not yet. Please, not yet.

"I really appreciate that quality about you, Connie." His voice took on a hollow tone. "Even though—"

"Something else worrying you?"

He laid down his fork and looked up. "Yes. A matter I'm not at liberty to discuss." He cleared his throat. "Connie, don't take it personally if you don't hear from me for a while."

The hash browns in her stomach staged a revolt. "Oh?" How could she *not* take it personally?

"Could we leave it at that? You'll understand soon enough."

Slowly she shoved her plate toward the center of the table. She felt like a fool. "Of course." But she didn't understand. Not at all.

SUNDAY EVENING, Connie transferred an armload of clothes from the washer to the dryer, hoping she'd have time after finishing her lesson plans to iron several blouses. Adele had headed off to bed immediately after that angel program she enjoyed, and Erin, who'd bypassed her youth-group meeting when Kyle had to go to some hastily called football team meeting, was studying.

Connie added a sheet of fabric softener to the load

and started the dryer, a tick of worry nudging her. Was it her imagination or did her mother tire more easily lately? She'd try to be more observant.

Annoyed with herself for the "poor me" attitude shadowing her since the puzzling breakfast with Jim, she turned on some mellow jazz and threw herself into pre-Civil War politics. By ten, she'd devised a pretty creative set of lesson plans, if she did say so herself, and now stood over the old wooden ironing board she'd set up in the kitchen, taking satisfaction from the smell of laundry-clean steam drifting from the crisp pleats of her white blouse. Unlike teaching, this was a job where you could clearly see your results. Hale Metzger, by contrast, was still a work in progress.

At the other end of the house, she heard Erin's door slam followed by the sound of long strides moving in her direction. Connie finished the blouse collar and arranged the garment carefully on a hanger. Erin burst into the room, her face flushed, her arms flapping distractedly.

"Now look what your Dr. Campbell has done!"

"*My* Dr. Campbell?" Connie hung the blouse with the others on a cupboard door pull. "What—"

"He's fired Coach Mueller!" Erin paced distractedly, shooting furious glances at her mother.

"Erin, what are you talking about?"

"You heard me. Your precious headmaster has fired him. Right before the play-offs."

Connie's mind was as fogged as the steam from the iron, which she absently unplugged. "Where did you hear such a thing?"

"From Kyle, of course. That's what the mysterious

team meeting was about.'' Erin hopped up on the countertop, her legs swinging against the lower cabinets. "Did you know?" Her look was accusing.

"Know?" Connie swiped back a hank of hair that had escaped her ponytail. "*Know?* I can't even believe what you're telling me. Why?"

"*Why?* Now, there's a question for you. Kyle said Coach looked like a thundercloud and wouldn't talk. Mr. Buxton hemmed and hawed about, you know, confidentiality and all, and Dr. Campbell copped out. A personnel issue, he said.'' Her heels beat a tattoo against the cabinet door. "No reasons, no explanations, no nothing. Just *adios, señor.* This just plain stinks. The guys on the team are furious."

"I can well imagine." Why would Jim do such a thing? Especially now?

"Kyle hoped to get a football scholarship. Who's gonna help him now, huh?"

"Honey, I know this is upsetting, but there must be a reasonable explanation. Maybe issues are involved we don't know about."

"How can you defend Dr. Campbell? My God, Mother, Coach Mueller has been at Keystone over twenty years, and the headmaster just came. He doesn't know squat."

"I'm not defending anybody, I just think we don't have the facts yet."

Erin's eyes turned cold. "That's just like you, all high and mighty." She jumped down to the floor.

Connie bristled, resentful her daughter could make her feel like some detestable primitive life form. "I know you're upset, young lady, but you don't have to take it out on me. *I* didn't fire anybody!''

Erin shot her a skeptical look. ''But your boyfriend did.''

''B-boyfriend?'' Connie grabbed her daughter by the arms and squared off. ''What's really bugging you? My two outings with Dr. Campbell—an old friend, I might add? Or Coach Mueller?''

Erin shrugged out of her mother's grasp. ''Both. But now that you bring it up, it's embarrassing to see how you look at Dr. Campbell when you think no one's watching.'' She opened the refrigerator, rummaged through the fruit bin and came up with an orange.

''Erin, you're being ridiculous. There's nothing going on with Jim—''

''*Jim,* is it?''

''What's gotten into you? I believe you yourself referred to him as—'' she searched her memory ''—a 'hot prospect.'''

''I was joking, Mother.'' Erin concentrated on stripping the peel from her orange.

''I've told you before. Jim and I were friends years ago. Yes, I've enjoyed helping him get settled, but that's all there is to it. And if he has fired Kurt Mueller, knowing what an unpopular decision that would be, he must have very good reasons.''

Erin threw the peel into the trash, walked away, then paused in the doorway to issue her parting barb. ''You know what, Mom? Shakespeare said it best. 'Methinks the lady doth protest too much.'''

Connie stared at the empty space where her daughter had stood. Her daughter? The young woman who had confronted her tonight was a stranger. Should she chalk up Erin's metamorphosis to adolescent angst, Kyle's shocking news or her own relationship with Jim?

Trembling, she set the iron on the counter and collapsed the wobbly legs of the ironing board. Had both her mother and daughter come to take her for granted? Good old Connie, no life of her own?

She picked up her blouses, flipped off the light and stood a moment in the dark, trying to collect her thoughts, to calm her unsettled spirit. And what about Jim? Was this what he'd referred to yesterday? Lord, didn't he know he was in Texas? That the last thing you ever interfered with was football?

AFTER THE AGONIZING session with Mueller and the no-win meeting with the football team, the final words Phil Buxton had spoken to Jim were "Might want to take your phone off the hook tonight."

Now, shortly after midnight, wearily brushing his teeth, Jim conceded that the coward's way had much to recommend it. About the only productive outcome of his marathon phone conversations had been the addition to his vocabulary of several colorful Texas expletives. It was hard to calm irate parents when he couldn't come right out and announce, "Your son's coach is an embezzler and compulsive gambler," though once, between calls, he'd enjoyed the brief fantasy of saying exactly that.

The board attorney, who'd sat in when Phil and Jim asked for Mueller's resignation, had cautioned them explicitly about what they could and couldn't say publicly—in essence, nothing. Raging and sputtering, the coach had charged around the boardroom like a staked bear. In the end, however, neither he nor his attorney could dispute George Carey's figures or the implications of the scene Jim had witnessed Wednesday night. He devoutly hoped he would never again have to terminate an employee under such unpleasant circumstances. It was painful to watch a giant, prideful man shrink into a cornered, desperate one.

The divorced coach attributed his problems to unmanageable alimony and child support payments and begged the school to protect his reputation. How could he get another job without a recommendation from Keystone? When Buxton offered to settle his gambling debt and secure counseling for him, Mueller had capitulated and signed his resignation letter.

But at the team meeting, his bruised ego semi-intact, he'd made no move to ease the difficult situation. "Were you fired, Coach?" Tommy Ben Watson had asked. Mueller had merely jerked his head at Jim, shrugged and muttered, "Ask him."

Jim swished some mouthwash around, spit into the sink and was wiping his face with a towel when the phone rang—again.

"Double damn!" Jim switched off the bathroom light and picked up the phone by his bed. "Jim Campbell."

"Go back to Boston, asshole!" The male caller slammed down the receiver, leaving the dead line humming in Jim's ear. Collapsing back on his bed, Jim threw a forearm over his eyes. Tonight was merely the opening skirmish. The battle lay ahead. He hoped it wouldn't be his Alamo.

ERIN, GLUM AND uncommunicative, sat in the passenger seat making a show of turning the pages of *Hamlet*. Connie studied her out of the corner of her eye as she drove them to school Monday morning. Her daughter's ensemble, black tights and a baggy black pullover, accentuated her pale complexion. Was she trying to make some kind of statement? A melancholy Hamlet-ess tossed about by the slings and arrows of outrageous fortune?

Connie, edgy after their confrontation last night, gritted her teeth. What had become of her supportive, loving daughter over the past few weeks? She could no longer attribute Erin's behavior to mounting academic pressures. Erin had been on the phone most of the evening until Connie had finally physically removed the instrument from her bedroom. Another maternal act guaranteed to endear her to her daughter.

Maybe she should extend a peace offering. "Do you want to stop for a sausage biscuit?"

Erin threw her a disgusted look. "Gross. I had a banana." She held the book up in front of her like a shield.

Connie was at a loss. Resignedly, she braked behind the line of traffic turning into the school and waited to inch forward. Why *had* Jim fired Kurt Mueller? She'd be the first to admit the coach had always struck her as a demagogue with little appreciation for academics, but he *did* win football games and was revered by his players. And Dr. Frank had seemed to get along with him. She hoped Jim's East Coast polish hadn't struck sparks with the good ol' boy network.

When they turned into the school gates, her empty stomach catapulted into her throat. "Oh, Lord!" she whispered, her eyes riveted on the straw-stuffed bespectacled figure, dressed in gray slacks, a blue blazer and school tie, dangling grotesquely from one gatepost. A crude hand-lettered sign stuck in the ground read Yankee, Go Home!

Erin looked up, then smiled a tight little innocent smile. "I wonder who could've done that," she drawled.

The effigy and the shoe-polished sentiments on the windshields of student vehicles were bad enough, but the worst statement greeted Connie when she walked into the upper school. With few exceptions, the students were clad completely in black. Her first-period AP seniors, grim faced and funereal, stalked into her classroom and fixed her with hostile eyes. She, like all the other school authority figures, was now the enemy. Barely controlling her irritation, she knew the first time a student uttered the word "establishment," she'd scrape her nails across the blackboard.

When the bell rang, she closed the door, then leaned against the front of her desk, her fingers laced in her lap as she surveyed the hushed class. "Well, do you want to talk about it?"

Jaime shifted uncomfortably, averting his eyes, and Melissa giggled nervously until Tara turned a scathing look on her. Nobody spoke. The computer hummed in the corner of the room and someone's stomach growled. Connie waited, trying not to let her anger surface. Over and over she reminded herself, *They're just kids. They feel betrayed.* But mob psychology was already at work, and it was scary.

"Okay, I interpret your silence as a no." With calculated deliberation, she rounded her desk, picked up the textbook and flipped it open. "Please turn to page 168 and write out the answers to the questions at the bottom of the page." Then she sat down, selected a stack of papers from her In box and, though the typed lines swam in front of her, began grading.

With the exception of the grinding of the pencil sharpener, the interruption by the office aide who brought Connie the official announcement of the athletic director's resignation and the explosion of sound when a book bag fell off a student's desk, the room was dead quiet for the entire fifty minutes.

When the bell rang, the students stood, efficiently gathering up their books and papers. As they left, Connie overheard Tara's breathless comment to the two girls at her side. "My father says Dr. Campbell is up to his fanny in you know what." Connie laid her red pen aside, closed her eyes and massaged her temples, wishing she'd eaten breakfast. It was going to be a long day.

"Mrs. W.?" She opened her eyes. Jaime stood quietly in front of the desk.

"Yes?"

"They're really upset. I tried to talk to some of them, but—" he shrugged "—you know how they are." He paused. "They like you. I think maybe by tomorrow... Well, you might ask again if they wanna talk about it."

She mustered a weak smile. "Thank you, Jaime. I may just do that."

"WELL, I MEAN if it could happen to Coach Mueller, why it could happen to any of us!" Jessie Flanders's hennaed head bobbed up and down. "None of us has tenure, you know." Fear showed in her watery blue eyes.

"I doubt this is about tenure," Pam responded dryly.

Connie watched her friend's hand hover over the box of doughnuts in the teachers' lounge before settling on one with those disgusting multicolored speckles. It was much easier to concentrate on Pam's doughnut selection than to listen to rampant paranoia.

"I mean can they do that? You know, just up and fire somebody?" Jane Ashford, the first-year chemistry teacher, scanned the group of faculty members.

"Honey, they can do whatever they want," Pam replied, taking a large bite out of her doughnut.

Connie couldn't let that remark pass. "But not without just cause."

"Do you think there is one?" Jessie asked.

"I don't know about you, sugar," Pam drawled, "but I've got to believe nobody in his right mind would fire a football coach from this place without a damn good reason."

"But...but—" Jessie's jowls quivered "—Mr. Mueller has been here almost as long as I have."

"I don't know him very well," Jane mumbled, "but the kids think he's great."

"C'mon, people. Get real." Pam picked up a napkin

and carefully wiped frosting from each of her fingers. "When was the last time Coach Mueller won a popularity contest in this room? Huh? The time he told Tommy Ben Watson he'd fix it so he didn't have to take the English test before the Rangeland game? Or maybe when he pulled two guys out of the chorus show because he wouldn't let them miss one Saturday game film showing for a rehearsal?"

"But the students... They're so upset. I don't know what to tell them." Jane, only six years older than her juniors, was wide-eyed.

Connie leaned over and patted her hand. "Kids always overreact to things like this. They're emotional. Our job is to stay calm and let the worst pass. And it will...eventually." Connie hoped her expression was more reassuring than she felt.

Jessie, who'd been lost in thought, roused herself and turned to Pam. "You mean like the time Mr. Mueller asked me to change a young man's grade?"

Several others, who had stayed out of the conversation, eyed Pam expectantly as she extended a flattened palm in Jessie's direction. "There. I rest my case." She shrugged eloquently, then picked up her textbook. "Folks, maybe, just maybe, this decision is long overdue. I, for one, will not lose sleep over the fate of our athletic director." She sashayed to the door, where she turned and made a sweeping gesture of farewell.

Pam had guts; Connie would give her that. She had a tendency to say what everyone else was thinking and didn't seem to care about the consequences. Though the tension in the room had eased with Pam's dramatic exit, Connie was still all nerves. Pam might not lose sleep. How Connie wished she could say the same for herself. Why, especially as interim head, *had* Jim risked such an unpopular decision? Pam's opinions had been right on, but the reality was that everybody overlooked the coach's idiosyncrasies when the league championship banner was hoisted to the rafters of the gym.

Surely Jim had his reasons. For his sake, she hoped they were good ones.

WHEN JIM LEFT the office late Monday evening, he noticed a beige BMW pulled alongside his car in the otherwise empty lot. As he approached, the driver's door opened and a tall thin man got out and slowly walked toward him. The man's face was shadowed by a large Stetson, and his body, conditioned and muscular, was encased in an expensive-looking Western-cut suit. "Campbell?" The question came at him like the strike of a rattler.

Jim stopped several feet away. "Yes. What can I do for you?"

"I'm Cleon Watson," he said, as if Jim was supposed to be impressed.

"I'm sorry I..."

"Tommy Ben's daddy."

The hotshot quarterback. "Of course. Your son's a fine player."

"He's fine, all right. And he'll be even finer when he's down there at UT startin' for the Longhorns." The man leaned back against the trunk of his car, his casual pose crafted to suggest a friendly little chat.

Jim, consciously relaxing his taut shoulder muscles, remained motionless. A reply didn't seem indicated.

From his jacket, Mr. Watson withdrew a cigarette and lighter. Clamping the cigarette between his front teeth, he cupped his hands and flicked the lighter. He took a deep drag. As he exhaled, he went on. "Yessir, 'at boy's got a great future. With his speed, his head for the game, an' one thing an' another, college coaches are already sniffin' around him."

Jim ambled to his own car and settled against the fender, where he could watch Watson. He waited for the punch line he sensed was coming.

"I'd sure hate to see a feller get in mah boy's way. Yessir—" he shook his head "—'at'd be a dadgum shame."

"Your point?"

Mr. Watson, blew a smoke ring and then, with satisfaction, watched it dissipate in the air. "A dadgum shame. So Tommy Ben's daddy here, you see, he's not gonna let that happen."

"No?"

"No. Mah boy needs Kurt Mueller. He's a damn fine coach. A winner. And, son—" he tilted the Stetson brim back, exposing an expression as cold as a nighttime desert floor "—he's got the connections, ya know what I mean? So, I'm not about to let you fire his ass." He shook his head. "No, sir."

"You're a little late." Jim kept his fists buried in his pockets.

"We'll see 'bout that. Bunch of us parents wanna have a meetin' with you, the board, hell, with ever'body. Open to the public, doncha know. I talked with Buxton right before I came over here. He said the earliest he can work somethin' out is next Monday night. 'Course, folks'll be mighty worked up 'bout missin' the Cowboys on *Monday Night Football*.'' He threw the cigarette down and took his time grinding it under his foot. Then he eased off the BMW and looked straight at Jim. "Less'n, of course, you could work out a reinstatement. Yessir. 'At'd be right fine."

Jim, too, stood erect, deliberately not extending his hand. "In that case, Mr. Watson, it looks like I'll see you Monday evening."

The man's lips thinned into a feral grin. "Count on it, son."

Jim waited while Cleon Watson rounded his car, climbed in, started the engine and backed out of his slot.

Only then was Jim aware that he had been holding his breath.

CHAPTER ELEVEN

As CONNIE ENTERED the upper school Sunday afternoon, Ralph, dressed in baggy gray sweats and scuffed running shoes, stepped out of his office into the unlit hall. "What are you doing here on the weekend?"

"I could ask you the same question."

"True." He frowned. "Jim and I are getting together to discuss tomorrow night's meeting. Jeez, for everybody's sake, I wish it hadn't come to this."

"It's been a rough week, all right." Even though she didn't know the circumstances of Mueller's forced resignation, Connie couldn't help wondering what Ralph would have done in Jim's position. Would he have played it safe?

Ralph gave an ironic chortle. "We've held our fingers in the dike despite the student council petition and the football team's boycott of the pep assembly. Not to mention, of course, stamping out rumors and fielding abusive phone calls." He rubbed a hand across his bald spot. "Yeah, 'rough' just about gets it. I'll be relieved when tomorrow night's behind us."

"For whatever it's worth, a group of upper-school teachers will be there supporting the administration."

"That's worth a lot. Except for Phil Buxton, several board members and me, you all may be the only ones rallying around Jim." His eyes lost their sparkle. "You won't believe some of the phone calls. These folks play hardball."

Connie felt a giant fist squeeze her chest. "Hardball?"

"It's Kurt's reinstatement or Jim's scalp."

She masked her alarm with a question. "And you wanted to be headmaster?"

He raised his eyes toward the ceiling. "The big guy upstairs was looking out for me, I guess."

"Lucky you." She shifted her tote bag to the other hand. "Listen, I plan to work in my room this afternoon."

"Why not at home?"

"I need peace and quiet, neither of which I can get there. Mother's lying on the sofa, watching *An American in Paris* at full volume, and Erin's treating me as if I were Medea reincarnated and single-handedly responsible for Coach Mueller's resignation."

He bowed in the direction of her classroom. "Then by all means, be our guest."

"Thanks. I'll need about three hours."

"Fine. If I leave before you do, I'll let you know."

As always when she was in the building after-hours or on the weekend, the empty halls, silent lockers and long shadows reminded her of a darkened stage just before curtain.

After dialing in the classical station on her transistor radio and spending an hour putting up her Civil War bulletin boards, she settled at the computer, her back to the hall.

In the middle of revising her Gettysburg lecture, she

heard the classroom door open. Ralph poked his head in.

"I'm off."

Connie looked at the wall clock. Five. She'd totally lost track of time.

"Jim's still in the building, though," Ralph said. "Be sure the outside door's locked when you leave."

She waved. "Thanks. I'm nearly done." She turned back to the monitor, but her hands remained in her lap. The peacefulness she'd cherished a moment before now seemed fraught with expectancy. *Jim's still in the building.*

They hadn't spoken since the breakfast a little over a week ago. Had he been trying then to warn her about Kurt Mueller's dismissal and the ensuing uproar? Or had he been attempting, gently, to distance himself from her? If the latter, he hadn't succeeded. Not counting Erin's baffling theatrics, she'd thought of little else but Jim during this past week. Almost as if she were two people—one, the old reliable Connie going through her routine; the other, a protective, confused woman...in love.

No! Stop it. She ran her finger down the page of the volume she was consulting, found the item she was hunting for and began typing again. A few more minutes and she'd be finished. Mother would be unhappy if she missed dinner.

Gettysburg. Dammit. Every time she pecked out the word, it was *Jim* she heard in her head. Jim and that memory she'd clung to for eight years. She rubbed her eyes, then bent to the work with a vengeance, her fingers flying.

A hand settled on her shoulder. Startled, she looked up.

"Didn't you hear me?" There Jim stood.

Swiveling in her chair, she accidentally brushed the book off the table onto the floor. "No."

"I didn't mean to frighten you." He had hold of her arms and was pulling her to her feet. "Are you okay?"

She was definitely not okay. "Fine." Instead of releasing her, he leaned over, searching her face.

"Sure?"

She swallowed, trying to stem the sensations warming her body. She nodded, avoiding his concerned eyes. Finally she managed to compose herself and look at him. "How about you? Are you all right? I've been worried."

His hands trailed down her arms as though he was reluctant to lose contact with her. He perched against the edge of the table. "The truth?"

"Yes."

"It's been holy hell." He removed his glasses and pinched the bridge of his nose. He looked exhausted. "I thought I knew what was coming. But I underestimated the size of the posse."

She sank back into her chair, even though, more than anything, she wanted to take him in her arms, tuck his head into the crook of her shoulder and caress his back. "What do you think will happen tomorrow night?"

A grim expression settled over his features. "A frontal attack with me as the target."

"What about the board?"

"Ah, the board." He smiled wearily, wet his finger and stuck it in the air. "Except for Phil and four or five others, it'll be a case of whichever way the wind blows."

Connie's heart plummeted. "I know you can't talk about the situation, but some of us think you did the right thing."

He slowly twirled his glasses by one earpiece. "That's what I love about you. You're always fair."

Had she heard correctly? *That's what I love about you?*

Before she could think of a noncommittal response, he repeated the phrase word by word wonderingly. "That's what I love about you." Carefully he set his glasses next to her printer, then grasped her hands and pulled her to her feet. "Connie, right now I want you so much it hurts." He drew her against his chest and held her tightly. Somewhere outdoors she heard the distant wail of a siren, but encircled in his arms, she felt warm, peaceful, safe. She felt his fingers drifting down through her hair.

She couldn't move or speak. It was as if he were physically drawing strength and comfort from her. And she wanted to give. Receiving could come later. Her cheek was pressed against the soft wool of his sweater, and over and over his fingers lifted, then dropped strands of her hair. Standing with her arms around him, she slowly stroked his back. She had no sense of the passage of time.

"You have beautiful hair," he murmured against her ear, his warm breath stirring tendrils. "It smells and feels just like I remember."

She slipped her hands from his waist and drew them up between them until she framed his chin, sandpapery against her fingertips. She tilted her head and found his eyes.

"Jim, I..." She couldn't quite seem to find her voice. "What can I do?"

He captured one of her hands and kissed her palm, looking at her all the while. "Nothing." Ever so gradually, he grasped both her hands and stepped back. "Stay clear, Connie. This situation is volatile. I don't want you anywhere near the fallout."

"But—"

He dropped her hands. "No 'buts.' I succumbed to weakness here, but it won't do you any good to be identified in any way—" his eyes bored in on hers "—in *any* way with me. Is that understood?"

"Are you trying to protect me?"

"Damn right. If this gets as ugly as I think it could..." He shook his head. "Connie, trust me. Do us both a favor. Stay away."

"I don't know if I can."

He picked up his glasses and hooked them over his ears. "You have to."

Something was going on here. The mixed signals again. The needful hug, followed immediately by his withdrawal. She turned away and fumbled with the pages in her printer tray. "You know I'm rooting for you."

"I'm counting on it." Then he moved toward the door. "It's getting dark. Let me walk you to your car."

AS CONNIE MOVED mechanically alongside Pam through the crowded gym foyer Monday evening, she couldn't help eavesdropping. Tommy Ben Watson's father's voice had the rasp of a power saw.

"Hell, Stewart, it's in the bag. You think this board's gonna let a coach as good as Mueller get away? When glaciers flow in Texas, mah friend." The smug smile on the man's face said it all.

She climbed clumsily behind Pam through the students and parents sitting in the bleachers until they finally reached the back row, where several other teachers had saved them seats. Connie leaned gratefully against the wall, clasping icy fingers in her lap. Folding chairs set up on the floor accommodated the overflow crowd, which buzzed with an ominous expectancy. At midcourt, tables had been placed end to end, with nameplates in front of each chair to identify the twelve trustees as well as Ralph and Jim. Even with the huge overhead blowers blasting warm air, Connie felt chilled, not from pregame excitement but from the anticipation of vultures circling.

Despite the appearance of normalcy—several men visiting casually near the water fountain, a frowsy-looking woman desperately trying to attract the attention of a friend, a couple of students giving each other high fives—the laughter sounded forced, the conversation subdued. Even the odors of old sneakers and stale popcorn, instead of communicating comforting familiarity, seemed to emphasize the seriousness of tonight's contest.

"You okay?" Connie felt Pam's fingers close over hers. She looked into her friend's concerned face.

"I don't know. This has the feel of a lynch mob."

"Wish I could disagree. My stomach's churning."

"So's mine." Connie licked her dry lips.

"With all the opinions flying around this week, you'd think at least some of the parents or students would've noticed the silence of the faculty."

"Nobody's even bothered to ask our opinion."

"And we sure as hell haven't been wearing black armbands. If it wasn't for the repercussions facing Ralph and Jim, I'd be dancing in the streets knowing that jerk was out of here."

Connie frowned, puzzled by the vehemence in Pam's voice. "Was he that bad?"

Pam curled her lip. "Bad? Connie, he treated his players like slaves, but that's not even the worst."

"What are you talking about?"

"I guess he never hit on you, huh?"

"Hit on me?" Connie was shocked.

"Mueller's an overbearing, abusive creep." Leaning closer, Pam whispered in her ear. "It took three well-aimed kicks, if you catch my drift, for him to get the message." Pam straightened up, crossed her arms and smiled forbiddingly. "He never messed with me after that."

While Connie was still digesting this new information, an electrifying hush fell over the crowd. The board members, looking straight ahead, their expressions neutral, entered from the locker room and walked to their seats. Some carried folders or legal pads. Jim and Ralph followed. Aside from the shuffling of chairs as the officials sat down, the hum of the blowers and the occasional cough of an onlooker, the room was silent.

Phil Buxton had remained standing, sorting through the file folder he'd carried in with him. He selected several pages, adjusted the knot of his tie and strode to the podium.

"This meeting has been called at the request of a group of patrons. The board has been asked to address concerns regarding the resignation of the athletic director. Let me start by reading a statement representing the board's position in this matter. Following that, members of the audience may step to the microphone in the aisle to comment or ask questions. Each speaker will be limited to two minutes. We request that you identify yourself and keep your remarks focused on this single issue."

He pulled a sheet of paper from the bottom of his stack. "Now, to begin—"

A belligerent-looking man wearing a gold Boosters' Club jacket stood and called out, "Where the hell's Mueller?"

Others quickly took up the cry. "Yeah, where's Coach?" "How's the man s'posed to defend himself?"

"May we have quiet, please." Buxton waited calmly. "Give us the courtesy of your attention."

One by one the hecklers sat down, though they were still poised like coiled vipers.

"Mr. Mueller, upon advice of counsel, declined to be present this evening." He looked out over the audience, as if assuring himself that it was safe to read the statement. "'November 17. In light of recent information that came to the attention of the board, the trustees have reviewed Kurt Mueller's employment record. In consultation with the school attorneys, the board voted to support the recommendation of Dr. James Campbell, interim headmaster, that Mr. Mueller be asked to submit his resignation from the Keystone School, effective immediately. His coaching responsibilities have temporarily been assigned to his assistant, Jack Liddy.'''

The board president paused to let isolated catcalls die. One of the trustees propped his elbows on the table, leaned over and, shading his face with his hands, stared at the notes in front of him. The woman at the end of the table nervously twisted the long strand of pearls around her neck. "Because of policies and laws concerning confidentiality, it would be imprudent for us to comment on the specific behaviors leading to this decision, other than to say that certain basic facts warrant the action taken. It should be emphasized that Mr. Mueller has cooperated with our request."

Connie's attention was riveted on Jim, who sat impassively, his hands folded on the tabletop. She gripped the edge of her bleacher seat. From the expressions on the faces of those parents sitting near her and the negative muttering spreading contagiously, Connie knew the crowd wouldn't settle for legal evasions. Most didn't want the truth; they wanted blood.

A razor-thin, bespectacled gentleman approached the microphone. "My name is Axel Martin. I'm an attorney and the father of four Keystone students." He paused for dramatic effect. "Was this a unanimous decision?"

"The necessary majority voted for termination," the board president responded.

"Any possibility you'll reconsider?"

"Not based on the facts available at this time."

The questioner's voice took on a malevolent tone. "After this evening, I hope the 'facts' will be seen in a different light. What we have here is an arbitrary decision to fire a man who's been at Keystone over twenty years, whose winning record as a coach is the envy of other schools and who is one reason our enrollment figures remain high. For the record, let's review Kurt Mueller's accomplishments." He pulled from his inside jacket pocket a folded paper from which he read an impressive list of championships, All-State players and win-loss records. He refolded the paper and stuck it back in his pocket before continuing.

"I've been asked to serve as a representative for a group of football parents, alumni and other interested parties. I'd like to call some of them to come forward."

Phil Buxton nodded. Among those lining up to speak, Connie recognized Mr. Watson, Kyle Drummond and Gleeanne Roth, Holly's mother.

Watson spoke first. "What I see here, friends, is vigilante justice." His eyes never left Jim. "We have us a part-time headmaster, a Hah-vahd man, mind you, who doesn't know diddly 'bout Texas and our football tradition." He turned sideways to look over the crowd. "Now, I don't know 'bout you, but I don't take kindly to this uppity interference. Where's the evidence, friends? What exactly *is* it that our fine coach is accused of?'' He faced the trustees. ''Now, I know a lotta you. You're mah neighbors, mah customers. But in this matter y'all have plain taken leave of your senses. A man has the right to face his accusers and we—'' he gestured at the crowd ''—have a right to know just what the hell's goin' on here.''

Phil Buxton tried to speak, but a chant from the football players—''Coach, coach, coach, coach!''—drowned out his words. He held up a hand. When the noise level slowly subsided, he leaned into the microphone. ''Mr. Mueller and his attorney appeared before a board committee. His rights and options were clearly spelled out. The board is not at liberty to discuss personnel decisions in a public forum. But let me assure you, this was not a decision made lightly or without sufficient grounds.''

Connie decided she had never seen a more uncomfortable-looking group of people than the trustees, few of whom were making eye contact with the speakers.

Kyle then made an impassioned plea on behalf of the football players. ''Here we are at play-off time. It's Coach Mueller who's brought us to this point. We have nothing against Mr. Liddy, but we need Coach.'' The chant went up again from the students. This time many adults in the stands joined in.

Smoothing her electric-blue mohair sweater over her slim hips, Gleeanne Roth stepped to the mike, her sculpted blond pageboy shimmering as she nervously fluffed it. ''My husband and I have been patrons of this school since our little Holly was in preschool. Keystone football has always been part of our family life. For Holly and the other seniors, this is just terrible. Why, it's ruining the year for them. I just don't understand what Coach Mueller could've done..." She paused to calm her trembling voice.

Pam leaned closer to Connie. "If she starts to cry, I'm going to upchuck."

"We all," she sniffled, "love him. Please reconsider this decision." She looked uncertainly about her, then affected an injured expression. "And I don't know what y'all's experience has been with Dr. Campbell, but I can tell you, he's not interested in sports. Why, two times, with no reason at all, he's canceled meetings with us cheerleader moms."

Buxton interrupted. "Please, Mrs. Roth, confine your remarks to the issue under discussion."

"Well, I'm hoping y'all will rethink this unfortunate step." She yielded her place to the next speaker, a beefy, red-faced man whose bristling eyebrows formed a bushy V.

"I'll tell you what I'll do if you don't reinstate Mueller. I'm takin' my kid outta here, that's what. We enrolled him last year and are paying big bucks for him to play ball for Coach. We're not payin' for some substitute." He jabbed a finger in Buxton's direction. "It's your call."

A buzz traveled through the onlookers. The speaker's son was the All-Conference running back.

Mr. Martin stepped up to the microphone. The crowd stilled. "As you can see, you have a problem here. Not the least of which is a message I received today from an alumnus who is one of Keystone's substantial donors. Should you stick with your decision regarding Mr. Mueller, he is withdrawing his offer of a generous gift to the athletic department.''

Phil Buxton didn't let him go any further. "With all due respect, Mr. Martin, the school is not for sale.''

Connie pounded a clenched hand on Pam's knee. "Yes!'' she whispered.

A tall, stooped-shouldered man whose reading glasses slipped down his nose approached the microphone and began speaking in a low voice. "Am I missing something here? It seems to me we elected these board members to exercise their best judgment. Frankly, I'm not sure it's any of our business what Mr. Mueller allegedly has or has not done. Am I the only one who reads the word *trust* in *trustees?*''

Connie and Pam joined in the isolated applause from the faculty section. The man turned around and smiled sadly at them before adding, "I, for one, am much more interested in the academic and moral dimensions of my son's education than in anything else. And so far, I've been quite satisfied with Keystone in this regard.'' He faced the board again. "Thank you for making what was, obviously, a difficult decision.''

He yielded the microphone to Axel Martin, who shot the crowd a disbelieving look. "How about hearing from some of the other board members, Buxton?''

The woman on the end turned pale; several others fiddled with pencils and papers. However, a man in an immaculately tailored suit, rose to his feet.

"Uh-oh. Greg Farley.'' Pam gripped Connie's hand.

Phil Buxton stood aside, as if reluctantly giving his fellow trustee access to the mike. "Axel, ever'body. Let me say this on behalf of my friends on the board.

Y'all elected us to make decisions. We don't always like what we have to do. But we try to do what's best for the school. Sometimes, like now, we don't agree. Personally, I like Coach Mueller just fine. But the board's voted. We oughta leave it at that.''

Before he could sit back down, a lone voice called from the crowd, ''How did you vote, Greg?''

Farley gave a who-me shrug, but before he could continue, Phil Buxton grabbed the mike. ''That question is out of order.''

Watson rushed to the floor again and pushed Axel Martin aside. ''I'll tell you what's outta order.'' His voice rose as he pointed straight at the headmaster. ''That's what's outta order. We were doin' fine here until Campbell arrived with his high-falutin' eastern ideas.'' He turned to the board president. ''Buxton, I believe you said Coach 'resigned'—'' he spit out the word ''—on the recommendation of Dr. Campbell. Well, I'm interested in hearin' what the headmaster has to say for himself, if there's anything he *can* say.''

Jim, his eyes glued on his accuser, slowly rose. Connie found her heart stuck in her throat.

Phil Buxton turned and said, ''Jim, you don't have to—''

Jim reached the microphone. ''I welcome the opportunity to respond.''

''Yankee, go home! Yankee, go home!'' Connie, along with everyone else, turned to the section where the football players sat. There was no mistaking the origin of the chant.

His face expressionless, Jim waited until the cry died a natural death. He looked slowly from one end of the gym to the other before speaking. "You have every reason to be suspicious of a newcomer. Keystone has a proud history and an admirable athletic program. Under Dr. Frankenberg's leadership you have grown and prospered. I'm sure it would've been more comfortable to continue the status quo. Frankly, when I arrived, that is exactly what I intended to do— to be a good steward until you selected a permanent headmaster. But circumstances altered my intentions.

"When I was hired, it was with the understanding that the board and, I would hope, all of you, wanted someone who would uphold the standards of the school. Among them is the issue of character." He turned to include the trustees in his glance. "It took character for this board to make a decision they knew would be unpopular with many of you. This was not an easy or capricious decision, but it was the right one."

Several audible scoffing noises echoed in the tension-filled gymnasium. Connie closed her eyes, willing Jim courage.

"This is also a caring school community. I care about Coach Mueller's welfare, just as you do. But I am charged with putting the best interests of the students above everything else. Though it may not be immediately obvious to you, I believe that is what I have done in making my recommendation to the board. And if I have to take the heat in this matter, that is a burden I will simply have to bear."

Amid a hostile silence, he resumed his seat.

Opening her eyes, Connie noted the spots of color on Jim's cheekbones. He was making every effort to contain himself. Whatever Mueller had done, Jim had obviously felt strongly enough about it to put his career on the line. She ached for him.

Mr. Watson approached the microphone. "Folks, we all heard that pretty speech. But I'm thinkin' Dr. Campbell needs to do more than take some heat. I'm thinkin' *he's* the one needs terminatin'."

Scattered enthusiastic applause and a couple of shrill whistles greeted his suggestion.

"We had no call for trouble till he arrived. I make a motion the board consider firin' *him*."

"Second."

"Second."

"I second that."

Rhythmic stomping began at one end of the bleachers and spread to the other end.

Phil Buxton tried vainly to restore order. "Ladies and gentlemen..." Greg Farley covered his mouth to hide a grin, and the woman with the pearls ducked her head. Ralph stared at his notes.

"They're crucifying him, Connie!" Pam gestured helplessly at the other faculty members, who sat mute. "We have to do something."

"Like what?" Heartsick, Connie recognized that there was little she or her colleagues *could* do. Could they run the risk of slandering the coach, of alienating both students and parents, of losing their jobs?

Jim sat quietly, letting the outcry wash over him. What must it be like to be the target of such rejection and derision? Especially when it was so undeserved.

Phil Buxton held his arms over his head. "Order. Order, please." His voice boomed over the speaker system. Those who had been standing reluctantly sat back down. "This kind of personal attack is inappropriate and counterproductive. Jim Campbell was hired to do a job. And as far as I'm concerned, he's done it."

"We can get rid of you, too," the beefy football father shouted.

Buxton ignored the interruption. "Among you, I'm certain are some fair-minded individuals willing to let this controversy play out. Emotional reactions and responses, such as we've seen here tonight, are understandable, but with time, I'm confident you will see the board and the headmaster have lived up to their charge to act in the best interests of Keystone School. This meeting is adjourned."

The football team walked out en masse chanting, "Coach, coach, coach." Several of the more vehement attackers converged on the trustees, gesticulating and venting frustration.

Connie sat rooted in her spot, watching Jim standing by himself. Even Ralph had joined the crowd moving toward the door. Jim waited, making himself available; but he might as well have been invisible. No one spoke or nodded to him. Finally he raised his eyes to the nearly empty bleachers, looked straight at Connie with an expression that pierced her heart and then shrugged before walking over to shake Phil Buxton's hand.

"Hey, babe, what're you going to do?"

Connie had forgotten Pam was still standing beside her. "Do? What do you mean?"

Pam put an arm around her shoulder and hugged

her. "I mean, your man's dying down there. He's all alone."

Connie didn't need Pam to tell her that. She already knew.

"It's fish or cut-bait time, sweetie. I don't want to hear all your excuses about Adele or Erin or the school. Go to him."

Every instinct urged her to do just that, and every societal restraint, even Jim's own words of warning yesterday, held her back. "I...I can't."

Pam's arm dropped to her side. "Then live with your regrets...if you can." With loping strides, she started down the bleachers toward the floor.

Connie followed her, the awful words hammering in her brain: "If you can."

CONNIE LET HERSELF quietly into the house. Her head was pounding. Bed. No papers, no lesson plans, no problems. Just bed. She hung up her coat and tiptoed down the hall. Her mother would be fast asleep by now. Erin's muffled voice carried through her closed door. She'd stayed home to cram for a test, so no doubt Kyle had phoned her about the meeting.

In her bedroom, Connie kicked off her shoes and shucked her skirt. Her skull was imploding with a grinding tension headache. She pulled off her sweater, laid it on the bed and neatly folded it. Then she gathered it in her arms and added it to the stack on her closet shelf. She couldn't help herself—her eyes strayed to the memento box. Pam's line seared her brain like a Times Square news flash: "Live with your regrets."

She crumpled to the floor of her closet, amid slippers, dirty laundry and fallen hangers. Isn't that what she'd been doing for eight years? Wishing undone her decision to set Jim free? Trying to protect herself from further rejection of the kind Colin had inflicted? Clinging to the memory of her one ideal summer?

And how is life as St. Connie, the self-sacrificing daughter and mother?

Jim. Did she love *him* or the fantasies he represented? The man was hurting. He was alone. Either she cared enough or she didn't. The throbbing of her temples told her tonight might be the defining moment before a lifetime of regret. Hugging her knees, she rocked back and forth. Dear Lord, did she have the courage?

Finally she stood, her stomach quaking, and walked to her desk. It was past time to take control of her life. From a drawer she withdrew two sheets of paper and began writing—one note to Erin and the other to her mother.

CHAPTER TWELVE

JIM OPENED the garage door into the kitchen. Damn, the phone was already ringing. He didn't know how much more he could take. He slung his suit jacket over a chair back, stripped off his tie and loosened his collar button. The answering machine could do its thing. But then he heard Cliff's voice. "If you're home, buddy, pick up. Otherwise, call me in the morning."

Jim retraced his steps, stopped the recorder and answered. "I'm here."

"Who the hell have you been talking to all week? I thought you'd installed a permanent busy signal."

Jim straddled a kitchen stool. "That's a great idea."

"You sound bushed. Everything all right?"

Jim slumped over the counter. "I've been better."

"Some kid cheat on the SAT?"

"Worse. I fired the football coach."

There was a long silence. "In *Texas?* You must be deranged."

Jim removed his glasses and set them down. "Thanks for the vote of confidence." Though friendly, Cliff's voice often had the power to reduce him to being kid brother again.

"What happened?"

Jim briefly recounted the particulars. "So I didn't have much choice."

"Doesn't sound like it. Firings are never pleasant. How are the natives responding?"

"If they were mounted, they'd drive me bare assed across the Red River."

Cliff chuckled. "That bad, huh?"

"Yeah, that bad. We had a big patrons' meeting tonight." Jim sighed. "There's a move to fire me."

"Jeez, what're you going to do?"

"Wait. The board president, who's a hell of a guy, is twisting in the wind with me."

"This could ruin your career."

"Tell me about it."

"Well, you can always come back to work for me."

Great choice. "Thanks, but I'm going to give this situation time. Emotions are running high. When the storm blows over, maybe I can salvage something."

"Other than that, Mrs. Lincoln, how did you enjoy the play?"

"That's the hell of it, Cliff. Keystone's a great school, and I really like Texas. You should see me in my cowboy boots."

His brother laughed. "It'd almost be worth a trip." He sobered. "Seriously, how are you?"

Jim cocked the phone against his shoulder and began unbuttoning his dress shirt. "Hanging in there. I didn't expect headmastering to be easy. I just hadn't expected it to get this hot this soon."

"If anybody can come through this relatively unscathed, it's you."

Jim's eyes watered. His brother rarely complimented him. "Thanks, Cliff, I appreciate your saying that."

After some family small talk, Jim hung up, dropped his shirt on a chair and disconnected the answering machine. He was through taking calls this evening, through listening to vitriolic, often anonymous, attacks.

Immobilized, he stared into space. Where had all his high-minded ideas taken him? He slipped off his shoes. Dammit all. He was right. It was a shame Kurt Mueller was a compulsive gambler, and Jim believed he needed help. But Mueller still had no business influencing impressionable kids.

Yawning, he picked up his shoes and started for the bedroom. The doorbell jerked him to alertness. Now what? They were going to come after him here? Irritation escalating, he dropped the shoes and flung open the door. "Now, look—"

Connie, dressed in jeans and a faded Keystone sweatshirt, her fists thrust into the pockets of a turquoise ski parka, stood on the porch, her eyes deep pools of sympathy.

"May I come in?"

The anger drained from him. "God, Connie, I don't think it's a good idea."

Her chin jutted out. "For whom? You or me?"

He couldn't deny his need. "You."

She stepped over the threshold, closed the door behind her and threw her arms around him. "Good, because I'm through letting you protect me. Jim, where I belong tonight is with you."

For the second time in a matter of minutes, his eyes

swam, but he didn't have much time to think about that. Her lips were too inviting, too full of proffered comfort.

JIM CRUSHED HER to him, and from his deepening kiss, he made his welcome obvious. Joy exploded in Connie, her doubts and fears vanquished. Warmth spiraled upward from her toes, and she knew, *knew,* she'd been right not to settle for anything less than this.

His lips planted tiny kisses across her cheek and came to rest on her temple, suddenly free from throbbing. Her headache was gone. And oh, what a blissful cure!

Nestled contentedly against him, she found his voice almost an intrusion.

"You'll never know how much I needed this." He sighed deeply, then, cupping her face, stepped back. "But you've got to leave. Now."

She grinned wickedly. "You may be my boss at school, but tonight I'm not taking orders. Tonight I'm the protector, remember?"

"Connie, I can't let you run this risk. Suppose someone from Keystone saw your car?"

She placed both hands on his shoulders and stood on tiptoes to look more squarely into his eyes. "I parked around the corner. Other objections? I'm equipped with answers."

"It's nearly midnight. What about your mother? Erin?"

"I've taken care of them." A white lie, of course. But she *would*—she hoped. "Bottom line, Dr. Campbell, do *you* want me here? Be honest, now."

He spanned her waist. "You know I do."

"Then shut up and let me take charge for a while."
She whirled away and walked into the living room.
There she examined the vaulted ceiling, the creamy
walls, the basic town house taupe carpet. The south-
western-chic decor and his New England antiques, fine
pieces all, fell short of appearing stylishly eclectic. She
turned and studied him where he still stood by the door
in his socks. "How about offering the lady a glass of
wine?" Never in her life had she so forcefully insin-
uated herself into a situation.

He grinned. "My pleasure. Chardonnay or caber-
net?"

"Chardonnay would be lovely." She gestured toward the green leather sectional sofa. "May I?"

"I'm still stunned you're here. Please. Sit down."

She slipped out of her parka, threw it on one end
of the sofa and relaxed into the cushions. He stood at
the minibar, his back to her. When he reached for the
wineglasses in the overhead rack, she eyed with appreciation the tautness of the white T-shirt stretched
across his broad shoulders, the way his slacks slipped
tantalizingly below his waist. He'd certainly kept himself in shape.

By the time he handed her the wineglass and sat,
one leg drawn up, facing her on the sofa, she'd started
to lose her nerve. She was *way* out of practice at seduction. She wasn't sure she could get the mechanics
right, much less the nuances. And should she even be
trying? The issue of children still lay between them.

Raising his glass, he clinked it against hers.
"To—" He faltered, his face suddenly pensive.

"To this moment." She lifted the goblet to her lips, but he reached out and stopped her.

"And to us." Once again, lightly, he tapped his glass to hers.

She took a sip of wine. Though the liquid soothed, her throat constricted. "Does this mean—"

He stretched his arm across the back of the sofa and played with a lock of her hair. "That there is an *us?*" He cocked one eyebrow questioningly.

"Yes."

He tilted her chin. She raised her lashes and looked directly into his forthright eyes. "There's always been an *us.* You know it and I know it." He brushed her cheek with his knuckles. "The question is, what are we going to do about it?"

She waited, sensing his need to think aloud, to answer his own question. She could tell him now, make this conversation academic. *Should* tell him now. But...one night. Only one. Was it too much to ask?

He dropped his hand to her shoulder. "I've known ever since that day I saw you in that ridiculous clown costume that I'd never really gotten over you. Come to think of it—" he rubbed his chin "—I may have been attracted originally to my ex-wife because she looked something like you. Same coloring, long hair. But we never clicked, no matter how hard we both tried. Emotionally, we were miles apart." He paused. "Nobody's fault, really." Tightening his grip, he pulled her closer. "What happened to us, Connie?"

"Back then?" Would she be able to tell it all?

"Yeah."

Her fingers worried a fold in her sweatshirt. "I think

I was on vacation from life. Colin had all but destroyed my confidence. He'd been like a god to me—witty, intelligent, worldly—and I couldn't believe he'd picked me. I mean, there I was, an impressionable grad student, and he was Dr. Colin Weaver, admired professor. Yet he *did* want me." Her voice fell. "For a while. Until a knockout coed came along. And then another. And finally, the one I caught him with in his office."

He pressed her head to his chest. She rested one palm on top of his heart. "Go on."

"My ego was at ground zero after that. Washington was an experiment, the one opportunity to try my wings. To be Connie Weaver, without the labels of wife, mother, daughter." She straightened and looked at him. "The one chance to release my inhibitions. But that woman you met that summer? She wasn't the real me."

His voice rumbled in his throat. "That's where you're wrong." His hand slid beneath her sweatshirt and his fingers rubbed gentle circles on her bare back. His breath was warm against her ear as his tongue traced her earlobe, sparking fire throughout her body. "That was more the real you than anything else has ever been."

His lips found hers and she responded instinctively, her body ripe and responsive. Could his words be true? She writhed against him, craving his fingers on her breasts, his mouth on the pulse point throbbing in her neck, his palms cupping her buttocks. Lord, how long had it been since she'd felt such heat, such abandon?

If, even lightly, he touched that moist, tender trigger between her legs, she would shatter.

The hungry kiss continued, probing and needful. She pulled his shirt out of his pants and let her hands slide over the firm flesh at his waist, then upward, brushing across his nipples, to his shoulders. He moaned, as he bent her backward into the sofa cushions, one hand trailing up her back, feeling for the hook of her bra. She was dying. It had been so long, so very long. And it felt so good.

"Oh, Jim, hurry." She reared up long enough to help him release the constricting bra, then fell back dazed, as his fingers found and caressed one engorged nipple.

"Connie, Connie."

Muffled against her neck, the words aroused her almost more than the ministrations of his hands and lips. She found herself squirming shamelessly against him.

Suddenly his hands stilled, and where heat had been, a cold—lonely and final—took its place. Releasing her, he sat up, arms stretched along the top of the sofa. "No. Not like this."

Her face burning, she hastily rearranged her clothing and scooted to a sitting position. There was that humiliating feeling again—rejection. "I'm sorry. I never should have..."

"Oh, honey, it's not you." Jim moved closer, warming one icy hand with his own. "If I made love to you tonight, I could never let you go."

Her heart thumped wildly. Didn't he understand? She didn't want him to let her go.

"I'd be taking advantage of you," he continued.

"No, I—"

His fingers moved slowly between hers, clasping and unclasping. "We're both too vulnerable. I never want you to think I took you only because I needed you, because I was hurting." He raised her hand to his lips, kissing her fingertips. "I wouldn't be much of a man if I didn't make our first time together again just about you and me. Not about Keystone or pity."

So much for seduction. "I didn't think it was about either of those things." Her breath came raggedly. "There's never been anyone for me since I met you." She stopped, unable to carry on. Love demanded an end to pretense, illusions. She gathered herself and forced out the words. "But...there's something you need to know. And a question I need to ask."

He played with a strand of hair that had fallen into her face. "Anything."

She closed her eyes, then opened them and squared around to face him. "Children? Do you still want...children?"

His hand stilled on her head. "Children? I've always wanted them. And if I'm not over the hill, I still do. I can't think of anything that would make me happier." She couldn't bear his hopeful expression or the void growing within her.

Now. "Jim, I can never give you children."

"What do you mean?"

"I had a hysterectomy even before Washington. I'm sorry. I should have told you then."

His face fell, then worry lines creased his forehead. "Then that's why...the letter?"

"Partly. It wasn't fair. I couldn't give you the one thing you most wanted."

"I don't know what to say."

"Don't say anything." She rose to her feet and scooped up her parka. "I'd better get out of here before I—"

The explosion of shattering glass just beyond the sofa shut off her words. Jim threw his body over hers and held her down. The harsh squeal of tires, raucous shouts and the grind of an accelerating engine hammered in her ears as she struggled to breathe. "Are you all right?" he whispered.

She was shaking. "Yes, I think so. What happened?"

He eased off her and stood, cold eyed, surveying the mess. She joined him. "Adolescent retaliation." He leaned over and picked up the rock lying amid the shards. "Look." He held it up. The two obscene words, scrawled in red paint, were unrepeatable.

"See? It's dangerous to befriend Jim Campbell." He set the rock on the coffee table and held the parka for her. "Connie, we need to talk about what you've just told me. Right now, though, you have to go. It's not safe here."

Robot-like, she inserted her arms into the sleeves and let him settle the parka around her shoulders. "Jim, I'm so sorry. For everything. Will you be okay?"

Like a patient father sending a child out to play in the snow, he slowly zipped her up and fastened the snap at her neck. "I think so."

He picked up his suit jacket from the back of the

chair and put it on. "C'mon. I'll walk you to your car."

She touched his arm, desperate for a reaction. "I could stay."

He ushered her to the door. "No, Connie. Not tonight." Then he turned her toward him, framing her face in his hands. "But...we'll see."

She couldn't trust herself to speak. She fought back scalding tears and nodded slowly. "Okay," she finally whispered.

ADELE'S EYES blinked open. What had awakened her? Yolanda? No, she was curled up at the foot of the bed. The front door opening? What time was it? She propped up on an elbow and tried to focus on the luminous dial of the bedside clock. One-thirty? Two-thirty? She couldn't make it out. The house was quiet. Had she imagined the noise? Dreamed it?

Whatever. She was wide-awake now. She switched on the lamp. After she'd scrunched up the pillows, she picked up her reading glasses, reached for her romance novel, extracted the bookmark and began reading. She fumbled back a couple of pages. She couldn't quite remember details of the scene she'd read earlier. Oh, yes. The heroine was ready to reveal her painful secret to the hero. She loved these parts where you never knew how the hero was going to react.

Was that the toilet flushing? Surely Erin wasn't still up. Something wasn't quite right. Maybe she'd better go check.

She threw back the covers and levered herself to the edge of the bed. There. She located her slippers. She hobbled across the room, gradually getting her legs under her. She reached the wall and flipped on the overhead light. What was that on the floor?

For support, she grabbed the doorknob before stooping to pick up the envelope lying on the carpet. Odd. Turning it over, she recognized Connie's handwriting. She tore open the flap. This couldn't be good news. Otherwise, why wouldn't Connie just tell her?

She withdrew the note and, breathing heavily, began reading:

> Mama, if you wake up and find I'm gone, I don't want you to worry. I'm at Jim Campbell's. It may be late when I get back.

Adele felt her heart thumping. This was crazy. The headmaster. Why would Connie be at his house in the middle of the night?

> He's in trouble and I'm going to him. I'm asking you to trust me on this.
>
> Remember Meg Ryan in *Sleepless in Seattle,* traveling clear across the country for Tom Hanks? I guess that's how I'm feeling. I have to go to Jim. Please don't worry. See you in the morning.
>
> I love you.
> Connie

Well, I never. Adele couldn't imagine what had gotten into her daughter. It wasn't seemly. Fooling around with the headmaster? A worse thought stabbed her

consciousness. What if Connie lost her job? Where
would they all be then? Who would take care of her?

She reread the letter. Meg Ryan? Did Connie feel
that strongly about that Dr. Campbell? Was she...in
love?

Adele's eyesight blurred. Shakily she retraced her
steps, then eased between the sheets and pulled up the
blankets against a sudden chill. In love? What else
would possess her normally sensible daughter to do
something so foolish?

Yes, Connie had known him a long time ago,
but...love? That was the only explanation for her odd
behavior.

Well, what was the worst thing that could happen?
Disgrace. Ruin. Yolanda pawed her thighs insistently.
But what was disgraceful about love?

Had Connie ever really been happy? Not with that
no-good Colin. And never in the way she and Edgar
had been. The sad truth was her daughter wasn't getting any younger, and except for Ralph, she'd never
had any chances.

What had she sacrificed for Erin, for her? Adele
pulled a tissue from under her pillow and blew her
nose. She'd been a burden to Connie, depriving her of
happiness.

The uncomfortable realization lodged in her throat
as the picture of Meg Ryan standing longingly on a
beach road observing Tom Hanks and his son replayed
in her head until, with Yolanda curled beside her, she
finally dozed off.

"MOTHER, how could you?" Erin stood in the bedroom doorway the next morning, waving Connie's

note in her hand, her brown eyes hot coals. "You went to Dr. Campbell's last night?"

Connie finished buttoning the starched white blouse, marshaling her thoughts. Somehow, in the morning light, her convictions were slipping away. No, dammit. It's now or never. She faced her daughter. "How could I what?"

"Take his side? Go to him? It's not bad enough he has to fire Coach Mueller and get everybody stirred up. Now he has to seduce you."

"Stop right there, young lady." Connie sucked in her breath. "Nobody seduced anybody." *Not for lack of trying, though.* "Jim Campbell is a friend of mine. Would you abandon a friend of yours who was in trouble?"

Erin took one step into Connie's bedroom, her lips curved in disbelief. "Sheesh. I've lived with the fact I have a mother on the faculty. But now—" she raised her arms helplessly "—I have a mother making a fool of herself. And not even in private. No, at Keystone for all the world to see."

Connie held herself in check. "Are you finished?"

"No!" Erin took a step forward. "It's disgusting. The whole school hates him, but you rush into his arms like some…" She searched for the right word.

"Like some woman in love?" Connie stared into her daughter's anger-bright eyes.

"Love? Give me a break."

Connie was across the room holding Erin by the arm before she realized she'd moved. "Is it so impossible to imagine?"

"Mo-other." Erin shook her arm free. "I don't understand you."

"No, I suppose not. My behavior must seem totally out of character."

"You can say that again."

"Well, you can jump to conclusions if you want. I'm not going to apologize." She walked to her desk and gathered her books for school. "Regardless of what I feel for Jim, I assure you nothing can come of our friendship, so you don't have to worry. Your little boat isn't going to get rocked." The truth of those awful words hurt.

"What'll my friends think?"

Connie slowly turned. "Whatever you tell them. No one knows about my errand of mercy."

"Well, thank God for that." Erin pivoted to leave the room but paused in the doorway. "Never mind taking me to school. Kyle's picking me up."

"Nothing happened, you know." Connie's words tumbled into the space vacated by her daughter.

And nothing was going to. Not after the crestfallen look on Jim's face when she'd finally confessed her barrenness.

CHAPTER THIRTEEN

ERIN'S ACCUSATIONS rang in Connie's ears. On top of worrying Adele and—she couldn't dwell on it—losing Jim, she'd alienated her daughter. Erin's absorption with Kyle, her drive to excel, her anxiety over college, helped explain the gulf growing between them. But nothing had prepared her for the intensity of Erin's censure this morning.

"Con-nieee, are you still here?" Adele stood in the hallway in a faded bathrobe, staring at her with concern. "You'll be late."

Connie glanced at her watch. Darn, she needed to get out of here. "I'm on my way." She scooped up her purse and headed for the door, then changed her mind. Might as well get it all over with at once. She confronted her mother. "Did you get my note?"

"Yes."

Connie searched her mother's face. "And?"

"I hope you know what you're doing." Her tone was surprisingly noncommittal.

"So do I, Mama. So do I."

She dashed out into the cold morning, her thin blazer little protection against the chill. Gusts of northerly wind swirled dead leaves around her feet. The car sputtered to life, and finally, several blocks from home, the heater kicked in, blowing hot air into her face. Her eyes, scratchy from sleeplessness, watered and her head pounded.

After returning from Jim's, she'd tossed and turned until morning. Her fantasy of one glorious night in Jim's arms was over. He wanted more than that. Deserved more than that—children, a whole family of them. She was beyond sadness. She felt only overwhelming emptiness.

As she drove through the Keystone gate, slate-colored clouds scudded across the expansive sky, their leaden curtain sealing off the sun. A wintry wind shook the car, and a few large raindrops splatted on the hood.

How could she face her classes? She was exhausted. The Mueller issue would be festering. Erin would avoid her. And if she saw Jim...?

She swallowed salty tears, overwhelmed by runaway emotions. Would she ever get things right?

Most of the students in her first-hour AP class had attended last night's meeting. Subdued, seemingly emotionally drained, they straggled in, their expressions veiled. She'd scheduled a lecture for today, but as she stood at the lectern, prepared to give it a go, Jaime Hernandez caught her eye. He stared at her. And suddenly she knew what she hadn't done last week, what she needed to do.

She put her lecture notes back in the folder, set the lectern aside and settled into a vacant student desk. "Let's sit in a circle this morning." One or two shot her a puzzled look, but, moving mechanically, they made the transition. "I think we need to talk."

Silence.

"All right, then. *I* need to talk." Several doodled nervously in their notebooks. "Corny as it sounds, I think of us as a family. We spend almost an hour a day together five times a week for nine months. For me, teaching is more than imparting information. It's a relationship. With you. And right now, I'm not comfortable in that relationship. Something has happened at this school to upset the trust between faculty and students. I don't like that feeling. Do you?"

Tara Farley studied her manicured nails and one of the young men across the circle cracked his knuckles. Jaime spoke up. "I don't." Heads swiveled toward the class president. "We don't understand about Coach Mueller. Why he's okay one day and not the next. Why Dr. Campbell would just up and fire him. Dr. Frank wouldn't have done that. We don't like change." Several heads nodded in agreement.

"Change is always difficult." From last night, she knew that only too well. "But what makes you think Dr. Frank wouldn't have made the same decision under the circumstances?"

"What circumstances?" Jared, a gangly student in the back of the room, asked, his sarcasm overt.

"What do you think they are?" Connie asked.

"I haven't a clue," the young man snapped.

Tara twisted her ponytail nervously. "I think Dr. Campbell's a jerk."

"At the minimum," Jared agreed.

"Wait a minute," Jaime interjected, his black eyes intense. "Maybe it's not as simple as it seems. Why would a new headmaster come in here and deliberately make a change he knows will upset the entire school?"

Bravo, Jaime. Connie waited.

"Because he's a jerk," Tara repeated.

"Your father's on the board. Did he intentionally hire a jerk?" Jaime's question closed down Tara's argument. "Did Mrs. W. or any other teacher, for that matter, have anything to do with Coach's resignation?" He scrutinized each face. "Why are we treating her like an outcast?"

Connie felt something warm and energizing filling the room.

Melissa Clayton shifted uncomfortably in her chair. "He's right, you know. We've been blaming everybody."

"Do you know why?" Connie asked. The question stopped them. "Could it be because you feel powerless?" She gave them time to consider the notion.

"Yeah. Nobody ever cares about our opinions," Jared said. "We're not stupid, you know."

"Of course you're not. But stop to think for a moment. Whose job is personnel?"

"The principal's?"

"The board's," Tara pronounced smugly.

"It's the headmaster's," Connie said. "So why *would* he make the decision he did, knowing it would be unpopular?"

After a prolonged silence, Jaime spoke up. "It could be we don't have all the facts. I mean, a guy wouldn't normally come here and self-destruct. Dr. Campbell's job is to look out for the school. He seems fairly bright, so maybe he's taking care of things we don't know about, shouldn't know about.''

Leaving no room for a counterattack, Connie picked up Jaime's argument. "Sometimes it's very difficult to stand on principle. To do the right thing, especially in the face of extreme opposition. History, however, is full of such examples. Thomas More, Nathan Hale, Martin Luther King. Isn't it easier to condemn than to compromise, to doubt rather than trust? Easier to throw stones than to consider facts?''

A waiflike young woman to Connie's left spoke. "Maybe we've reacted with our emotions instead of our reason. It's almost like…" She faltered. "Like mob psychology. You know—" she glanced around at her classmates "—like the union violence we studied.''

A few looked up with interest.

"We're smarter than that," Jared scoffed.

"Are we?" Jaime's question hung in the air until the bell shattered the quiet.

As the seniors left the room, Jaime patted Connie on the shoulder and said, "Thank you.''

Melissa paused beside Connie's desk, then spoke. "I've got some thinking to do, Mrs. W.''

Connie remained in the student desk, letting the good feelings wash over her, realizing they would have to sustain her for the rest of the day.

WHILE HE STAYED home waiting for the glazier to arrive to repair the broken window, Jim mulled over Connie's bombshell. He could see the pain it had caused her to tell him about her hysterectomy. He wouldn't fool himself. He'd been disappointed. In truth, he had never given up the hope of having children of his own. In idle moments, when he'd realized he was serious about Connie, he'd questioned whether she'd want more children, given Erin's age, her age. But he'd glossed over answers he didn't want to think about. Now, for both their sakes, he couldn't afford the luxury of wishful thinking. No. He had to search his soul. Where were his priorities?

The glazier arrived and efficiently replaced the broken glass. Then, running behind schedule, Jim barely made it to the midmorning assembly in the middle school. When he finally reached his office, Harriet handed him the mail and an ominously large stack of phone messages. She nodded toward his office. "Phil Buxton's waiting."

More trouble? "Thank you. Hold my calls, please."

He stepped into his office, slowly closing the door behind him. "'Morning, Phil." Buxton looked up from the sofa where he sat, balancing a cup of coffee on his knee. "Don't get up." Jim tossed the mail on his desk, drew an armchair near the sofa and sat down. "You took a lot of flak last night. How're you doing?"

"Nothing a good night's sleep and a six-month vacation in the Caribbean wouldn't cure." Phil gestured toward Jim's desk. "You read any of that yet?"

"No."

"Get ready. Some of it's undoubtedly hate mail."

"I'll just add it to the pile I've already received. Did you, by any chance, have nighttime visitors?"

Phil's eyes narrowed. "Yes. You, too?"

"A rock through the window."

"Lord. My fence was spray-painted." He set his cup on the end table. "Think it was kids?"

"Probably. Adults are usually more circumspect."

"Any idea who?"

Jim recalled the triumphant look Hale Metzger had shot him when Cleon Watson had called for his resignation. "I have no proof, but according to Ralph, young Metzger is the ringleader of a group of fellas who are running wild."

Phil's shoulders sagged. "I was afraid you'd say that."

"Because of his father?"

"Leonard Metzger's capable of making waves."

"If we catch Hale?"

"Do what you'd normally do."

"Good. That's the support I need." He paused. "I imagine some of the trustees would like to see me gone."

"They're after me, too. But, Jim, this storm should pass—eventually. We did the right thing in terminating Mueller."

"I know."

"Believe it or not, I've received occasional calls from parents concerned about the type of program Mueller was running. I suspect when the hotheads lose steam, we'll hear from others who support our decision."

"I hope so."

When Phil rose to his feet, Jim stood, as well. Buxton held out his hand. "I came by this morning to tell you to hang tough, Jim. If you nail those kids, do whatever you need to. You've got my support.''

Jim gripped Phil's hand and gave a rueful smile. ''That means a lot. It's getting kind of lonely up here.''

''We hired you because we thought you were a man of character. Nothing's happened to change my opinion.''

After Buxton left, Jim picked up the first letter. ''Dear Dr. Campbell,'' it read. ''I may be in the minority, but I want you to know that not all of us were pleased with the way Mr. Mueller treated our sons. We don't mind discipline, but some of his methods bordered on the psychologically harmful.''

Would wonders never cease? Unfortunately, though, Mueller's vocal supporters had stifled voices like these.

By midafternoon, after he'd fielded a dozen phone calls—two favoring the coach's termination, ten against—events of the past twenty-four hours began to wear him down. Jim could feel the edges of his self-control fraying, replaced by a dull, consuming frustration. Not a productive place to be. He checked the thermostat. The office was uncomfortably warm and stuffy. Muddy thinking could result from the volatile combination of exhaustion and discomfort. He needed to get the hell out of here.

He put on his tan raincoat and, after telling Harriet his destination, headed across campus toward the lower school, the raw north wind invigorating him. Whenever he felt overwhelmed, he found renewal with the little folks. He needed them now. Their unconditional affection, contagious enthusiasm and innocence served as reminders of the sacred mission of educators. Protesting football players, angry parents, vicious personal attacks—these were replaced by sunny faces, eager questions and the reassuring smells of colored markers, damp plastic raincoats and paste.

A toothless, freckle-faced boy, backpedaling at the end of a line of second graders moving toward the lower-school gym, called out, "Hi, Dr. Camel."

"Hi, yourself." Automatically Jim found himself grinning.

"Wanna come watch us play dodgeball?"

Jim hunkered down. "Could I play, too?"

"We-ll." The youngster, hands on his hips, eyed Jim skeptically. "I dunno. Are ya any good?"

"It's been a long time, but I think I can do it."

The boy shrugged. "I guess. C'mon." The instant Jim felt the warm, sticky hand take hold of his, the screws clamping his stomach released. Right now, proving he could dodge a ball and hit a moving target was his most important mission.

Apparently he acquitted himself satisfactorily with the second grade, because he was invited back to the classroom for refreshment time. Sitting on the tiny chair, his knees mere inches away from his chin, he sipped his chocolate milk, nibbled on a graham cracker and felt happier than he had in days.

When he strolled back across campus later, the rain had stopped. Finally he permitted himself to think again about last night, about Connie. Did she have any idea how much her coming to him had meant? How tempted he'd been to forget the risks? To lose himself till morning in her inviting mouth and warm body? He'd wanted, just for a few hours, to let himself go. He slowed his pace. No children. He had to decide now. To weigh his desire for children against his love for Connie. He couldn't have both.

Turning up his collar against the wind and burying his fists in the raincoat pockets, he sat on a concrete bench outside the middle school. There was no question in his mind that he loved her, always had. The exuberant young seminar student of Washington, D.C., had matured into an attractive, steadfast, selfless woman. That selflessness was one reason he loved her, but also part of the problem. Her responsibilities to her mother and daughter came first. And despite last night's momentary passion, he suspected it would be difficult for her to commit to him. Unless, of course, he could convince her he wanted her more than he wanted his own children—and that he wanted Adele and Erin, too. But before he did that, he'd have to be absolutely sure himself.

Hell, he couldn't even think about commitment when he didn't even know if he'd have a job beyond the next board meeting. All he knew was that in the midst of this turmoil, the one constant was Connie.

What would you do if you could be assured no one else would ever know? Out of the blue his own question confronted him. If no one would find out? He didn't even have to think about the answer. He'd go to Connie and love her senseless. The measure of a man's character. Foolishness or ultimate wisdom?

The middle-school bell reverberated and the building erupted with scores of youngsters swinging book bags perilously and playing spontaneous games of tag as they waited for their rides. He'd been so preoccupied he hadn't noticed the long line of vehicles idling in the drive. He rose to his feet and stood for a moment watching the car pool scene.

Dr. Camel. So much for illusions of self-importance.

ERIN DASHED in late from school, went to wash her hands and then slid into her accustomed seat at the dining-room table. The rigid set of her jaw, her overly polite mannerisms and the way she deliberately avoided Connie's eyes were cool reminders that nothing had changed since this morning.

"Have some aspic, Erin." Adele passed her the salmon pink gelatin.

"No, thanks, Gramma." She lifted a forkful of pot roast and sniffed it, then took one tiny bite.

"Don't you like it?" Adele looked worried.

"It's an animal product."

"Of course it is," Adele snapped. "So?"

Erin's fork clattered to the plate. "I'm thinking about becoming a vegetarian."

"Oh." Adele's chin quivered. "I always thought you liked my pot roast."

Strained silence lasted for several moments. Connie's appetite vanished, and Erin daintily moved meat and potatoes around on her plate, eating hardly anything. Adele lifted food mechanically to her mouth, her huffiness evident in her stiff posture.

The small wall clock chimed the quarter hour. Connie laid down her fork. "I think we should talk about it."

"'It'?" Her mother looked from Connie to Erin.

"Last night."

"May I be excused?" Erin shoved back her chair.

"No." The one syllable hung in the air, adding to the tension in the room.

Erin leaned back, folded her arms and doggedly stared into space. Bit by bit, Adele tore her bread into tiny pieces.

Connie felt a helplessness approaching panic. She plunged in. "Jim Campbell is someone I care about." She registered the roll of Erin's eyes. "As you know, I met him in Washington that summer I attended the fellowship program. Frankly, I was in love with him then."

Erin finally looked at her. Her mother's jaw gaped.

"Except for a series of circumstances there's no reason to go into now, I might very well have had a relationship with him." She turned to her daughter. "What would you have me do, Erin? Pretend he never existed or that that summer never happened?"

"Mo-ther, he's the headmaster, for Pete's sake."

"Exactly how does that change anything?"

Erin sneered. "I can see it all now. Headline in the school newspaper." With a flattened hand, she underlined the imaginary words: "History Teacher And Headmaster Get It On. It's humiliating, not to mention everyone hates him because of Coach Mueller."

Connie felt the fingernails of one hand biting into her other palm. "Let's take those comments one by one. First of all, suppose we did 'get it on,' as you so delicately phrase it. Would that be so terrible?''

Erin gave her an incredulous look, as if the question defied consideration.

''He is a decent, caring man whose company I enjoy immensely. Am I not entitled to a life?''

''Of course you are, dear.'' Her mother turned to Erin. ''Dr. Campbell seems very nice, but—''

''If you're worried about what people will think,'' Connie continued, ''how is my seeing Jim Campbell any different from dating Ralph Hagood?''

''Mr. Hagood would never have fired the coach.''

And that's exactly why Ralph was never the man for me. ''You don't know that. What is bothering you the most, Erin? The fact I have a friendship with Jim or the fact he requested Coach Mueller's resignation?''

''I don't know.''

''Well, you might think about it. I'm not going to do anything hasty or foolish. But I can't live the rest of my life worrying how other people will react. I've done that for way too long.'' The declaration of independence felt good. ''And as for the situation with Mueller, you might try talking to some of the other seniors, Jaime or Melissa, for instance.''

Erin neatly folded her napkin and placed it on the table. ''May I go now?''

Connie's shoulders sagged. ''I suppose.''

''But what about the pecan pie I made for dessert?'' Adele looked hopefully at her granddaughter.

''Full of butter and sugar, Gramma.'' She stood and, her head high in the air, walked out of the room.

"Pecan used to be her favorite." Adele shook her head. "I don't understand the child."

"She's upset because her mother actually has passionate feelings. Mothers aren't supposed to react to hormones."

Surprisingly, Adele's eyes twinkled. "Passion?"

Connie leaned over and covered her mother's veined, wrinkled hand. "And what do you think about all this?"

"I'm a bit confused. A little anxious." Adele hesitated. "But I want you to—what does Erin say?—go for it. There's too little happiness in the world. You deserve the kind of fun Edgar and I used to have." She winked. "He was quite a man, you know."

Connie's voice dropped. "Oh, Mama. I think Jim is, too. But I think it's too late."

Her mother squeezed her hand. "Erin's a good girl. She'll come around. She just needs time."

Connie lifted her fork and took a bite of pie she didn't want. *If only it were that easy.*

"IT'S *HIM*." A look of disapproval on her face, Erin stood at Connie's bedroom door later that evening. She nodded at the phone. "For you." She turned abruptly and shut the door more loudly than necessary.

Connie lifted the receiver. "Jim?"

"Hi." His voice sounded like warm honey. "You busy?"

"Er, no. Have you had a rough day?"

"The usual complaints and calls for my head. Otherwise, though, this was a very fine day."

Her heart sank. He sounded satisfied. Had her admission given him a welcome out? "Oh?"

"Yeah. I spent the afternoon in the lower school. To remind myself why I wanted to be a headmaster. You know, it's not about angry parents or one bad coach. It's about kids."

"They can be pretty great, can't they? Although right now, I wouldn't give you a plugged nickel for mine."

"Trouble?"

"Erin can't quite forgive me for last night."

"Understandable." Then he chuckled. "I imagine she's not used to her mother having a life of her own."

"To say the least. And, Jim, since she dates a football player, you have a clue where you stand with her."

"About two rungs above an ax murderer. But—" she could almost see him stretching his arms "—my shoulders are broad."

As her stomach dizzily descended to the vicinity of her knees, she decided to force the issue. "Jim, why did you phone?"

"As a matter of fact, to say I'd come to a conclusion. About us."

"Oh?" She wasn't surprised. But it still hurt.

"Today Phil Buxton called me a man of character. If that's true, I owe it to everyone at this school to model the values I believe in. To act in public, as well as in private, out of my convictions."

Her hopes vanished. She gripped the phone, steeling herself for the words she knew were coming: *We can't go on.* "Jim, I understand. I should have told you about the hysterectomy long ago. It will end right here. I promise.''

"What are you talking about?" He sounded genuinely puzzled.

"You and me, of course."

He laughed. "I see I haven't made myself clear. I love you. Any man worth his salt puts that above everything else. I refuse to apologize for caring about you and wanting to spend time with you."

She could scarcely breathe. "Jim, your dream of babies—"

"You come first."

"But the trustees, your future..."

"What will be, will be. Listen, I have an important question to ask you."

"What?"

"May I come over? I have the strongest need to hold you. Now."

CHAPTER FOURTEEN

WHEN CONNIE HAD announced Jim was coming over, her mother smiled a funny little smile and discreetly retired. Erin, however, laid it on. "He's coming *here?* I've got a big calculus test tomorrow, and you expect me to concentrate?" She'd marched off in high dudgeon.

Now Connie stood in the doorway waiting, her thoughts and emotions swirling. Just when her dreams were about to come true, she couldn't evade those long-ago words: "Can't you just picture the two of us in a big old house overflowing with babies? Lots of them?" A lump rose in her throat. No matter how he protested, if she truly cared about him, she couldn't deprive him of sons and daughters.

Jim's car pulled into the driveway, and he loped up the walkway. When she opened the door, he flung his arms around her, pulled her tight against him and buried his head in her neck. "Oh, God, Connie. You feel so good."

Slowly he straightened and caught her face between his hands and stared at her as if he thought she might vanish. Then his hungry mouth came down on hers, his lips seeking satiation. She hung on to him, limp and breathless. The power of his body, the tenderness in his lips, erased every caution. When he raised his head, he smoothed her hair back and whispered in her ear, "Being a man of character has great rewards."

Someone had to be realistic. She pulled away to look into his eyes, glazed with desire. "Don't forget the risks."

He drew her close once more, holding her against his chest. The rhythm of his breathing, the steady beating of his heart did little to calm her nerves. "I love you. The only risk is losing you."

She bit her lip and felt tears pooling in the corners of her eyes. It was tempting to remain sheltered in the comfort of his embrace, to pretend everything was all right.

Instead, she took him by the hand and led him to the living-room sofa. "We need to talk."

He settled beside her, a bemused smile on his face as he studied her features. "I don't know if I'm in the mood for 'serious.'" He nibbled her neck. "I had something a little more…elemental…in mind." When he straightened, he brushed a forefinger across her lips, then sat back. "Your mother? Erin? My job?"

Connie, stalling, nodded.

He picked up her hand and began speaking in a low voice. "I would never ask you to choose between me and your family. Your mother, Erin—they're part of who you are. The way you care for them is one of the reasons I love you. I realize I may have to do a sell job with them. After all, they've had you all to themselves for a long time. I'm an unexpected development. But it'll all work out with time."

From Erin's room, Connie heard the familiar music

of an exercise tape and the thump-thump of her daughter's step aerobics. Connie received the message loud and clear—Erin was working off hostility. And if she didn't get an A on the calculus exam, it would be Connie's fault.

Jim continued. "As for the job? I won't kid you. I like it at Keystone. I think I can make a difference here. Not everyone is anti-Campbell. We've arranged for professional counseling for Kurt Mueller to address some personal issues. The team seems to be uniting behind Coach Liddy and they have a good chance of winning the district play-off game Saturday. Things are tense now, but Phil thinks the storm will blow over. And if it doesn't?" He wrapped a tress of her hair around his finger. "We'll consider our options. My placement firm is already sending my credentials out as vacancies arise."

For the second time tonight the thought came. *If only it were that easy.*

"After Erin graduates, would you consider moving?"

Her head snapped up. "What are you saying?"

"I'm asking you to marry me."

For an instant, she lost herself in his sea-green eyes. *If only…* Her throat scratchy from unshed tears, she abruptly rose to her feet, needing to put distance between them.

"Connie—"

"Just give me a minute." She walked to the window and stood, hugging herself against the pain rooted, like a noxious weed, in her stomach.

She sensed him rise, then felt his arms encircling

her from behind as he rocked her back against him. His warm hands settled on her arms. "Take your time. Just let me hold you."

With a monumental effort she choked back the instinctive "I love you." There were other words she had to utter. Ones that would end it all. Steeling herself, she slowly turned and gripped his arms for support. "Jim, I can't marry you."

He looked bewildered. "Why not?" His voice sounded distant.

"I'm sorry. I never should have let us go this far."

"What are you talking about?" She felt his hand stroking her neck as if trying to slow the pulse throbbing just under the skin.

"You're not too old, Jim. You can still have a whole backyardful of kids." She found his eyes through the mist of her own. "Just not with me."

He ran his hands down her back, cupping her to him. He spoke softly. "Connie, I love children. And yes, a big family was a dream of mine. But that was never the basis of my love for you." His voice turned husky. "It's all about you. Just you. Without you, the rest would be meaningless."

Ignoring the fingers still moving gently over the sensitive skin of her neck, ignoring her insistent need for him, she whispered, "Jim, I can't ask you to make that sacrifice."

"You're not. Will you please think about it?" His lips quirking in a sad, lopsided smile, he traced away the tear sliding down her cheek.

The thump-thump of step aerobics was a pale echo of the thundering in her chest as she moved out of his embrace to speak the painful words. "No, Jim. It has to stop here and now."

"MRS. W., YOU sure look, uh, I dunno, different today."

Brad Scanlon scrutinized her face the next morning. What was it about this kid? Did he possess a sixth sense?

Connie looked up from her desk, out of the corner of her eye watching the sophomores drift into second period. "That bad, huh?"

"Yeah. I hope it's nothing serious."

Nothing serious? Try a broken heart.

She rubbed her eyes and tried to concentrate on the world history lesson. Opening her textbook, she stood and called for attention, noticing Stanley Henderson scuttle into his seat just as the bell rang. His first day back. She held her breath.

"Hey, wuss, where ya been?" The chatter stopped. Several boys in the back snickered. Stanley's face was flame red.

Keeping eye contact with the students, Connie slowly lowered the book to her desktop, then deliberately took her time rounding the desk to stand directly in front of the class. She let the students stew, then finally spoke. "I do not know who said that. I do not *want* to know, for I would think very little of such a rude, immature individual." Hale Metzger, his chin propped on his folded hands, ignored her. Jerry Rutherford studied the historical time line tacked high on the wall behind her. "However, let me make myself clear. From now on, in this classroom, all of you will respect the dignity of every other person here. That means being courteous and maintaining control of yourselves. History has not treated selfish rulers or bullies kindly." She paused, her jaw clenched. "Neither will I."

She reached behind her and picked up the text and somehow made it through a subdued discussion of the Holy Roman Empire. Stanley kept his eyes glued to his book. He gripped both sides of his seat; his thin body slowly rocked back and forth throughout the class period.

When the bell rang, Metzger and his buddies sauntered out, walking with that cocky stride that cries out, "Look at me. I'm special." Connie gritted her teeth. Interestingly, Jerry Rutherford lagged behind the group, as if uncertain whether to join them.

Stanley had waited for his tormentors to exit. Then, wearily, he gathered his books, rose to his feet and scurried out of the room. Connie started after him, but Brad waylaid her. He looked nervously down the crowded hall, then spoke quietly. "Mrs. W., I'm glad you said, you know, what you did in there."

"I meant every word."

"Yeah, I'm glad. Most of us, well, we don't like that kinda crap any better than you do."

"Brad, do you have any idea who's involved in harassing students?"

He stood on his toes, studying the students moving noisily toward their next classes. Then, turning away from her, he said, "Maybe."

"But you won't say?"

"That'd be squealing."

There it was. The student code of silence. *Never betray a peer, no matter what.* She took a chance. "Is it Hale?"

"You mean him and the football guys?" He hoisted his backpack to his shoulder. "You never heard it from me, Mrs. W." Then he joined the tide moving down the corridor.

Now she really did feel sick.

THE MONDAY AFTER Thanksgiving break, Connie relaxed in the back of her classroom, watching part of Kenneth Burns's Civil War video series with her sixth-period junior American history class. As the black-and-white images of old photographs reeled by, she reflected on the past few days.

Uptight was too mild a description for Erin, who, immediately following the Thanksgiving meal, had blanketed the dining-room table with her college application forms, determined to complete them during the four-day weekend. She'd sat tensely studying the applications, then had disappeared into her bedroom, where she'd churned out essays on the computer, many of which she'd immediately trashed, her perfectionism driving her to a frenzy. Connie could get her to eat scarcely anything. But by Sunday evening, the application checks had been written, the pages assembled for each college and the packets ready for the addition of teachers' recommendations.

The fact that the football team had lost the play-off game the previous weekend and, as a result, Kyle had accompanied his parents out of state for the holiday hadn't added to Erin's good humor. Was it too much to hope that now, with her college applications behind her, Erin would be easier to live with?

The rumors, not checked by the break, continued to spread throughout the school—about Jim's high-handedness, Kurt Mueller's alleged indiscretions and the random acts of vandalism targeting those responsible for the coach's dismissal. But even with those unpleasant distractions, Connie was relieved to get back to her routine. Shaking her preoccupation, she tried to refocus on the film.

When the harsh staccato of the fire alarm sounded, Connie jumped. The students sat for a moment, stunned, then scrambled to their feet. She stopped the video and directed them toward the pre-established fire exit. Something about Ralph's voice on the loud-speaker alerted her. This was not a routine fire drill. She grabbed a cardigan off the back of her chair and followed the students outside, where they stood shivering in the winter cold. In the distance she heard the insistent sirens, then saw the fire truck turn in the gates. Jim, Ralph and the upper-school secretary stood anxiously on the sidewalk in front of the building. Several firemen jumped off the truck and huddled in conversation with them. Then Jim and Ralph disappeared with the firemen into the building. Jim's expression, even from a distance, was ominous.

Ginny Phillips, hugging herself against the chill, sidled up to Connie. "It's a bomb threat, Connie. I was in the office when the call came in."

Connie's stomach twisted. Ever since the Oklahoma City disaster, what used to be an annual rite—calling in bomb threats—could no longer be chalked up to youthful mischief. The penalties now for such actions were stiff. "What did the caller say?"

"It was a male. Basically his message was, 'Reinstate Mueller or else.' Then he mentioned a bomb planted in a locker."

"Was it a student?" Connie was sick with disappointment.

"That's what Ralph thinks. It was a pretty stupid trick, if you ask me, because since November 1 the office has had caller ID on the phones."

"Good, I hope they catch whoever did it."

The milling students began to grumble as they realized they wouldn't soon be returning to the warmth of the building. Several ran in place and one enterprising teen tossed a Frisbee he'd somehow carried out with him. When Connie was convinced her lips had turned blue, the middle-school P.E. teacher beckoned to them. "Everybody move to the gym, please." No one needed a second invitation.

As Connie herded the students along, she couldn't help worrying about Jim. Surely this call was a hoax. But what if it wasn't?

In the gym, the coaches threw out some basketballs, prompting a couple of spontaneous games. Other students huddled on the bleachers, chatting or completing homework assignments. After a restless half hour, the chant went up, "Home, home, home." Connie couldn't blame them for being impatient. It was already beyond time for the last-period class to begin.

Pam joined Connie and Ginny. "I don't think we're going anywhere for a while."

"Oh?"

"On my way over here, I saw Ralph come out of the building to talk with a police officer who'd just arrived."

"What do you think's up?" Connie asked.

With a satisfied smile, Pam stretched out her legs and lounged against the row of seats behind her. "I think they're gonna pin somebody's hide to the wall on this one."

Finally, Jim appeared and dismissed the students for the day. As he blended with the dispersing crowd, Connie watched him following a group of sophomore boys. She, Pam and Ginny found themselves close behind. When they moved outside, Connie observed Jim adroitly cut Hale Metzger off from his buddies and edge him toward the administration building. Jim muttered something indistinguishable.

Pam, who'd been closer, whistled. "Boy, did you hear that?"

"What?"

"Our headmaster just told young Mr. Metzger to keep his mouth shut and to follow him straight into his office."

None of them, however, had any difficulty hearing Hale's whining retort. "Hey, man, what're you pickin' on me for? I didn't do anything."

Never had Connie seen Jim so grim.

WHY DIDN'T ANYONE make tapioca anymore? Adele puttered in the kitchen, examining the contents of the cupboard. Erin was getting skinnier every day. Maybe a little pineapple tapioca would be just the thing to tempt her. She heard the front door slam.

"Hi, Gramma," Erin called from the living room. "We got out early today. I caught a ride with Mallory. I'll be in my bedroom studying."

That's all the child did these days. Except for that Lyle boy, she hardly spent any time with her friends. Adele was all for good grades, but her granddaughter had gone overboard.

She leaned momentarily against the counter. Mercy, she felt exhausted for some reason. But not too tired to whip up the tapioca.

Later, pouring the warm, thick mixture into a bowl, she smiled, remembering the complimentary glass storage containers that used to come with new refrigerators. Now everything was plastic and the darned things warped in the dishwasher. Yet they called it progress. Just like flour sifters. Where could you find the old-fashioned kind with the crank on the side? No, now they had squeezers, not made for arthritic fingers and wrists. Or, worse yet, the sifters were electric! Imagine. An electric flour sifter! Ridiculous.

After putting a lid on the bowl, Adele looked up to see her granddaughter walking toward her, her face ashen, tear-streaked. In her trembling hand she held a letter.

"Good Lord. What's the matter, child?" Adele's fingers went instinctively to her chest. Something was terribly wrong.

"He can't do this." Erin's eyes flashed fire. "It's not fair."

"Who?"

"Dad." She shook the letter before throwing it down on the counter. "How could he?"

Adele put an arm around Erin's shoulders and led her to the small kitchen table. "Gracious, sit down, honey. Tell Gramma what's wrong."

"He's leaving Vanderbilt."

Adele racked her brain. Why should that upset Erin so much?

"Oh, Gramma, don't you get it? Maybe Vanderbilt was my only chance to go out of state. To get away from here."

Oh, dear. "But can't you just go wherever he's going?"

"Japan!" Her tone was bitter. "He's accepted an appointment at some university there. I didn't wanna be *that* far away."

Adele felt her chest constrict. What could she do to help her granddaughter?

"He's agreed to match whatever half my tuition costs would be at a Texas state school."

"That sounds generous enough."

"Oh, right. Gramma, Texas in-state tuition is nothing compared with out-of-state schools." Her shoulders shook. "What am I gonna do now?"

A cramp raced down Adele's arm. She stood up. She needed her pills. The late-afternoon sun pouring through the kitchen window blinded her; she couldn't see the door. She grabbed for a breath of air. Her lungs ballooned against her ribs. She couldn't breathe. The sun sprouted fuzzy gray edges, and from somewhere far away, she heard a sound like a blob of pudding hitting the floor.

"Gramma!"

Someone was shouting at her. Who? she wondered,

as she sank to her knees, a spasm of pain knifing through her chest.

JIM HAD ARRANGED several chairs in a semicircle around his desk. Young Metzger, his face an indifferent mask, was seated across from him beside his father, whose cold eyes followed Jim's every move. Next to Jim sat a detective from the bomb squad. Ralph and his secretary filled out the group.

Jim shuffled some papers on his desk, then looked up. "Mr. Metzger, we have reason to believe that your son has been involved in the past in harassment of other students. However, we have no proof of that. Today, though, evidence points to the conclusion that he called in a bomb threat and is responsible for planting a mock bomb we found in the locker area."

"Like hell," young Metzger brazened.

The older man placed a restraining hand on his son's shoulder. "Quiet. Let me handle this." He glared at Jim. "Before this outrage goes any further, I'd like to know what gave you the preposterous idea my son would do such a thing."

Jim deferred to the detective, who briefly explained. When the call had come in, the quick-thinking secretary had written down the caller's phone number, and then asked him to repeat himself while she recorded the message. "We traced the call to the pay phone at the convenience store across the street."

Hale stared belligerently at the detective. "Couldn't have been me. I was in class."

"What class?" Jim asked, although he'd already checked the boy's schedule.

"Art."

"And did Mr. Egan let you out to get a drink, go to the bathroom, run an errand?"

"No. I was there all period."

"Then how is it you don't know Mr. Egan is sick today and a substitute covered his class?"

The teen coolly eyed Jim. "I forgot."

"How convenient," the detective muttered dryly. He turned to the upper-school secretary. "Could you repeat that message for us."

Her voice shook. "He said that a bomb would go off at 2:40 p.m. in the locker section unless Coach Mueller was reinstated."

"Ma'am," the detective continued, "do you have a sign-out sheet when students leave campus?"

"Yes, we do."

"Any one sign out shortly before the call came in?"

"A sophomore girl with a dentist's appointment and Jerry Rutherford."

Hale shot the detective an I-told-you-so look. "Apparently you got the wrong guy."

"I don't think so. We checked with the teachers. Seems the Rutherford boy was in class all afternoon. But you weren't."

The detective handed the secretary a sheet of paper. "Does this look like Jerry Rutherford's handwriting?"

"I really couldn't say. Jerry usually prints, but this is cursive."

"Thank you, ma'am." The detective leaned forward, his elbows on his knees, fingers laced. "Son, lemme explain exactly what could happen here. A bomb threat is a serious offense. If we prove you phoned it in, you're facing legal action.''

"I didn't do anything, I tell you.''

The detective rubbed a finger under his nose. "Lemme spell it out for you and your daddy. We're brushing down the locker and the phony bomb for prints, we're checking the handwriting on the sign-out sheet against samples of yours and Rutherford's writing, and if necessary, the crime lab can do a voice analysis of the answering-machine tape.'' He paused. "At this point, I think I'd better read you your rights.''

Leonard Metzger leaped to his feet. "Just a damn minute here.''

The detective stood and approached the irate father. "Sir, we need to take your boy down to the station. You can follow us.'' He turned to include Hale in his gaze. "I think you both better be careful what you say.'' He pulled a card from his jacket pocket and, scarcely glancing at it, read the Miranda statement.

The older Metzger turned on Jim. "Are you just gonna stand there and let 'em haul my boy off to jail?''

Jim faced the man. "Sir, this is beyond my jurisdiction now. What final action the school takes will have to await the detective's findings. Meanwhile, until this matter is cleared up to our satisfaction, I am suspending your son indefinitely .''

"You can't do—''

Jim looked straight into the blazing eyes. "Yes, I can. If you wish, we can make arrangements for Hale to keep up with his schoolwork and take final exams so he doesn't lose credit for the semester, but under no circumstances is he to set foot on this campus without clearing it with me in advance. Understood?"

Leonard Metzger's lips thinned and he spit his final words. "Go to hell, Campbell."

The detective stretched out his arm to usher father and son out of the building. "We'll be in touch, Dr. Campbell."

"Thank you, Lieutenant."

Ralph clapped a hand on Jim's shoulder. "Tough business. I think they've got the kid dead to rights."

"I just wish Keystone could have done a better job with him."

"It's difficult when parents aren't willing to let kids take responsibility for their actions." He squeezed Jim's arm. "Don't be too hard on yourself."

Jim turned to the secretary. "This can't have been pleasant for you. Thank you."

After they'd all left, he slumped into his desk chair, knowing that whatever happened as a result of this incident, the boy's future hung in the balance. He would either get the scare of his young life and make a turnaround or his bitterness and bravado would ruin him. He prayed the boy would get some help before it was too late.

But at least it hadn't been a real bomb. His other kids were safe. Absently he pulled at the knot of his tie and picked up a stack of résumés for the athletic director's position. The pressure was on Buxton and the board to name a replacement. He tossed the first one aside. Not enough coaching experience. The second was from a fellow he'd known vaguely from the East.

He was scanning the man's letters of recommendation when the phone rang. Marking his place, he answered. "Jim Campbell."

"Thank God you're there." Pam Carver sounded frantic.

"What's the matter?" He realized he was on his feet.

"Connie just got a call from Erin. Adele's had a heart attack."

"Where is Connie?"

"On her way to the hospital."

"Is anyone with her?"

"Just Erin. The doctor told Erin it's serious. They're running tests now." She hesitated. "I could go, but I think it's you Connie needs."

"I'm on my way." After getting the name of the hospital, he threw on his suit jacket and dashed for his car, cursing the miles between him and his destination.

CONNIE STARED at the institutional blue of the overcrowded intensive care waiting room. She remembered reading somewhere that blue was a soothing color. No doubt the pastoral landscapes hanging from the walls were also designed to be calming. It wasn't working. Her stomach was in knots, and the acrid smell of old coffee did nothing to help. When she'd arrived at the hospital, she'd had a brief visit with her mother in the emergency room. Adele's gray face had frightened Connie even more than Erin's frantic phone call to the school office. The ER physician had referred the case to a cardiologist, then aides had trundled her mother off on a gurney with no word about when Connie could expect to hear more.

Whoever had designed the waiting-room chairs had obviously never had to spend any time in one. She couldn't decide whether to sit or stand. Throwing her dog-eared copy of *People* on the chair-side table, she closed her eyes, leaned back and forced herself to try to relax.

"We got here as soon as we could pick Bryson up from day care," a man brayed. Her eyes snapped open. A couple carrying a fussy toddler, whose diaper clearly needed changing, rushed toward the couple sitting in the corner. Connie coughed, then stood and walked to the doorway, searching the hallway for Erin, who had gone to the snack bar for drinks. Empty.

Poor Erin. She'd borne the brunt of the emergency—calling 911, riding in the ambulance, describing the heart attack to the ER physician.

The smock-clad auxiliary member manning the reception desk summoned her to the phone. Pam minced no words. "Jim's on his way." Connie's knees turned to water. How could Pam know Jim was the last person she wanted to see? It would hurt too much.

She concluded the conversation, then sat back down, her heart racing. A frazzled-looking young mother rose and switched on the television. Cartoons. Bugs Bunny's buck-toothed grin mocked the solemn concerns of the room's occupants.

"Here, Mom." Erin handed her a plastic cup. The carbonated beverage was a welcome improvement over the coffee. "Any word yet?"

Connie shook her head. "I don't imagine we'll

know much until tomorrow. The doctors will have to review the test results." Studying her daughter, she took another sip of her soda. Erin looked wiped out. "Honey, why don't you take the car and go on home? There's nothing you can do here."

"I can be with you."

Connie choked back a sob. "I appreciate that, but I'm all right. You'll be more comfortable at home."

"Mom, how will you get home if I take the car?"

"Pam just called. Jim's coming. He can bring me."

"Jim?" Erin's lip curled. "The headmaster?"

Connie nodded, watching her daughter's pale face take on a fiery hue.

"Mother, exactly how serious is this thing with *Jim?*" She placed scornful emphasis on the name.

Why now? This was neither the time nor the place to have this discussion. She sighed. "Not serious. He's merely a friend."

Erin grabbed her purse. "Whatever. I'd just be in the way. First, Dad jumps ship, and now you're acting weird. I'll see you later." Before Connie could react, Erin was out the door.

Connie considered going after her, but what would that accomplish? She could make allowances for Erin's emotional state—worry about her grandmother, jealousy over her mother's attachment to Jim, but— What had she said? "First, Dad jumps ship." What was that all about? Lord, neither of them needed a Colin complication. She set down the cup, her fingers chilled from clutching the icy soda during her confrontation with Erin. She squeezed her eyes shut. *Oh, Mama, what's happening?*

"Connie?" She felt warm hands on her own, felt herself being pulled from her seat into a bear hug.

"Jim? Thank God." Her legs went limp with relief as she felt herself supported by his strong embrace.

"Shhh. It's okay. Let it go." She raised a hand to his shirtfront, surprised to feel the dampness of her own tears. He stood quietly, letting her dissolve against him. Her outburst surprised her. She hadn't realized how near the brink she'd been. She felt his lips brush her forehead. "I'm here, Connie."

Such welcome, bittersweet words. She raised her tear-stained face. "I'm sorry. I mean, Pam had no right to bother you."

A soft smile lit his face. "She had every right." Before she could pull away, he kissed her tenderly. "Now, sit down and tell me what's going on."

He helped her into the chair, then handed her a crisp white handkerchief. She wiped her tears and blew her nose. "Sorry."

Before she could begin her story, a middle-aged, expensively dressed woman with dark eye shadow and carmine lipstick who'd been sitting across the room advanced toward them. "Dr. Campbell?" She fixed an appraising stare on him. "Aren't you the Keystone headmaster?"

Jim stood. "Yes. Have we met?"

Her lips smiled, but her eyes were gray agates. "Not officially. I'm Geraldine Farley. My husband's on the board."

"Of course. Nice to meet you."

The woman turned to Connie. "And if I'm not mistaken, aren't you Tara's history teacher?"

Connie's tongue was paralyzed. She nodded.

"Interesting." Mrs. Farley drew out every syllable.

"I'm sorry to meet you under these circumstances," Jim said. "Do you have a relative in intensive care?"

"No. I was just keeping a friend company. I'm leaving now, but—" her insincere smile broadened "—I couldn't help noticing the two of you." She paused for emphasis. "You know—how *cozy* you seem to be." With a flick of her wrist she waved farewell. "'Bye, now."

Connie leaned her head against the wall and closed her eyes, shriveling inside with a sudden, visceral foreboding.

CHAPTER FIFTEEN

BLOCKED ARTERIES. Angioplasty! When the cardiologist gave Connie his diagnosis the following morning, she panicked. "And if that doesn't work...?"

"Bypass surgery would be indicated."

She'd insisted Erin go on to school—no point her waiting around worrying—but now she wished she were here. She'd never felt so alone. The waiting room was a claustrophobic second skin, and each tick of the wall clock lasted an eternity. Finally, late that afternoon, the doctor arrived and beckoned to her from the doorway. Standing suddenly, she felt light-headed from dread. Only force of will kept her from falling.

"Your mother came through the procedure just fine, Mrs. Weaver. We're reasonably confident, at this point, that the angioplasty did the trick."

She called Erin to deliver the good news, then stayed at the hospital for two rotations of intensive-care visitation. Despite the formidable network of IVs, catheters and oxygen lines connected to her mother, Connie was amazed by the difference in her appearance. Instead of its usual sallowness, Adele's complexion was a healthy pink. An astonishing improvement.

All the way home, Connie offered prayers of

thanksgiving. The doctor had indicated the hospitalization would be brief and he wanted Adele participating immediately in the hospital's cardiac rehabilitation program.

As soon as Connie arrived home, she gave Erin an update, then retreated to her room, undressed, pulled on an old flannel nightgown and scrubbed off her makeup. Ralph called to reassure her about her classes and to urge her to take off as many days as she needed. But so close to final exams, she hated for the students to have a substitute. Wearily, she brushed her teeth, wondering how she was going to transport her mother back and forth to the hospital for rehab.

Finishing in the bathroom, she remembered Ginny had asked her to call with a report. Her friend answered on the first ring. Quickly Connie filled her in.

"Are you okay, Connie?"

"Exhausted, but relieved."

"I hope you're taking some personal leave."

"A few days. I hate to let the students down at this time of year."

"They'll survive. Your family's your first priority now." The guidance counselor's commonsense voice was reassuring.

"I know." She propped her elbow on the desk and rested her head in her hand. "Ginny, was Erin okay today?"

"I talked with her sixth period. Understandably, she was upset about your mother." Ginny hesitated a moment, before slowly continuing. "Connie, is something else bothering Erin?"

Connie bolted upright. "Why do you ask?"

"She wants me to delay sending out her college applications."

"Delay? I don't understand."

"It has something to do with your ex-husband."

Connie felt pressure building behind her eyes. Amid all the confusion, she'd forgotten to follow up on last night's cryptic remark. "Colin?"

"Apparently, from what Erin tells me, he's reneged on the amount he's willing to provide for her tuition."

"What do you mean reneged? Why hasn't she told me?"

"She didn't want to worry you right now. She told me she's reconsidering where she's applying."

Connie sighed bitterly. "Leave it to Colin to destroy his daughter's hopes."

"I know you have a lot on your mind, but I think you need to talk with her."

"I will." Another layer of gloom descended.

"Connie?" Ginny paused. "What's your opinion of Tara Farley's veracity?"

"Tara?" She strangled on the name.

"She's spreading the craziest stories about you and Dr. Campbell. I think that may be part of what's eating at Erin, too."

"Oh, Ginny." Connie closed her eyes. "Tara's not crazy. Is this about what her mother witnessed yesterday in the waiting room?"

"No point in beating around the bush. It's all over school that he was kissing you—in a *very* friendly manner."

"It's a misunderstanding." Connie fumbled for an explanation. "You may as well know that at one point several years ago, Jim and I were close. So the kiss, well, it looked like more than it was. Jim and I...that's all in the past."

"Connie, I believe you, but..."

"From what you say, it's messy."

"I'm afraid so. Oh, Connie, that's all you need. Try not to worry." After promising her support, Ginny hung up. Connie replaced the receiver and cradled her head in her arms. Where was the birthday fairy now?

From Erin's bedroom came the soft lyrics of Celine Dion. Connie vacillated. Should she try to discuss the college situation? The ugly rumors?

Celine Dion faded away, replaced by some unfamiliar male vocalist. College application deadlines were only a few weeks away. Of more immediate concern, she owed Erin an explanation about Mrs. Farley. She walked down the hall and knocked lightly.

"Come in."

Connie stepped inside. The stuffed bears on the quilt-covered bed looked oddly out of place in the room illuminated only by the blue gray light of the computer monitor. Erin consulted a textbook lying beside her on the computer table, then continued typing, finally stopping to look at her mother. "Whaddaya want?" She squinted, her brows knitting with irritation.

"I think we need to talk. It's getting close to deadlines for your applications."

"Tell me about it."

Erin thrust her the single typed page of Colin's letter, then turned away to brush her hair. One stroke, two strokes...measured, heartbreaking stoicism. He was leaving in January for a guest professorship in Japan. Unfortunately, he went on to say, he would be unable to attend Erin's commencement. His next words carried an indifferent finality:

> Vanderbilt, of course, is no longer an option for you. Since in-state tuition at Texas schools is so reasonable, it makes sense for you to go to one of your fine local universities. You can count on me for $3,500.00 a year for your college expenses.

Connie stared at the letter. Erin, her back to her mother, continued drawing the brush through her hair.

"Oh, honey. Unbelievable."

Erin's thin shoulders lifted, then fell. "I don't want to talk about it."

"We have to talk about it."

The brush clattered to the floor. "Not now, Mother. Leave me alone, will you? I have to study."

"I know you're disappointed about your father, but that doesn't mean you can't go ahead and apply out of state. Maybe you'll get a scholarship or a financial aid package."

"Well, we certainly can't count on that, can we?"

Connie longed to gather her daughter in her arms, but no matter how much Erin might inwardly welcome a hug, the self-contained high-school senior in front of her would reject any gesture of maternal affection.

In a toneless voice, Erin continued. "Over Christmas break, I'll get my Texas apps done. It's not the end of the world, you know."

"Oh, honey."

The don't-oh-honey-me look was unmistakable. Connie felt like weeping with frustration. "Do we need to talk about the rumors Tara's spreading?"

Erin pivoted and faced her. "I had a swell day. Kids staring at me, whispering behind my back. Kyle finally had to tell me what was going on. Is it true? Were you and *Jim* sucking face in public?"

Connie's patience snapped. "That's a disgusting thing to say." She rose to her feet. "I'm sorry you were embarrassed. I would never deliberately hurt you in that manner. Now, so the record is absolutely straight—yes, Dr. Campbell was at the hospital, and yes, he kissed me—rather platonically, I might add. Am I involved with him? Regrettably not."

"Well, that's at least a relief. Is that all? I really need to study."

Connie knew a dismissal when she heard one. "Yes, Erin, that's all."

Connie closed the door silently and leaned, defeated, against the wall. She was sick and tired of responsibility, of guilt, of…dammit, self-pity.

ADELE WAS RELEASED from the hospital the following Sunday, scared but looking healthier than she had in months. Tomorrow, when Connie started back to school, a licensed practical nurse would come in to help and the senior citizens' van would take her mother to and from rehab. Connie settled Adele on the living-room sofa, set Yolanda in her lap, covered her with a soft blanket and handed her the TV remote control. "Enjoy, Mama. *Carousel* ought to be just what the doctor ordered."

"Thank you, dear. I love that part about June bustin' out all over. Great dancing." She shooed Connie away. "I'm fine, really. Go on and grade your papers or whatever."

"You're sure?" It was still hard to leave her mother, even for a few minutes.

"Positive." The music of the overture drowned out Connie's protest.

THE WINTRY WIND outside did little to prepare Connie for the chill of the curious stares and whispered innuendos greeting her the next morning as she walked down the hall toward her classroom. Snippets such as "There she is—you know, the head's girlfriend" and "Wow, I never thought of Mrs. W. as a hot chick" made it difficult for her to carry her head high. While a few of her students expressed concern about her mother, most viewed her with prurient interest, as if she had a scarlet *A* branded on her chest. It took every bit of restraint not to defend herself.

Defend herself? Why should that even be an issue, particularly when neither she nor Jim had done anything to feel ashamed about?

Fortunately, her long absence meant her classes had a lot of catching up to do prior to final exams the following week. Enough of her students were grade conscious that she could mask her embarrassment and frustration with the routine of teaching.

Between class periods, she dashed to the teachers' lounge for a cup of coffee. Her arrival stopped conversation. Only the words "...and he's been such a talker about character" drifted into the silence. Jessie Flanders and two others scrambled for the door and the remaining teachers began an animated discussion about their Christmas shopping. Over their heads, Connie spotted Pam giving her a what-can-you-do shrug. Cheeks burning, Connie filled her mug and beat a hasty retreat. Pam caught up with her out in the hallway.

"Don't mind them. You've given them something to talk about besides how overworked and underpaid they are."

"Ginny warned me, but I had no idea it would be this bad."

"Half the women are jealous and the others are silently saying, 'Bravo.'" Pam placed a hand on Connie's shoulder. "In the long run, they all know you. They understand you wouldn't do anything to compromise yourself. Right now they're just feeding off Mrs. Farley."

"What's she saying, Pam?"

"She's a regular one-woman fount of information. And since she's chairman of Saturday's Holly Ball, you know, Keystone's annual lah-de-dah fundraiser—" she rolled her eyes and bent her hand at the wrist "—she has a built-in audience of gaga moms. Believe it or not, here's what she says." Pam adopted her best outraged matron tone. "'Why, isn't it shocking, simply shocking, that our headmaster talks a good game about character, but acts like a rutting bull? We can't forget our children are being influenced by those two.'"

Connie groaned. "That bad, huh?"

"Not really. Most people are wise enough to consider the source. 'Sensationalism' is that woman's middle name."

"I wish I felt reassured."

"Look. What you and Jim do on your own time is nobody's business. And from where I sit, he's doing a great job as headmaster. *Adios,* Kurt Mueller. *Auf Wiedersehen,* Hale Metzger. And last I looked, my friend, there was no policy forbidding fraternization. Relax. This, too, shall pass."

"Thanks, Pam. I hope you're right. But I need to tell you, it's over…between Jim and me."

Pam paused at the door of her own classroom. "Are you crazy? I don't know what's stopping you, but here's my two cents' worth. Stay in the ball game. Go for it!" She winked saucily as Connie continued down the hall.

If only she *could* take her friend's advice. But she couldn't play fast and loose with Jim's needs. Accepting the criticism and judgment of others was no longer the issue. Now she'd never be put to the test, never know if she possessed the courage to confront a Geraldine Farley.

When she reached her classroom, she was puzzled to find a plain envelope on her desk with only "Mrs. W." written on it. Once she took roll and quieted her study hall, she slit the envelope open and withdrew a carefully folded sheet of notebook paper. Immediately she recognized Stanley Henderson's precise printing:

My parents have decided I need to live in San Antonio with my grandparents. I want you to know I appreciate everything you tried to do for me. Your a good teacher and I learned alot from you. Most of the kids here were alright. But a few were mean. Especially to a guy like me. So I won't be back after the semester. Thanks for being such a nice lady.

Your friend,
Stanley

Sadly she remembered her earlier thought: *We can't save them all.* She didn't know whether to pound her fist on her desk or cry. Instead, she took out some personal stationery and began writing Stanley a note wishing him well.

JIM SCANNED the copy of the police report on his desk, then handed it to Ralph, who was sitting across from him. Faced with overwhelming evidence and severe penalties, young Metzger had confessed to his culpability in the bomb-threat incident. Now the school had to decide whether to press charges.

After reading the document, Ralph set it back on the desk. "They've got him cold."

"Buxton's left what happens to Hale up to us."

"That's a tough call. Maybe I've been in this business too long, but if there's a way to help the kid, I'd like to see us try."

Jim checked his watch. "His father's due here in a couple of minutes. Shall we see what he has to say?"

"Sounds good. The father's the key, I think."

"I agree. The youngster has to know everyone

means business—his family, the school, the authorities."

Harriet tapped on the door, then admitted Leonard Metzger, dressed in an immaculate business suit.

"Have a seat, Mr. Metzger." From behind his desk, Jim gestured to the vacant chair next to Ralph. "How can we help you?"

Mr. Metzger pulled nervously at his French cuffs. "I want you to drop the charges and readmit my son to Keystone."

Jim fingered the police report. "Let's take those issues one at a time, starting with dropping the charges. We have patrons who justifiably feel your son recklessly endangered others. They want to see justice done."

"What kind of justice crucifies a fifteen-year-old?"

Jim folded his hands and eyed the man. "Naturally, I am concerned for your son. But I have to weigh his actions against my responsibility to other students and their parents. What Hale did was not only thoughtless, it was malicious."

Metzger's face flushed. "He's just a kid, for God's sake."

Ralph leaned forward. "Does that mean he shouldn't know right from wrong?"

"He's said he's sorry. What more do you want?"

"What we want," Jim responded, "is to see some evidence on his part of contrition. And we'd like to know if you plan to get him help."

"Help? What kind of help? Oh, no, you're not talking about some wacko shrink?"

"As you know, we suspect this is not the first such incident involving your son."

Metzger gripped the arms of the chair. "Are you talking about that Henderson kid?"

"Among other things."

"Like?"

"Like a rock thrown through my window the night of the patrons' meeting."

That seemed to take some of the wind out of Metzger's sails. "My kid? You're outta your mind!"

"Truthfully, I don't know who did it. But Coach Liddy overheard some football players, including your son, talking about it."

"That doesn't mean a damn thing! You just said there were others."

"Mr. Metzger, are you here today to blow off steam or to work with us to try to help your boy?"

The man's chest slowly deflated before Jim's eyes. "I don't know. I thought he was just full of wild oats. But—" he shook his head "—ever since the boy's mother died last year, he's been hard to control."

"Maybe his actions are a cry for help," Ralph suggested.

Beads of perspiration edged Metzger's hairline. He looked at Ralph, then back at Jim.

"Let me make a couple of suggestions," Jim said. "First, it sounds as if therapy is indicated. Second, he needs to have boundaries at home—strict guidelines, a set curfew, penalties for getting out of line. That would be up to you."

"Are you saying I'm a bad parent?"

"It's what happens from now on that counts," Jim said quietly.

Neither administrator spoke, letting the troubled father mull over the suggestions.

"And *if* I got him help, laid down the law, spent more time at home with him?"

Jim caught Ralph's eye, saw the brief nod, then continued. "If we had such assurance, we would be prepared to drop charges. As for the second matter, Hale's reinstatement at Keystone, that's a bit trickier because it impacts other students as well as their parents. Because he has acknowledged guilt, I have no choice according to school policy but to suspend him for the entire second semester."

"The hell you say!" Metzger started to rise, then slumped back.

"He could attend public school to finish his sophomore year. Then we would be in a position to re-evaluate your request."

"If I might offer a suggestion." Ralph faced the man. "Several of our troubled students have profited from a good outdoor wilderness survival program. You might consider that for summer."

"You're sure you can't let him back in sooner?"

"I realize how distressing this is," Jim said, "but in the long run, I think Hale will profit most from having to accept the consequences of his actions." He stood and extended his hand across the desk. "Keep us informed. We all have your son's best interests at heart."

Mr. Metzger stood, adjusted the buttons of his suit

jacket, nodded, then, ignoring the proffered hand-shake, walked out of the room.

Jim slowly sat down, then turned to Ralph. "Well?"

"Masterfully handled. It could've been a whole lot worse."

"I hope the kid makes it. He's desperately seeking attention. The funny thing is, he has a lot of leadership potential, if it could be harnessed constructively."

"I know." Ralph fingered his bald spot. "You did the right thing. We can't forget about the other kids just waiting to see what they can get away with, or the parents who'd raise holy hell if we let Metzger back in right away."

"This is definitely not the fun part of headmaster-ing."

"No, it isn't. And if I might say so—" Ralph fidg-eted in his chair "—I don't imagine the rumors about you and Connie are much fun, either."

Jim looked up, in an odd way relieved Ralph had broached the subject. "No, they're not. Particularly when some are vicious, unfounded. I can take it, but Connie..." He shook his head.

"She's a wonderful person."

"I know."

"Are...are you in love with her?"

Seeing the pain and concern in his principal's eyes, Jim realized that at one time Ralph's feelings for Con-nie had probably gone beyond friendship. He deserved nothing less than total honesty. "Yes, I am. I know how much she values your friendship, as do I. So I need to tell you this. She comes first with me. Before anything else, Keystone included.''

Ralph's face relaxed into a smile. ''Good. That's all I wanted to hear.'' He hoisted himself out of the chair. ''On my desk is a letter ready to be mailed to Phil Buxton. I'm withdrawing my name from consideration for the headmaster's job.'' Jim's eyes widened in surprise. ''But the letter doesn't stop there. I'm endorsing you for the position. Based on what I've seen, I think you'd make a first-rate replacement for Dr. Frank.''

Jim rounded his desk, reaching for Ralph's hand, which he clasped firmly. ''I can't thank you enough for your vote of confidence. It means a lot. But—''

''I don't need the pressure of interviews like the one we just had. I'm happy at the upper school. Why sacrifice that? You're the man for the job.''

''I hope I get the opportunity to justify your confidence.''

''So you've hit a few rough spots.'' He dropped Jim's hand and moved toward the door. ''Trust the board. Most of them are pretty fine people.''

LATE THAT AFTERNOON Jim sat in an alcove of the nearly deserted school library, working on his remarks for a new admissions brochure. Would it be his first and last such endeavor? Despite Ralph's generous gesture of withdrawing his name, Jim knew the board was reviewing applications for the position of headmaster, his included. Given everything that had happened, what were his chances realistically? A lot depended upon the board's assessment of his judgment.

He set down his pen and leaned back, glancing

around the modern, well-lit facility. Three middle
schoolers crowded around one of the computer ter-
minals and across the way two debaters photocopied
page after magazine page for their files. He enjoyed
getting out of his office, finding quiet spots across
campus where, free from intrusive phone calls, he
could observe the comings and goings of students, remind himself just what was at stake.

The thud of a book falling from the stacks behind
him, followed by what sounded like a whole shelfful
tumbling to the floor, snapped him out of his reverie.
Alerted, he stood, listening. At first it was quiet. Then
came the sharp intake of a cry, followed by desolate
whimpers. He walked around the stacks—and stopped
dead.

There, crumpled on the floor, surrounded by books
and strewn papers, sat Erin, holding her stomach and
rocking back and forth, sobbing uncontrollably.

Slowly, so as not to alarm her, he touched her shoulder. "Erin?"

She stopped rocking long enough to look up at him
through watery eyes. Then, as her tears continued to
flow, she covered her face with her hands and huddled
over her knees. When he touched her tentatively again,
she jerked away, hiccuping out a "No."

He hunkered beside her, waiting while she gasped
for air and tried to regain control. Finally, he spoke.
"Let me help you with these things." He began piling
up the books and gathering the scattered contents of
her notebook.

When he finished, he sat on the floor beside her.
She settled back on her heels, swiped at her eyes and

drew a tissue out of her backpack. She did her best to blot her runny mascara, then blew her nose.

"Need to talk about it?"

Her look said "With *you?*"

"That was a major meltdown. How can I help?"

She shifted to a sitting position, drawing her knees up to her chest. "Nobody can help."

"I know I might not be your first choice, but I'm the one who's here, and I'm a good listener." Every few seconds, with a shake of her shoulders, she inhaled, trying desperately to control herself. He folded his hands between his knees and waited.

When she spoke, he had to lean forward to catch the words. "It's not really you." She wadded the tissue between her fingers. "It's everything. I'm just stressed out."

This wasn't the first senior he'd seen crack under pressure, and she'd had more than her share of that. "Talking might help."

"I've been so worried about Gramma."

"That's understandable."

"And I want Mom to be happy, I really do, but..."

"We've embarrassed you."

She looked up at him. "*I* understand you two are right for each other. It's just...it's hard, you know, to hear your friends talk about your mom that way."

"And to think about sharing your mom with a man?"

She released her knees and slowly let her legs slide to the floor. "I'm not really that selfish."

He smiled gently. "Of course you're not. For what it's worth, Erin, I love your mother very much. I would never intentionally do anything to hurt her...or you.''

She hit her thighs with balled hands. ''I hate this place. It's nothing but a gossip mill. People can be so cruel.''

''Yes, they can. I'm sorry you've had to bear the brunt of the talk.''

''If I wasn't so worried about Gramma and final exams and my college screwup, I'd probably have ignored my friends or told them to go to hell. But everything's happening at once.''

''Your grandmother should be fine, and your mother and I will weather this crisis. But what about you? Let's start with final exams.''

''I have to ace them.'' There was desperation in her voice.

''Why?''

''I've got to have straight As to be valedictorian.''

''That's important to you?''

''Very.''

''What's the worst thing that would happen if you weren't?''

''I'd miss out on some college scholarships. I'd let myself down.''

''With your record of academic achievement and participation in activities, your scholarship chances are excellent with or without graduating first in your class.''

''You think?''

''I know.'' He winked. ''Years of experience.'' He sobered. ''Let's get to the more important consideration. Your perfectionism.''

"You think *that's* what it is?"

"I do. And you know what?" He paused until she looked at him. "The world isn't crazy about perfect people, especially ones too busy to have any fun. When's the last time you blew off a test to go to a concert?"

She hung her head. "I don't know."

He tipped up her chin. "Erin, are you happy?"

Her eyes filled with tears. Finally, she shook her head and whispered, "No."

"We headmaster types can't help giving advice. Take what I'm going to say with that in mind. You're pushing too hard, being too hard on yourself. Relax. Take time to play, to enjoy your friends, so you can look back on this senior year as special. It happens only once, you know."

She dug out another tissue. "But what about college? I don't know what to do."

"With the right attitude, you can be happy many places. Your mother's told me you want to go out of state. Are you trying to escape home? Get away from the same old friends? To test yourself? Think about your motivations, Erin. And take your time. You don't have to decide everything today."

He stood, picked up the stack of books and began reshelving them. Behind him, he heard her tamping down her papers. Then she clicked open the notebook rings to reinsert the pages. He turned and watched her, noticing how her shoulder blades poked through her tunic top. "When's the last time you had a double-dip ice-cream cone?"

She stood up, a tiny grin softening her features. "What?"

"You heard me."

"Gosh, I don't know."

"Well, whaddaya say we go to the Dairy Delite and the two of us pig out?"

"Chocolate-almond royale?"

"You're on."

She giggled shyly, slung her backpack over her shoulder and walked beside him out of the library.

CHAPTER SIXTEEN

JIM SAT AT HIS DESK Wednesday morning, preparing the agenda for the upcoming board meeting. Decisions needed to be made regarding the athletic director's position and the headmaster search. And there was a food service issue that still hadn't been resolved. He shoved the sheet of paper aside. Golden winter sunlight streamed through the windows, a welcome reprieve from the overcast skies of the previous two days.

How was he supposed to concentrate on school business when his thoughts kept straying to Connie? To her polite but distant reactions when he'd called several times to check on her mother? She'd sounded almost brusque, but a shakiness in her voice fed his hopes. Was she doing it again? Sacrificing herself, her own needs, just as she'd done for Adele and Erin, for what she thought he needed? Children?

Children. He wouldn't kid himself. His best-of-all possible worlds was populated by four, maybe even five, long-legged, tan kids dribbling basketballs, climbing trees, playing tea party in a huge backyard, their faces lighting up when he approached. "Daddy, come see!" they would shout. And he would shoot a basket, build a fort, sit in a playhouse, with a tiny china cup balanced on his knee. Okay. But where was

Mommy? Always the fantasy stopped here—with the soulful blue eyes, the long wind-tossed hair, the graceful, tapering fingers of the only woman he'd ever loved. Connie. Connie, who loved him enough to give him freedom to have his children. Damn. How could he make her see the dream was nothing? That without her, he was nothing?

"Dr. Campbell, there's a young man waiting to see you."

Jim hadn't heard Harriet's knock. He looked up. She smiled knowingly. "You said not to interrupt, but in this case, I think you won't mind."

Harriet was an old hand, and he trusted her judgment. He swiveled toward the door. "Send him in."

A broad-shouldered, distressed-looking youth wearing a varsity letter jacket entered tentatively, then stuck out his hand. "Sir, remember me? Jerry Rutherford. Do you have a minute to talk?"

Jim stood, shook the boy's hand and indicated a chair. "Certainly, son. What can I do for you?" Harriet's instincts were right on target.

Jerry sat forward in his seat, his hands clenched between his knees. "I came to thank you."

"Thank me?"

"Yeah. It coulda been me, you know—the bomb threat thing."

Jim settled back, steepling his fingers. "Why wasn't it?"

"Something you said. Remember the assembly, when you spoke?"

Jim nodded.

"At the time I thought what you said was a bunch

of bull.'' He shifted uneasily, his face flushed. "I limed Henderson's yard. Not just me, you understand. But I was there.''

"Go on.''

"You know what you said about what you'd do if you knew nobody'd ever find out? Except for the guys I was with that night, nobody knows. Not my parents or my teachers or you. Till now.''

Jim held very still. "So why are you telling me?''

Jerry looked down and fiddled with his jacket zipper. "Because all along somebody important *did* know. Me.''

It was hard to tell in the harsh light, but the boy's lashes seemed to glint in the sun. Jim waited.

"I thought I was so cool.'' He looked directly at Jim, his eyes transparent with honesty. "I was wrong. I'm ashamed. I've called Stanley to apologize.''

A knot in Jim's throat made it difficult to speak. "It takes a big person to admit a mistake, Jerry.''

"Yeah, well I don't want you to be proud. I want you to tell me what to do, how to make it right.'' His voice trembled.

"I wish I could, son, but I can't. You were involved in a malicious, senseless act against an innocent party who has suffered because of it. You made a decision and there have been consequences, more serious probably than you ever could have imagined. It's not the past you can do something about.'' Jim paused. "What have you learned? That's what counts now.''

Jerry wiped his palms on the knees of his jeans. "I guess that I have to live with myself. That when things get tough, the only person I can count on is me.''

"So is that why you weren't involved in the bomb threat?"

"I guess. Metzger had kinda joked about it, but I didn't take him seriously. I mean, jeez, after Oklahoma City... But the more he kept talkin', the more I kept thinkin' of that story you told. About the two runners. It coulda been me, you know, joining hands with Metzger, thinkin' we were hotshots phonin' in that bomb threat." He swallowed convulsively. "But, Dr. Campbell, I'd rather cross the finish line feelin' proud."

Jim rounded the desk and placed a hand on the boy's shoulder. "You have, Jerry. You have."

The boy stood up. "I gotta get to class, but I just wanted to tell ya." He zipped up his jacket and stuck his hands in the pockets. "Don't go someplace else, Dr. Campbell." A faint smile broke across his face. "I hope you stick around. You rule!" Then he ducked his head, walked quickly from the office, past a smug-looking Harriet and out into the sunshine.

Beaming, Jim gave Harriet a salute, strolled to his office window and watched Jerry Rutherford, head held high, cross the campus. He felt like pumping his fist in victory. Every now and then, a miracle happened. And it was the miracles that kept him going. God, he was proud of that kid!

And then it hit him. The answer! This time he *did* pump his fist in the air before turning to give Harriet her instructions.

ADELE, huffing and puffing on the stress-test machine, felt ridiculous. Shorts! At her age. Every time she looked down at the treadmill, she was repulsed by her withered thighs, knobby knees and blue-veined legs. Betty Grable, whose pinup had decorated GIs' lockers throughout the forties, was undoubtedly rolling in her grave. And then the little white bobby socks and those clodhopper workout shoes! But even this humiliation was better than the alternative—bypass surgery.

The young therapist, looking like a million bucks in *her* exercise outfit, kept shouting encouragement. "Way to go, Adele! Just a few more minutes." Easy for her to say. Across the room, Adele spied a balding gentleman whose beer belly hung like a deflated inner tube over the band of his sweatpants. He didn't look so hot, either! The dress code here was some devious plot on the part of doctors. Embarrass the patients into reform!

"Okay, Adele." The machine whirred to a blissful stop. Adele took a few deep breaths before the sucker punch of the therapist's next words. "Time for your walk." Balefully Adele eyed the oval wooden course. "Start slowly, then see if you can work up gradually to a faster pace." If she didn't die first.

Slowly she put one foot in front of the other, aware that the loudspeaker was booming music designed to spur the patients along. Glenn Miller. "Pennsylvania 6-5000." Briefly her eyes filled; big band music always made her ache for Edgar, for his arms around her, deftly guiding her on a crowded dance floor, convincing her they were the only couple who mattered. When her vision cleared, she realized she'd almost collided with a short, trim gentleman with a gray military mustache, who had lapped her, then whirled around to backpedal along just in front of her. "New here?"

She nodded. "New, but I don't know how long I'll last."

"It's hard at first, but when you get the hang of it, you'll feel so much better. I try never to miss." He held out a hand. "I'm Vernon Wray."

She barely squeezed out the breath to answer. "Adele Vail."

He shook her hand, then abruptly stopped walking. "Wait a minute." He furrowed his brow, pulling her aside to avoid a collision with Tire Belly, who passed by them wheezing and sweating. "Edgar Vail? Adele and Edgar Vail?" A grin melted his features.

"Why, how did you—?"

"Dance contests. I remember Grand Lake, Oklahoma. You and your husband really knew how to move around the floor."

She smiled sadly. "That was a long time ago."

"You still dance?"

"No."

"Let's see what we can do about that. Dancing's great exercise."

And before she could gather her wits, he'd circled her waist and was fox-trotting her along the course, joining in with the vocalists for the refrain of "Pennsylvania 6-5000."

Adele thought she might faint, but when she looked up at Vernon, grinning down delightedly, her feet took wing.

AFTER LUNCH, Connie checked her mailbox in the office. A cryptic phone message from Adele, announcing that in the future Connie could cancel the senior citizens' van service to rehab, lay on top of an envelope from the headmaster's office. When she read the announcement from Jim's secretary, she threw up her hands. Another meeting. Meetings in and of themselves were bad enough at this time of year, but being with Jim tested her resolve to the limit.

"Something wrong, Mrs. W.?"

She didn't even have to turn around. She'd know that voice anywhere. "Just a few technical difficulties, Brad. Nothing for you to be concerned about."

"Okay. Just checking."

Solicitude. She'd give the kid that. She looked down again at the summons: "Dr. Campbell would like you to join him and a few others at 2:30 p.m. today in room 14 at the lower school for the first meeting of the Long Range Planning Committee."

On top of everything else, there went her prep period!

HAD SHE MADE a mistake? This was the kindergarten room. Little bodies huddled around a water table, fingers happily splashing. Two girls bent head to head over a jigsaw puzzle, and a redheaded boy with a bumper crop of freckles, his arms spread wide to simulate plane wings, buzzed around the room in aviator's goggles. Connie pulled out the letter and looked at it again. 2:30 p.m. in room 14. And above the door were the numerals 1 and 4. Tentatively, she poked her head into the room.

A roly-poly imp of a woman rose from the carpet

where she'd been kneeling to help an adorable Oriental girl learn to tie her shoe. "Hi, Connie. Welcome to chaos. It's free-choice time."

"Miriam, I—"

"Yes, you're in the right place. Well, almost, anyway." She grinned. "The meeting's in the Big Yellow House."

"I beg your pardon?"

"Over there." The teacher pointed to a vividly painted playhouse, constructed of two refrigerator cartons, complete with tiny curtained windows, beneath which were window boxes full of colorful plastic flowers. "The door's on the other side."

Connie pointed at herself. "Me?"

"Oh, yes. You." With a smile, Marian turned back to the child waiting patiently at her side.

For no reason she could explain, Connie felt a sudden attack of nerves. Approaching the waist-high doorway, she could hear the chatter of children's voices. "You be the daddy this time, okay?" "If you can't behave, baby, I'll put you in time-out."

Stooping, Connie edged into the house.

"She's here, Dr. Camel. She's here!"

Sitting cross-legged on the floor, a chef's hat on his head, a frilly apron barely covering his dress shirt and tie, Jim just grinned at her. "So she is."

"Sit down, Mrs." A small hand tugged on her skirt. "You can be da wittle sister."

Connie crumpled to the floor. "But the meeting…?"

A dark-skinned boy with a mass of black ringlets

crawled over to sit in front of her. "You guys, we can start now. She's here."

The way the children said "she" made her feel like visiting royalty.

A tiny blonde, missing her two front teeth, spoke up. "Thith ith the meeting, right, Dr. Camel?"

Over the children's heads, Jim looked at her with such love that she was momentarily disoriented. "Yes, this is the meeting." He settled an arm around a little boy with a cast on his leg. The youngster snuggled against him, sucking his thumb. "The Long Range Planning Committee," he added by way of emphasis. "And these fine boys and girls have agreed to serve on the committee. Right?" The kindergartners giggled. "Ryan, here—" he smiled down at the boy practically sitting in his lap "—thinks I'm king of the school."

"Dr. Camel's the king, all right," Ryan agreed.

"But-but-but," the blonde said, "a king needths a queen."

"A queen?" *Surely he's not... Surely he didn't...* Connie pursed her lips and peered at Jim, who seemed to be deliberately ignoring her and focusing, instead, on his little "committee."

"Where do you think the king should look for a queen?"

"At the school!" the curly-headed cherub cried out.

"That's a very fine idea, Mason. And if the king found a queen at the school, where would the king and queen find children?"

The little blond girl, whose hand had entwined with Connie's, bobbed up and down on her knees. "Here!

Right here! Why there's—'' she paused as if counting
''—prob'ly twenty-fousand forty-'leven of us!''

''Well, then, Ms. W. There's your answer.'' Jim
readjusted the contented thumb sucker to reach behind
his back. Then he glanced around at the wide-eyed
children. ''Okay, gang, whaddaya think? Who's my
queen?''

Amid finger pointing and a cascade of giggles, the
tiny voices squealed, ''*She* is! *She* is!''

And sure enough, she *was* visiting royalty because
Jim pulled a gold foiled cardboard crown from its hiding place, crawled across the room, knelt before her
in his ridiculous hat and child's apron and placed it
reverently on her head. Then, as the children quieted,
he sat back on his heels and searched her face before
whispering, ''I *have* a whole schoolful of children.
What I *need* is my queen.''

Connie's mouth quivered as she swiped at the tears
running down her cheeks.

He leaned forward, pinning her between his arms.
''Now, are you going to tell me you don't love me?''

Her tear-clotted answer was barely audible. ''No.''

A small body skittered around them to the small
cutout doorway. ''Mith Randall, Mith Randall, heth
kithing her!''

And so he was, deliberately, recklessly, wonder-
fully. Her arms found their way around his neck.

Across the Big Yellow House, through a euphoric
haze, Connie heard a boyish voice. ''I don't think I
wanna be king, do you, Mason?''

''No! Kissing's yucky. Let's go play trucks.''

FROM THE KINDERGARTEN Jim dragged her along, insisting she wear her crown every step of the way, through the lower-school gym, where the fifth graders were playing double Dutch, into the middle-school art room, where seventh graders worked elbow-deep in papier-mâché, and finally on to the upper-school chorus room, where they stood in the doorway listening to the special ensemble singing a dreamy version of "People Will Say We're in Love."

Connie smiled. "Is this mere chance, or did you pick this song?"

"Let's just say I had a bit of last-minute help influencing their selection."

"From?"

He circled her waist and maneuvered her on into the room. "There."

On a stool to the left of the accompanist, Erin sat, mouthing the lyrics to her mother.

"Jim, I don't believe it."

He chuckled. "It's all about miracles, Connie. All about miracles—of which your daughter is one." He ushered her back into the hall. "So whaddaya say? How's about a date?"

It was all happening too fast. "A date?"

"Yes, it's only fitting that the queen of the school, the future Mrs. Jim Campbell, accompany the king to the Holly Ball Saturday night."

Her instinct was to cry out "Wait!" The gossip, his job—

As if sensing her reservations, he held her by the shoulders and looked deep into her eyes. "Trust me, Connie. I love you. You love me. It's the honest thing to do. The finest example we can set is to love.'' He squeezed her gently. ''You have the courage. I know you do.''

Did she? Could she walk out on that uncertain plank, leaving behind the only life she'd known, to jump with him into the uncertain waters of the future?

He was asking something important of her. To commit—publicly, permanently.

CONNIE WAS FINDING IT next to impossible to concentrate on preparing her semester exam questions so dazed was she by this afternoon's unbelievable events. She could almost see the birthday fairy touching her sparkly wand to the Big Yellow House. But would the magic carry her through Saturday-night's public ordeal? She'd accepted Jim's invitation. The Holly Ball would mark their first official public appearance as a couple. If only she could stop the panic rioting in her thoughts.

''Mom, can I come in?'' Erin stood in the doorway, her fresh-scrubbed face glowing.

''Always.'' Connie shoved her papers aside and turned her chair around. When Erin perched on the edge of the bed, Yolanda jumped up beside her, as if wanting to be one of the girls. ''That was quite a production you and Jim worked up today.''

''It was fun! He's a cool guy.''

''Good heavens! Do I read approval in that?''

Erin pulled up her legs, hugging her knees to her chest. ''You sure can. But, Mom, I feel kinda ashamed.''

''Oh?''

"I really misjudged him. Just like most of the other kids, I went with the crowd. I didn't give him a chance, ask the right questions."

"You did the best you could with the evidence you had."

"Maybe. But all of us just assumed Coach was right and Dr. Campbell was wrong."

"Hey, honey, I think you're going to have to get used to calling him 'Jim.'"

Erin beamed. "I can handle that. I really like him, Mom."

"What's made you change your opinion of him?"

"First of all, Kyle and some of the guys are talking now about how they like Coach Liddy, how he treats them like human beings. When I asked Kyle what he meant by that, he said Coach Mueller was always moody, didn't really care about his players as people."

"So the lesson is?"

"Don't make snap judgments. Take time to gather all the facts."

"You're a fast learner, all right—definitely valedictorian material."

"Mom, it won't be the end of the world if I'm not."

"It won't? Since when?"

"Since a double-dip chocolate almond royale ice-cream cone."

"What are you talking about?"

"*My* date with Dr. Camp…Jim." Erin laughed. "Mom, you look so funny. Pick up your chin. I had a meltdown in the library Monday. You, Jim, Gramma, Coach Mueller, college, *beaucoup* tests and papers. I just lost it."

Connie moved quickly to sit beside her. "Oh, honey."

"No, Mom, it's all right. Better than all right. Jim helped me see a lot of things about myself, about college, about you." Erin turned to face her. "Mom, I remember what you said the other evening when I was being so cranky. You know, about how you would have liked to be involved with him. I like him, Mom. Marry him. It's okay with me."

Connie drew up her knees and sat facing her daughter, feeling as though they were two best friends at a sleepover, with Yolanda an interested third party. "I won't embarrass you?"

"Only if you come to class with a hickey!"

Connie picked up a pillow and made as if to throw it at her wonderful daughter.

Erin raised her hands in front of her face. "No fair. Save that for Mom's Weekend at UT."

Connie convulsively pulled the pillow to her chest. "What did you say?"

"Ha! Gotcha, didn't I? Do you think I'm trotting off hundreds of miles and missing all the fun of you and Jim when I can stay in Texas? And be closer to you?"

The tears welling in Connie were cut short by the phone. Erin jumped off the bed. "I'll get it. It's probably Kyle."

Connie hugged the pillow, stunned, delighted by Erin's bombshell.

"Just a minute, please." Erin covered the mouthpiece with her hand and turned, wrinkling her nose in puzzlement. "It's for Gramma. Mom, who's Vernon Wray?"

ON THE WAY to the Holly Ball, Connie sat quietly against the car door, her stomach nothing but ice slivers. Now that the time had come, there was no turning back. Geraldine Farley, Gleeanne Roth and the fathers of football players, who might not be as forgiving as their sons—all would be waiting for them at the country club. Waiting for Jim to make another mistake. A mistake called Connie.

She glanced over at him, breath-takingly handsome in his tux. He was humming along with the carols on the radio, seemingly unconcerned about the looming debacle. But even as fear lanced through her, she knew she'd suffer anything to stand beside him tonight— and always.

"You'll never guess who came by the house today," he said.

"That being the case, I'll let you tell me."

"Oh, you spoil all the fun."

"Okay, Willie Nelson."

"Way off."

"Brad Scanlon, checking on me."

"Warmer."

"I give up."

He put an arm around her shoulder and pulled her as close as the seat belt would allow. "Kurt Mueller."

"You're kidding."

"Nope. He wasn't exactly charm personified, but he did thank me for giving him a wake-up call regarding his gambling addiction. You may have guessed that was his basic problem. Says he's trying to get his act together. Still hopes for a recommendation from Keystone.''

''What do you think?''

''I think we'll have to wait and see, not only about him but about whether I'm still here when the time comes.''

''Jim—'' He cut her off. ''We'll be fine. Here or elsewhere. What's important is that we're together.'' He pulled up in front of the club, got his check from the parking attendant and helped her out of the car. ''Scared?''

''Terrified.''

''They'll never know what hit 'em. Besides, you look fabulous in that ivory gown. C'mon.'' He tucked her hand over his arm and escorted her into the ballroom, glittering with flocked trees, mirrored snowflakes and white poinsettias. Loud laughter, the cinnamon scent of holiday potpourri, the clink of ice in drink glasses, the conversations crescendoing around them—Connie swallowed hard and clutched Jim's arm for support. The crowd jostled them as they made their way toward the wine bar. Phil Buxton greeted them warmly, then leaned over, said something to Jim and winked broadly. After he excused himself, Connie asked, ''What was that all about?''

''I called Buxton today and told him about you and me. He approves.''

''One out of five hundred isn't bad.''

They stood off to one side sipping their wine, watching as slowly, head after coiffured head, turned discreetly to size them up. A murmured, ''I can't believe he has the nerve..." floated to their ears. "Well, you know what I heard..." Jim circled Connie's waist and led her toward the dance floor, where the band had just started their first set.

Suddenly, Connie realized they'd never danced. Could she follow him? Would she make an even bigger spectacle of herself with the entire Keystone patron body looking on? As Jim pulled her into his arms, a buzz started around the room. Connie sensed the heads turning.

"C'mon, honey, you're doing fine," he whispered in her ear.

Lightly, as if without a thought, she found herself being danced around the floor as though they'd been partners for years. They fit together so perfectly she could almost forget where she was.

"Keep this up and I'll tip the band to play 'People Will Say We're in Love.'"

She pulled back. "You wouldn't!"

"It's true, though. We are in love. And I'd rather they'd say that." With a flourish, he turned her and hugged her closer, bending her slightly toward the floor as the song ended. When he stood her back up, she let go of his hand and turned to leave the dance floor.

Just then, Geraldine Farley, svelte in a hip-hugging emerald velvet sheath, blocked her way. In one diamond-beringed hand she held a highball glass that appeared to contain straight Scotch. "Well, as I live and breathe. If it isn't our headmaster and his date." She leaned closer to Connie, the unpleasant odor of whiskey on her breath. "You know what I think, *Ms.* Weaver? I think you're both about the biggest hypocrites I know.''

"Mrs. Farley, if you'll excuse me—" Connie tried to step around the woman, who grabbed her by the arm.

"*Excuse* you?" Her voice rose wildly. "I don't think so. You're teaching my daughter while you're screwing the headmaster." A hush fell over those standing within earshot, a hush that rippled and spread throughout the room.

Jim took hold of the woman's arm to disengage it. "Come on, Connie, you don't have to listen to this."

Mrs. Farley tilted back her glass and sloshed Scotch on her dress. "And *you!* Dr. High-and-Mighty Campbell. Character? You wouldn't know character if it bit you on the—"

"I think you'd better stop right now." Indignation, hot and pure, goaded Connie on. "You've had too much to drink, and you don't know what you're saying."

"Connie—" Jim put a hand in the small of her back.

Connie looked at Jim a moment, then made up her mind, once and for all. "Let me handle this, Jim." She faced the woman, then slowly looked around at the crowd, pressing close, standing silently. In that flash, Connie saw that most looked more curious than hostile. Briefly, as if for reassurance, her fingers sought the cameo around her neck.

"Mrs. Farley, you have made a most damaging accusation. And whether you would say this to me under other circumstances or not, I don't know. I'll never know. But Jim Campbell is a fine man. He would never, by thought, word or action do anything to jeopardize this school, its students or its faculty.''

"I don't have to listen to this!" Mrs. Farley's face was rigid.

"Yes, I'm afraid you do," Connie continued. "You have impugned my character and that of Dr. Campbell. Did you see us kissing in the hospital? Yes. Are we in love? Yes. Do we intend to marry? Yes. Have we done a single thing to be ashamed of? No. Friendship, romance, respect and love are values our students need to see modeled, not belittled." Connie paused for breath, her heart pounding. Geraldine Farley's mouth suddenly sagged.

Connie threaded her arm through Jim's and said in a voice that carried across the room, "This man has honored me by asking me to marry him and I have accepted. Most of you know Jim as a man of principle. I hope you will find it in your hearts to rejoice with us in our happiness." Suddenly she felt a serenity surpassing any she had ever known. Tara's mother no longer seemed daunting, merely pathetic. "Mrs. Farley, I'm sorry this incident had to be so public, but I will never be sorry to stand beside this wonderful man. Good evening." Legs trembling, she started across the room, her chin high, Jim's arm supporting her. When she dared look up at him, it was like that first time in the gym all over again when she'd thought her knees had turned to jelly. He was that handsome, that dear! Even now, a tiny grin ticked the corner of his mouth.

He leaned over and whispered, "Way to go, champ!"

Before they reached the edge of the dance floor, somewhere from the back of the crowd, Connie heard one person clap. Then another. Unbelievably, the sound grew until she was blushingly aware that almost everyone was applauding them. It was the most wonderful music she had ever heard! "Jim, I—"

He stopped, turned her to him and, in front of everyone, kissed her slowly, deliciously, lingeringly. When he raised up, the applause had grown to a roar.

But all she heard was "It's for you, darling, my precious queen of the school."

EPILOGUE

HAZY WISPS of peach-colored clouds filtered the rays of the setting sun. It was the kind of balmy Texas evening made to order for a commencement ceremony. Connie stood under the shade of a pecan tree outside the administration building waiting to line up with the faculty. Once again the rite of passage, an occasion that never failed to move her profoundly. The orneriest boys were forgiven, the in-jokes and special times forever consigned to memory, the hopes and expectations left, for fulfillment, to the future.

Pam, her academic gown zipped up, her mortarboard riding at a jaunty angle, approached. "Hey, Mom. Thinking about Erin?"

"Yes. And the others, too. Where does the time go, Pam? Do you remember that folk song 'Turn Around'?"

"About a woman watching her daughter grow up?"

Connie sang the chorus softly. The last note hovered in the air. "It seems like only yesterday she took her first step. I can't believe it's all over."

"It's not, Connie." For once, Pam was being totally serious. "It's commencement."

"You're right. The beginning."

"And your family sure knows how to do begin-

nings. Erin's starting college, you and Jim are new-
lyweds, Jim's been hired as permanent head and, if
I'm not mistaken, frisky Adele has a new lease on life,
too.''

Connie laughed. ''Vernon is a gem. Wouldn't you
love to be a fly on the wall when he and mother go
on their ballroom dancing cruise next month?''

Pam raised her arms over her head, snapping her
fingers flamenco-style, and hummed, ''La Cucara-
cha.''

''Ladies, ladies, line up, please.'' Jessie Flanders,
senior sponsor, was in her element, the sleeves of her
academic gown flapping like bats' wings from her
waving arms.

''I think she means, 'Places, everyone,''' Pam intoned. ''Here we go, kiddo.''

From the stadium came the majestic opening strains
of Elgar's ''Pomp and Circumstance.'' The music
alone always stirred Connie, but this year the lump in
her throat came even more readily. At the head of the
procession was dear Jim in full doctoral regalia. Behind her and the other teachers, the long line of seniors—their gold gowns reflecting the fading sunlight,
their crimson tassels dancing from their caps—included her suddenly and mysteriously grown-up
daughter. *Colin, you have no idea what you're missing.*

She fell into step with the algebra teacher and,
through a veil of tears, marched into the stadium to
her seat, where she and the rest of the faculty remained
standing to pay tribute to the graduates as they passed.

Erin, her honor cords hanging around her neck, was

near the end of the procession. She looked expectant,
confident—everything any parent could hope for.

The music concluded, followed by a shuffling of
programs and the clatter of people settling into their
seats. In the end zone, the flag fluttered in the faint
breeze; the brilliant evening star poked a hole in the
dusky canopy of the sky.

The greetings, the guest speaker, the choral number,
all passed in a blur. Then it was Erin's turn. Connie
watched her smooth her gown and then, clutching her
notes in one hand, mount the podium.

Erin paused nervously, as if suddenly aware of the
throng she faced and of the momentousness of her
role. Then, quietly, she began. "Dr. Campbell, distinguished guests, faculty, family and friends. It is a priv-
ilege to stand before you representing my classmates,
who have honored me by selecting me to speak here
this evening.

"We have labored in classrooms, created in studios
and theaters, been judged by ability, aptitude and performance. Ultimately school is about learning—not
just the prescribed curricular material, but about life.
And school is about preparing, not just for college or
the workplace, but for life. Tonight I'd like to share
some of the lessons I've learned at Keystone."

Connie caught Jim's eye and basked in the flood of
his approval. Erin's voice gained strength, conviction,
as she continued.

"First, I have learned that although we may strive
to achieve lofty goals, others may win. Earlier in the
year, I wanted desperately to be valedictorian. I struggled, competed and sacrificed some good times along

the way. But tonight I stand here as an honor graduate, not as valedictorian. It is Bruce Silverstein who deservedly achieved that recognition, and I congratulate him. Did I fail? In November I might have said yes. Now I tell you I did my best. None of us fails if we can say that.

"In some ways this senior class has had a tough year, and we didn't always understand why things happened the way they did. We thought it was our right to know—that the administration owed us explanations. It was 'us' versus 'them.' We forgot to trust. I've learned that sometimes I have to walk in faith, waiting for answers to reveal themselves. I can't always be in control. I didn't like this lesson, but I can testify to its value.

"Judging others too quickly. Jumping to conclusions. Acting on assumptions. Following the crowd. We learned a lot, didn't we, from what didn't work, didn't feel right?"

Connie slowly ran her thumb over the simple gold band spanning her ring finger as she watched this remarkable young woman hold the audience captive.

"I've learned that one has to be careful in seeking greener pastures. Faraway places can broaden our knowledge and understanding, but we should never forget the enriching possibilities that lie in our own backyards.

"Caring, character, curiosity. I've learned a great deal about each in my years at Keystone. But if I were asked what was the most important lesson of all, I would speak to you of heroes. Of heroines. We toss that word 'hero' around too lightly, applying it to rock stars, millionaire athletes, those who make dramatic rescues. By that epithet we honor talent or feats of strength, agility, daring.

"But I hold up to you a different kind of hero. From my family and from this faculty, I have learned that true heroes are men and women who possess character, who day by day live the courage of their convictions, who know right from wrong and are not afraid to make the difficult choice of right. Heroes act beyond lip service. They demonstrate their caring for others in everything they do."

Connie noticed Erin hesitate, then saw her look directly at Jim before turning to smile straight into Connie's eyes. "The single most important lesson I will carry with me from this place? It's simply this. One principled person standing alone—the keystone—holds a community together."

Erin stepped away from the podium, and as she made her way past the dignitaries, Connie saw her pause to grasp Jim's hand before she returned, amid the applause, to her seat.

And then, as one, the seniors rose, their hopeful young voices blending in the alma mater. Just when Connie thought she might lose it totally, she spotted in the stands the familiar face of Brad Scanlon, who was looking right at her. He held his clenched hands over his head, champion-style. Even from this distance, she could read his lips. "Ya look great, Mom!"

Connie smiled contentedly. The sages were right. Life *does* begin at forty!

MEN at WORK

All work and no play?
Not these men!

July 1998

MACKENZIE'S LADY by Dallas Schulze

Undercover agent Mackenzie Donahue's
lazy smile and deep blue eyes were his best
weapons. But after rescuing—and kissing!—
damsel in distress Holly Reynolds, how could
he betray her by spying on her brother?

August 1998

MISS LIZ'S PASSION by Sherryl Woods

Todd Lewis could put up a building with ease,
but quailed at the sight of a classroom! Still,
Liz Gentry, his son's teacher, was no battle-ax,
and soon Todd started planning some
extracurricular activities of his own....

September 1998

A CLASSIC ENCOUNTER
by Emilie Richards

Doctor Chris Matthews was intelligent, sexy
and *very* good with his hands—which made
him all the more dangerous to single mom
Lizette St. Hilaire. So how long could she
resist Chris's special brand of TLC?

Available at your favorite retail outlet!

MEN AT WORK™

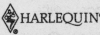HARLEQUIN® Silhouette®

Look us up on-line at: http://www.romance.net   PMAW2

HARLEQUIN SUPERROMANCE®

There are some men you just can't help loving…

Jesse Amorado is one of them. Great-looking and sexy, of
course. More important, though, he's a man of strength, of
loyalty and honor. A man who cares about his family, cares
about his community—the town of Coyote Springs, Texas.
A man who fights for what he believes in… A man who
lives with intensity—and loves the same way.

A MAN CALLED JESSE
by K. N. Casper

You can't blame Tori Carr for falling in love with
Jesse Amorado. Even if they're business rivals.

HARLEQUIN®
Makes any time special™

Available in October 1998—
wherever Harlequin books are sold.

HSRLTM

Look us up on-line at: http://www.romance.net

HARLEQUIN SUPERROMANCE®

S

FINDERS, KEEPERS

Is a detective agency that specializes in
finding lost loves, friends, family, etc..

If Noah had been adventurous enough to discover
the world and himself, he could be adventurous
enough to visit an agency that specialized in finding
lost lovers. But meeting Maggie Tyrell, proprietor,
was an adventure in itself. However, Maggie
wouldn't be deterred from the task at hand—even if
Noah wanted her to call off the search. *Even if it
meant her heart would break...*

Found: One Wife
Harlequin Superromance (#809)
October 1998

by Judith Arnold

Available wherever Harlequin books are sold.

❄ HARLEQUIN®

Look us up on-line at: http://www.romance.net   HSRFKOW

Intense, dazzling, isolated...

THE AUSTRALIANS

Stories of romance Australian-style, guaranteed to
fulfill that sense of adventure!

This October, look for

Beguiled and Bedazzled

by **Victoria Gordon**

Colleen Ferrar is a woman who always gets what she wants—
that is, until she meets Devon Burns, who lives in the very
secluded Tasmanian bush. He has a proposal of his own, and
the question is: how far will Colleen go to get what she wants?

*The Wonder from Down Under: where spirited women win
the hearts of Australia's independent men!*

Available October 1998
at your favorite retail outlet.

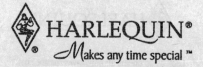

HARLEQUIN®
Makes any time special™

Look us up on-line at: http://www.romance.net   PHAUS4

HARLEQUIN SUPERROMANCE®

9 MONTHS LATER

DEBORAH'S SON

by award-winning author
Rebecca Winters

Deborah's pregnant. The man she loves—the baby's
father—doesn't know. He's withdrawn from her for reasons
she doesn't understand. But she has to tell him. *Wants* to tell
him. She wants them to be a family.

**Available in October
wherever Harlequin books are sold.**

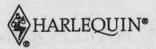

HARLEQUIN®

Look us up on-line at: http://www.romance.net

HSR9ML

SEXY, POWERFUL MEN NEED EXTRAORDINARY WOMEN WHEN THEY'RE

Destined for Love

Take a walk on the wild side this October
when three bestselling authors weave wondrous stories
about heroines who use their extraspecial abilities to
achieve the magic and wonder of love!

HATFIELD AND McCOY
by HEATHER GRAHAM POZZESSERE

LIGHTNING STRIKES
by KATHLEEN KORBEL

MYSTERY LOVER
by ANNETTE BROADRICK

Available October 1998
wherever Harlequin and Silhouette books are sold.

HARLEQUIN®
Makes any time special ™

Silhouette®

Look us up on-line at: http://www.romance.net   PSBR1098

HARLEQUIN SUPERROMANCE®

COMING NEXT MONTH

#806 A MAN CALLED JESSE • K.N. Casper
Love That Man!
Jesse Amorado is a proud man determined to preserve his
community—the barrio in Coyote Springs, Texas. Developer
Winslow Carr has other plans for the area: tearing it down.
Winslow's daughter, Tori, is now a partner in the firm and is
an even greater threat to Jesse's peace of mind. Because Tori
makes him think of other kinds of partnerships—the kind that
last for life.

#807 A FATHER'S VOW • Peg Sutherland
Hope Springs
Will Travers left Hope Springs almost ten years ago. Accused
of a crime he didn't commit, he tried to make a life for himself
in another city. But now he's faced with raising his son on
his own, and he realizes there's no better place to do that
than his hometown. Even if it means facing his accuser,
Libby Jeffries—the only person who can help him make
enough sense of the past to give his son a future.

#808 DEBORAH'S SON • Rebecca Winters
9 Months Later
Deborah loves only one man—a man she expected to marry.
But Ted Taylor rejected her for reasons she doesn't understand.
Hard as it is on her pride and her heart, she *has* to see him
again, has to tell him she's pregnant with his son.

A deeply emotional story by the author of *Until There Was You*.

#809 FOUND: ONE WIFE • Judith Arnold
Finders, Keepers
Noah had been adventurous enough to discover the world—
so he could certainly be adventurous enough to visit an
agency that specialized in finding lost loves. But meeting
Maggie Tyrell, proprietor, was an adventure in itself. Noah
soon discovered he was less interested in finding the woman
he *thought* he'd loved than in finding out more about the fiery
self-styled love detective!